The Parker Sisters, Childish Things

Thelonious Legend

Copy and Story Editor Melanie Scott

Story Editor Alisha Grauso

Cover Art Alona Russ

Mo powers mo problems for the Parker sisters. It's a new year but the same drama. Do your homework, keep your rooms clean, and try not to get killed or kidnapped by mercenaries. But there some new players to the game. Players as unique as the Parker sisters. The bar has been raised, and the game is afoot.

This follow-up to the fast-paced sci-fi thriller Sins of Father the Parker Sisters has leveled up. But so have their enemies. So while juggling boyfriends, new superpowers, kidnapping plots, they still have no idea who is after them. But they are getting closer.

Roxane Gay, Bad Feminist "I would rather be a bad feminist than no feminist at all."

Dr. Maya Angelou "There is no greater agony than bearing an untold story inside you."

Dedicated to Delores Williams 1948 – 2014
Mom, I see you every day in your granddaughters. Your compassion for others. Your intellect. Your laugh. It's a new day, mom, but the struggle is constant, and we are still fighting the good fight. We hope to make you proud.

Fonzo Williams 1970 – 2021
They tell me God works in mysterious ways. That everything happens for a reason and that you are at peace. But Fonz, I miss you, man, and I grieve for the memories we didn't get a chance to make. Rest easy little brother, and I'll see you on the other side.

To my daughters,
We live in a time when commercialism and capitalism is camouflaged as Democracy while our leaders demagogue to divide us in a transparent attempt to retain power. I have no idea what the future holds but do not be afraid to take the path less traveled. You might change the world.

To my wife,
How did we get here? Luck? Providence? Fate? Does it matter? We've come a long way from riding our bikes around North Omaha. Looking forward to what the next chapter in our life brings because we've been blessed.

Prologue

"Are you going to expense that?" U.S. Marshal Russell asked US. Marshal Harris.

The hotel phone rang, interrupting the conversation. They both paused to look at Carlos as he answered. The line evidently went dead, as Carlos hung up and continued to flip through channels while glancing around the no-frills room. It consisted of one main area with two beds, a flatscreen TV, a sofa with a rollout bed, and a bathroom near the door entrance. Carlos laid claim to the bed closest to the window. Although it faced the parking lot, Carlos liked to sleep with a breeze on him. And, God willing, he was hoping to get a good night's sleep finally.

"I told you. I do all my expenses at once and don't itemize. If you itemize, you have to stick to the caps for each meal," Harris explained to the younger and more fit Russell. Harris touched the pen to his tongue as he continued to work on the *New York Times* crossword puzzle. The older Marshal then shook the pen a few times as he sat on the bed and leaned against the backboard. For three days of driving and checking in and out of hotels, Carlos had entertained himself by betting whether he would ever see his smirk turn into a smile, but it never did. It was a maddening game, but it kept Carlos occupied in place of a phone and other devices.

"We can do that?" replied Russell as he punched the pillow and readjusted his position on the couch. He had been in a constant state of motion for the last twenty minutes, in a frustrating attempt to get comfortable. Carlos watched the younger Marshal, wondering if he would acknowledge he was too tall for that couch. Carlos also found it ironic that his security detail openly discussed gaming expense systems while protecting him before he testified against his former employer for gaming and defrauding the government in military contracts.

"In that case, I'll call back and order the ribeye too," Russell said, shifting positions again. The Marshal's refusal to use the rollout bed feature led Carlos to believe his security detail's competency was inadequate.

"Too late. I told you not to get that omelet for breakfast. You'll go over now," Harris replied, touching the pen to his tongue again. His using a pen to do the *Times* crossword gave Carlos some hope. However, Carlos still second-guessed himself for listening to that hacker and dropping dime on his employer. It all seemed stupid now. Reckless. But at the time, being rewarded millions as a whistleblower was not a difficult decision. The hacker told him there was a False Claims Act that allowed whistleblowers to receive up to thirty percent of funds recovered from fraudulent or criminal activity. And thirty percent of a billion-dollar contract was generational wealth.

"We still on for next weekend?" Harris continued, now peering at Russell over his reading glasses.

"Are you serious? Last time I went to a game, your son didn't even play." Russell stood and looked at the couch as if he wanted to throw it out the window. He lay back down with his feet dangling over the armrest in a position that even made Carlos uncomfortable. Tired of playing the no-smile game, Carlos closed his eyes and dreamed about how he would spend his money. First, two new gravestones for his parents, who had worked every day in the fields to provide him and his sister a better life. They both were immigrants who died when he was in college and never got a chance to see him graduate, and their sacrifices realized. The second was to pay for his little sister's wedding. She had honored him by asking him to give her away, and he would be honored to return the favor. He would honor her and his parents by paying for her wedding and paying off her student loans. She was an OBGYN nurse and had racked up crushing student debt. And lastly, buy his Abuela a big house in the suburbs with a maid. A white maid.

"But he might start. His coach likes his attitude and says he is getting better every day. Plus, there will be a lot of hot single moms there," Harris persisted, and the comments made Carlos smile. For the last three days, Carlos had listened to Harris brag about his son's athletic potential. But, based on remarks from Russell, that was more wishful thinking than anything. And Carlos knew soccer. Carlos played in college on a scholarship before he got hurt. And through all his years of playing, he never saw a lot of hot single moms. But maybe that was a suburb thing.

The phone rang with the light, indicating it was the front desk again, and Carlos was hopeful. Although they checked in late, they were able to get their order in before the kitchen closed. In an exhibition of defiance, Carlos quickly answered the phone. Carlos was instructed not to answer the phone, but hunger and boredom gave him courage. And he was relieved his body would get a break from eating McDonald's before he settled in for the night. "Hello?"

Harris frowned at Carlos, then shrugged. "Tell them if my steak is overcooked, I'm sending it back," he said, before refocusing on his crossword.

"Well, hello, Mr. Alvarez! What a pleasant surprise. So, the Marshals are allowing their charge to answer the phone? Interesting. And did you get the ribeye too, Mr. Alvarez? You might as well. It's not like you are paying for it. At least not directly."

"Who is this?" Carlos asked.

Harris sat up. "Give me the phone, Carlos."

"Consider me a friend, Mr. Alvarez. A friend of the family. As a matter of fact, I have someone here who would like to say hello…"

"Carlos?" A different voice now. One with a fearful tone.

"Anita?"

Harris jumped out of bed, snatched the phone from Carlos, put it to his ear, and slammed it down. "We have to move. We've been compromised," he announced.

Carlos was stunned. *Why would they have my sister?* Harris yanked Carlos up by his arm. "Move it, Carlos!" Carlos felt the fingers dig into his arm and knew it should hurt, but he was numb to it. He felt warm breath on his cheek as the Marshal yelled instructions at him. The blood rushed into his face as he nodded and put on his shoes. Both the Marshals grabbed their guns, and Harris spoke rapidly into his cell phone. "Sir, we've been compromised. No! I mean, no, sir, too exposed. Yes, sir, I agree. Yes. Yes, sir, I will."

Russell was at the door with gun in hand. Harris chambered a round and grabbed a revolver from his ankle holster. He now had a weapon in each hand, and his perpetual smirk had changed into a frown. "Carlos, keep up!"

Russell peeked out the door, fully opened it, and looked around, whispering, "Clear!"

Harris then passed Russell as he went into the hallway. Carlos lost sight of him but heard him also say, "Clear!"

"Let's go! Carlos, let's go!" Russell said as he snatched Carlos by his collar and pushed him into the hallway. Carlos' legs were heavy, and his feet were numb, but they managed to move on autopilot. Harris was waiting for him at the end of the hallway with the exit door open. The movement helped Carlos. He realized he was in danger. His sister was in trouble. And all this was because of the hacker. Carlos had been content being an accountant working for a company with health benefits. But he was told he had to do the right thing. And that it would change his life. So, he did. Now he was in a dimly lit hallway in a rundown hotel with unseen bad guys hunting him.

Russell passed Harris and entered the stairwell. They were four floors up and methodically descended every floor, making sure to 'Clear' it before moving on. They crept and stopped when they got to the bottom level. Once they stopped moving, Carlos became a vessel of fear. It whispered into his ear, telling him the Marshals couldn't protect him. It told him to run. It told him he needed to get away and save his sister. He squeezed his eyes shut and tried to silence the doubt. He grabbed the cross he always hung around his neck and said the Lord's Prayer for courage. He convinced himself he was doing this for the greater good and to provide for his family.

Two new gravestones, Abuela's new house, sister's wedding, sister's student debt

Russell opened the door and scanned the parking lot. He nodded for Carlos and Harris to follow. It was after ten in the evening, quiet and still. The flickering light of the hotel sign gave the parking lot a haunted look. As they advanced, their shadows danced, then froze, then danced again. There were only seven cars in the parking lot. Carlos didn't know if the vehicles provided cover or ambush opportunities for the unseen *El Fantasma*. He heard the hum of distant traffic that he could not see through the rolling hills. The gas station and McDonald's across the parking lot had no activity.

Carlos knew the hotel was on the route to his court appearance, and the Marshals wanted to avoid crowds; however, they could not have picked a better place for an ambush. But Carlos was going to make it through this. He was his parents' dreams realized, and he would not die in a parking lot. He repeated his new mantra to himself over and over to stay focused and calm his fears.

Two new gravestones, Abuela's new house, sister's wedding, sister's student debt

There was one parked car between them and their vehicle, which was fifty yards away. There were another two hundred yards of open space before the on-ramp and their escape.

Two new gravestones, Abuela's new house, sister's wedding, sister's student debt

Then it hit Carlos. "Anita! They have my sister!" The words came out louder than he intended. His voice scared him and reverberated in his ears as it washed over the parking lot. All three froze as if his voice had awakened El Cucuy. Even their shadows stopped to listen.

Russell grabbed him by the arm and whispered, "They don't have your sister. They're messing with you. Now, come with us if you want to live!" Carlos winced, but he understood. He had to make it through the night, and a new life waited for him in the morning.

Two new gravestones, Abuela's new house, sister's wedding, sister's student debt

"Stay close behind me, Carlos," Harris instructed, and his smirk was back, which gave Carlos hope. Maybe after all this was over, Carlos might get to see him properly smile. Harris took off on a brisk walk, leaving the cover of the parked car, and headed for their vehicle and their salvation.

"Go!" Russell pushed Carlos in the back. His mouth was dry, making it painful to swallow. Following Harris, he attempted to mirror every step like he did when he followed his father's footprints in the sand when he was a kid. Although the night air was cool, Carlos was sweating, and his every sense was magnified. The hum of distant traffic, the smell of McDonald's. His dancing shadow now to the side of him, taunting him, daring him to walk faster. Carlos grabbed his cross and kissed it.

Two new gravestones, Abuela's new house, sister's wedding, sister's student debt

Russell coughed behind him, and Carlos turned in time to catch him as he stumbled into his arms, dropping his gun. Carlos heard himself say, "It's going to be OK, man. It's going to be OK. You going to check out some hot single moms next weekend, remember?" It was an out-of-body experience. It didn't seem real. Carlos turned to yell for help but felt a sudden sharp burning session in his lower back as his legs gave out, sending them both crashing to the ground.

Russell opened his mouth to say something, but the light in his eyes dimmed and went out. His mouth stayed open with warnings left unsaid. "No! No!" Carlos screamed to everyone and no-one. Carlos released Russell and tried to stand, but his legs wouldn't listen. He couldn't even feel them. Tears in his eyes, he turned to Harris for help. Harris was on his knees. His mouth was reflexively opening and closing. His eyes looked confused. He swayed for a minute and then fell face-first to the concrete with his guns scattering in opposite directions. *Never saw him smile.*

His legs useless, Carlos pushed himself up by his arms to get a better view. A red stain was forming in the chest area of his shirt. *Bullet hit my spine.* His arms shaking from holding his weight, Carlos tried to steady himself. His vision blurry, he saw a figure approaching, fading in and out of focus. Carlos had been a good kid. Studied hard, stayed out of trouble, and got a degree in accounting. But El Cucuy came for him regardless. The gunman was not El Cucuy. The hacker was. The hacker baited him. The hacker played on his greed. The gunman was just an instrument. But Carlos was not ready to give up yet. He had too much to live for. Grunting, Carlos attempted to reach Russell's fallen gun. He couldn't move. He tried to scream for help and coughed up blood. The gunmen were only steps away. Carlos realized he had lost a game with secret rules not known to people like him. He had tried to do the right thing and got beat. He struggled to kiss his cross and then closed his eyes.

Two new gravestones, Abuela's new house, sister's wedding, sister's student debt

***

"Not feeling this, Slim. They got us ghosting civilians now? Three hots and a cot isn't worth this, bruh. But I guess it is what it is. Hit the cleaners, and let's be out." Goldie talked as he put two bullets in the back of the accountant's head and briefly held up his new silencer to admire his modifications. The silencer worked as designed, sounding like a soft whistle, but he shook his head. Probably not a big enough market to make modifying silencers a legit side hustle. He unscrewed the silencer, placing it in his pocket and the gun behind his belt at the back. He kept his head up to scan the area as he bent down to wipe the blowback blood on his loafers and pick up his shell casings. He was getting too old for this.

"You been talking that same mess since we got back in the world. But look where we at? And the cleaners on the way," Slim replied while putting bullets in the back of Harris' head and retrieving his casings. "And your silencer is rad, but don't start," Slim added, smiling.

Goldie smiled back. Wasn't too many killers Goldie trusted. Killing warped reality and damaged souls, making most dysfunctional without medication, be it prescribed or otherwise but him and Slim were built different. And Slim was one of the better marksmen he ever served with. He had just hit three targets from over two hundred yards out in under ten seconds. That was special. But they were both special. Different. Goldie and Slim lived everyday lives, escaping damage caused by the fog of war and the taking of lives. They were a unique breed of killers who could kill and then have a cup of cappuccino without their hands shaking. That was a rarity. "Let's bounce, Slim."

Slim nodded as he readjusted the strap on his guitar case, which contained his long-range sniper rifle. Goldie grimaced. He didn't want this. But he didn't have a lot of marketable skills. He was a five-foot ten-inch Black man with a bronze complexion and hazel eyes who had sold his soul a long time ago. Now he was seeking an exit strategy. He smoothed the oversized, nondescript polo shirt he wore to hide his muscles and gun. He had contact lenses to hide his eyes. Muscles drew attention. People remembered muscles for some reason. Slim didn't have that problem. He was a six-foot three-inch gangly white guy with Chinese tattoos and a long blond ponytail. He looked like any hipster in any city in America, making him virtually invisible. Goldie had to work harder. People noticed muscular black guys with hazel eyes, so oversized shirts and contacts were a must.

"Slim, I'm serious. Did you see our next assignment? We babysitters now? Isn't right. Plus, we're working with that crazy chick from Kabul. I'm going to reach out to Sarge because you know he got that phat assignment. Heck, he already hooked up Big Mac. And remember Perry? Dude is out in Hollywood getting paid as a consultant for war movies and stuff. He said he might be able to put us on."

"I'm happy for Patch and Big Mac, but babysitting rich folks isn't my thang. I didn't know you talked to Perry. I thought he bit it in Jalalabad? But if you got the hookup, that be rad cause I don't trust myself if we got to work with that crazy chick. Some friends from my first tour died because of her."

"Forget her. I'm working on something. And everybody thought Perry died, but he just lived in Nebraska for a minute. But, as I said, he in Cali now, and I'm with you on the babysitting rich folk, but anything must be better than this, right? I'm just waiting for Perry to get back to me and see where that goes."

"Hook it up, hook it up. But how are we getting out of our contract?"

Goldie turned around, noticing the bodies were already gone, and a white ACME Cleaning van was headed for the on-ramp. The cleaners were quick. "Don't worry about the contract, Slim. I'll take care of that," Goldie said as he and his friend disappeared into the rolling hills.

Chapter One

"Stop blowing that whistle! I'm getting up already!" Eve yelled. Gwen was in Eve's bedroom, standing over her while Eve put her head beneath a pillow.

"Let's go, Princess! You were supposed to be downstairs five minutes ago! I'm adding fifty more pushups to your workout!" Gwen shouted. She then snatched off the covers and ran out of the room, barely escaping a thrown pillow.

Gwen smiled as she marched into Ana's room. It was six in the morning. Gwen had been up since five, counting the seconds. Sleep no longer came easy to Gwen. Watching your older sister almost get stabbed to death by a giant mercenary would do that to you. But it was more than that haunting sequence that chased sleep away. Eve had been spectacular and fearless in that fight. She attacked a grown man trying to kill her with a savagery and skill that Gwen didn't think she could ever match, leaving her feeling inadequate and restless.

Gwen blew her whistle again while standing directly over a sleeping Ana. "Come on, dork! Gotta put some muscle on them bones."

Ana moaned and turned away from Gwen. "Exit my room. I am still recovering from yesterday. My muscles do not respond to resistance training as rapidly as you or Evelyn."

"Listen… I will not have this type of negative attitude on my squad! Be downstairs in five minutes, or I'm throwing you out the window!" The girls' bedrooms were on the second level of a six thousand square foot Victorian home with twelve-foot ceilings. If Gwen did throw her younger sister out the window, she would have time to think about her negative attitude before hitting the ground.

"Your constant threats no longer hold sway over me. Furthermore… OK! OK! Put me down! Unhand me! I'll be down in five minutes! I promise!" Ana pleaded as Gwen picked her up and carried her over to the window like a suitcase.

Gwen dropped her, sending Ana crashing to the floor on her stomach. "See ya downstairs in five, dork!"

"I hate you!" Ana screamed as Gwen ran out of the room and slammed the door.

"Hey! It's too early for this mess! Gwen, stay out of your sisters' rooms! And stop slamming doors!" Gwen's father, Barry, screamed down from their parents' bedroom in the loft.

"Wasn't me!" Gwen yelled back. She spent the next twelve minutes eating four eggs, four toasts, two bananas, two glasses of orange, and a protein shake. Gwen's need for calories had decreased by more than half in the last month, and she now only spent ten to eleven hours sleeping as opposed to twelve or thirteen. She felt like a typical teenager. Except for the fact she weighed over three hundred pounds, was super-strong, had an older sister that was a super-fast ninja, and a younger sister who was a super-smart billionaire with a secret lab beneath the basement. Also, they had a billionaire civil-rights icon as a grandmother, who *Time* magazine just voted the most admired woman in America. Again. But other than that, a typical teenager doing advanced martial arts training in the morning with her sisters.

"OK, we good? Everyone got a good sweat?" Gwen asked her sisters between breaths twenty minutes after barging into their rooms. All three sisters were in their sizeable rectangular basement facing each other. Eve nodded, Ana shrugged, and Gwen turned to face one of the three walls of mirrors. She bounced on her toes, and threw a few punches and kicks before turning back to face her sisters. "Let's do this…" The sisters then unrolled a wrestling mat to cover the hardwood area of their mother's dance studio before they geared up.

Eve winced while she stretched. "Did you make the updates, Ana? My ribs are still sore." Gwen had managed to finally notch a win against Eve a couple of days ago, connecting on a kick that sent Eve cartwheeling into the wall. Eve had used her super-speed power nine minutes earlier, making her easier to hit and making her reaction time almost normal before she could recharge.

"Evelyn, as you know, Gwendolyn's kicks have been measured at 9,300 pounds per square inch. Any padding that could fully negate that would be too restrictive and compromise our speed and flexibility, which I know you prioritize. Nevertheless, I have made modifications that allow for a higher rate of absorption and displacement of impact while incorporating a micro-spring technology that stores kinetic energy it can't displace."

Gwen raised her hand. "Bro, is it me, or did you just describe Vibranium? Better be careful, fam. King T'Challa is going to send the Dora Milaje to snatch your edges."

"That makes absolutely no sense. How does one even go about snatching edges?"

"Are you two idiots finished? And Gwen, you better up your game. With your strength, you should be kicking over 10,000 PSI every time. So, you and I are spending extra time today to work on your hip rotation, and if you don't hit 10,000 PSI by the end of the week, *I'm* snatching your edges."

Gwen frowned. "Whatever, Princess." But she knew Eve was serious. While Gwen and Ana were doing two-a-days, with sparring in the morning and strength training in the evening, Eve was doing three-a-days, if not more. All summer, all she did was workout, read, talk to Tyler, workout, read, talk to Tyler. It was an early Christmas miracle that Gwen had been able to land a blow. She was not looking forward to spending extra time getting kicked in the face by her older sister. Gwen would rather hang out in Ana's stinky bat-cave helping with the planning while being watched by her creepy mutant ravens.

"Whatever? Well, you better bring it because I'm not holding back," Eve said as Ana helped them with the straps of their sparring gear. Their gear consisted of three full-bodied unitards with impact sensors. They also used extra padding inspired by their old Tae Kwon Do sparring equipment. They wanted to be as safe as possible because some of their sparring matches got intense.

After the girls had all their gear on, Ana checked her notepad and gave a thumbs up. "We are good. Cameras are online." The sparring area had twenty-one robotic cameras located in the corners, ceilings, walls, and floor.

Gwen took a deep breath. "OK, Princess; it's me and you first round. Ana, set the timer for two minutes with a thirty-second rest. It's you and me next round, Ana, and don't forget your mouthpiece this time, dork."

"I am a nerd!"

"Moving on, we get a three-minute rest. Then we both attack Eve for ninety seconds. Two-minute rest, then you and Eve both attack me, two-minute rest, then me and Eve beat you down. Then we run it back."

"Let's do it," Eve said, putting in her mouthpiece.

Ana yawned.

Eve and Gwen faced each other and bowed. Eve carried one twenty-eight-inch bamboo stick in each hand. She was experimenting with Kali, the Filipino art of stick fighting, to provide more reach and keep Gwen at a distance to mitigate her strength.

Ding-ding

Eve and Gwen circled each other, with Eve bouncing on her toes and continually switching foot position from southpaw to conventional while alternately twirling the sticks in each hand. The constant movement was frustrating to Gwen and forced her to reassess her plan of attack continually. Losing patience, Gwen bit down on her mouthpiece and charged forward, using a pawing jab to gauge distance for an overhand right. She wanted to press the issue and go for her second win in a week.

Eve dipped under Gwen's jab and pivoted while striking Gwen twice in the head and twice in her ribcage before she could react. Gwen shook her head to clear the cobwebs. *That girl is fast!* But Gwen weighed over three hundred and thirty pounds and was super-strong. She needed to leverage her weight and strength better. Eve was just so good with angles and spacing.

Gwen started bouncing on her toes to switch things up. She had yet to figure out how to mesh and blend different fighting styles as Eve did. Even Ana had got good with her staff in record time. As if to prove Gwen's point, Eve kicked her in the chest, knocking her off balance and back a step. She then spun, hitting Gwen twice in the head and twice in the ribs with her sticks. Gwen shook it off, and when Eve spun again, Gwen managed to land a kick in Eve's back between her shoulder blades. Eve became a blur of motion as Gwen's kick sent her airborne. But before Gwen could catch her breath, Eve had bounced off the wall and come back at her. She broke a stick over Gwen's head then caught her with a knee beneath her chin.

Gwen dropped to a knee, dazed and seeing stars. It took a few seconds to gather herself while Eve helped her to her feet. Gwen managed to smile through her pain and frustration. "You got me. I didn't even see you coming off the wall. How are you feeling?"

"I'm good. I'm OK," Eve said between controlled breaths. When her power first manifested, it took Eve over two hours of recovery before using it again. Now she was able to use it after an hour or less.

"Cool. Let's check the tape," Gwen said as she and Eve huddled behind Ana, who edited camera footage from every angle to create a video of the best view of their match.

"A few more seconds, sisters, just capturing the metrics, now doing a bit of analytics and… OK, here we are," Ana said, finishing typing with her patented dramatic flourish that always annoyed Gwen.

The video showed Eve becoming a blur after Gwen kicked her. Ana backed it up and slowed it down so they could see Eve's movements. In contrast, while Eve appeared to move at average speed, Gwen was frozen. Eve twisted, turned, and flipped in the air so that her feet touched the wall of mirrors while her body was parallel to the ground. Eve launched off the wall and back at Gwen without ever touching the ground. Gwen's foot was still in the air from kicking when Eve broke one of her bamboo sticks over the top of her head. Eve also connected with a knee beneath Gwen's chin before flipping over Gwen's back, landing on her feet and pivoting away as Gwen fell to the ground. It was amazing. It didn't look real.

The fact the mirror didn't shatter when Eve made contact was a testimonial to how smart her dorky little sister could be. Ana had the mirrors specially designed and installed after the first couple of accidents, but Gwen still found it amazing.

Ana ran it back a few times while providing the metrics. "Evelyn, your heart rate peaked at one hundred and twelve beats per second, which is more than five times a hummingbird's heart rate. Your external body temperature peaked at one hundred forty-seven degrees. How are you feeling?"

"Winded, but OK."

Ana nodded. "Excellent. Your body temperature has already lowered to one hundred and nine degrees, and your heart is currently at sixty beats per minute. Remember, it is essential that you continue to work on your breathing and resting heart rate, which would allow you to recover quicker. Also, as I mentioned, there is a school of thought that suggests we only have a finite number of heartbeats, so it might be vital for your long-term health from a longevity perspective as well."

Gwen rolled her eyes. "But how hard did I kick her?"

"Your kick measured at two thousand one hundred pounds per square inch. Eve was able to avoid the brunt of it thanks to her super-speed kicking in."

Eve shook her head. "I was sloppy. We need to do some extra rounds. Everything still feels forced."

"Princess, no-one has time for extra rounds. Ana and I have a life! And we still have stuff to do before school starts!"

"We're not going to get better if we don't practice!" Eve replied. Last year, after the Parker sisters' powers manifested, their cellular structure began degrading, slowly killing them. This forced them to look for a cure. Eventually, they were saved by their father's college friend, David, who showed up in the nick of time with an antidote. They got the antidote and barely escaped a trap by mercenaries who were after David. And during their search for a cure, the sisters uncovered murders, fraud, and embezzlement. They were determined to bring the guilty people to justice. That was why they trained so hard.

"Hey! What's going on?" their father yelled from the stairs. He had on his work uniform, as his daughters sarcastically referred to it. It consisted of a long-sleeve, button-down bluish shirt and tan slacks.

"Pops! You should see the move Eve did!" Gwen said, feigning enthusiasm because Eve made the move on her.

"Oh, I'm late for work. Send it to me, and I'll check it out over lunch."

"Barry?" their mother said as she joined their father on the stairs.

"Oh, and girls, stop jumping out the window. We talked about this. And clean this house. Or if you're bored, help Jen and Claire with their lemonade stand. They're raising money for their fencing team or something."

"But Pops, that is part of our super-hero training!" A few months back, the girls escaped mercenaries by jumping out of a window thirteen stories up. Unfortunately for Gwen, she didn't have much body control and got knocked out when she hit the ground, almost getting them captured. So now Gwen and Eve had incorporated free falling and landing on their feet from heights into their practice. It took Eve a couple of hours to consistently land on her feet no matter how she jumped or fell out the window. It took Gwen two weeks, practicing every day, before she consistently landed on her feet. And because of the strength and density of Gwen's bones and the strength and the elasticity of Eve's, they no longer used the air mattress to cushion their landing. Ana, however, still refused to try it.

"Are those new cameras?" their father asked, stepping off the stairs and towards the sparring area.

"Why, yes, they are, Father. They arrived last week, but it took me a couple of days to make the necessary modifications and upgrades. Now we can track Evelyn's movements when she is moving at super-speed."

"Really? Show me."

"Barry, it's time for us to go."

"Right, babe. Girls, no more jumping out the window. I mean it. Someone could see you, and that's the last thing we need. And straighten up the kitchen and your rooms because I'll be checking when I get home."

"Gotcha, Pops. Don't leave the front door open, and don't make a mess."

"That's not what I said, Gwendolyn. Stop being cute," Barry said as he climbed the stairs.

"Uh, didn't you have that on yesterday?"

"No, this is my first time wearing this shirt. I got it last weekend. Remember?" The girls' mother, Michelle, always gave their father a hard time about the way he dressed. He was the Vice-President of Infrastructure at a medium-sized company but still, he dressed like he was an entry-level programmer, according to their mother.

"Uh, my sister and I are going shopping tomorrow. I think I might have to spruce up your wardrobe."

"Oh, so now you not feeling my style?"

"I think you're taking liberties with the word 'style,'" Michelle said, as both parents disappeared upstairs.

"Come on, dork, it's me and you," Gwen said, putting her mouthpiece back in. The sisters spent two hours sparring before Ana and Gwen tapped out to take a break and eat breakfast.

Bzzz, Bzzz

"Hmm, David received the funds and is going dark because other people are looking for him," Ana said, looking at her phone.

"What do you mean? And I thought we agreed that all the drones in the neighborhood was suspicions and your ravens were going to start taking them out?" Eve asked as the three sisters sat at the breakfast bar, eating and recuperating.

"The birds are still in training and not ready to go live. And as I have mentioned before, there is more than one entity searching for David. The race to stabilize the process so it can be monetized has been joined."

"And they think David has stabilized it. Like he did with us?"

Ana nodded. "Indeed Evelyn."

"Well more entities sounds like more targets to me. And what are we doing about it? Aren't we supposed to be looking for David too? And going after the bad guys? We just can't let them kidnap people and experiment on them. I mean the ones we discovered were soldiers with families who thought they died for their country when they really died for profits. We can't let that ride. Grams has been fighting against this stuff her entire life. This fight is in our DNA. We have to do something."

Gwen clapped sarcastically. "Great speech, Princess. If you don't get an Oscar you was robbed. But it's more complicated than that. We are still trying to maintain our anonymity, right?"

"Excellent word choice, Gwendolyn."

"Thanks, Ana. I get one new word emailed to me daily, and I've been trying to work them into conversations. You know, it's never too early to start thinking about the SATs."

"I concur, Gwendolyn, and…"

"Are you two finished? What are we doing to stop the bad guys?"

"Look, Princess, I know you want me and Ana to find bad people for you to beat up, but super-hero work isn't easy. Let her know what else we discovered, Ana."

"David thinks he is speaking with Father and told Father that we should be careful."

"And you know this how?"

"Because she is a genius super-hacker? I mean, have you ever met Ana? And we thought it be a good idea to kind of put some parental control on Pops' phone and other devices. The last time he tried to help he led us into an ambush. Plus, David is shady and I don't want him asking for help from or even talking to Pops. Anything that dude is involved with is definitely illegal and we need to keep him as far away from Pops as possible."

"But that's not what parental controls are!" Eve shouted.

"Evelyn, Gwendolyn is correct. Having access to Father's devices allows us to limit his exposure to David and other nefarious elements. It also allows us to mitigate any potential legal exposure he might get into and, as Gwendolyn said, while protecting Father from himself. And it seems Father is searching for David as well, but with David going dark him locating David is not a concern at this point."

"What? How come no-one told me?"

"Are you kidding me? Make it make sense! Unless it's kicking people in the face, you're always too busy! We tried to get you to come down to the lab last night, remember?"

"Evelyn, we just received the correspondence last night, and David is desperate. If it is even him. However, he needed money, so I sent him two hundred thousand in bitcoin…"

"And…?"

"Will you let her finish, Princess?"

"David intimated that things have heated up. That entities are becoming desperate to monetize the process…"

"And…?"

"Jeez, Princess, let her finish."

"That includes us, Evelyn."

"Translation—we probably don't have to work so hard looking for the bad guys because they might be coming for us. And we need to get ready for that," Gwen said.

Chapter Two

Barry was running late, so instead of making coffee, he rinsed out his thermos and filled it with lemonade. His daughters had finally listened to him and agreed to help their neighbors Jen and Claire earn funds for their team fencing trip. Making lemonade and assisting neighbors was the type of regular activity his daughters should do more often. After a year of super-powers, knife-fights, and miracle cures, a lemonade stand was a welcomed respite.

Barry stepped off the elevator and gritted his teeth for what was to come. The company's servers had crashed a few months back. Now Barry as the VP of Infrastructure, was tasked with migrating everything to the cloud to mitigate future crashes. But the most challenging part of the project was explaining to leadership what the cloud was and how it worked.

"B-dawg! My main man. What's crackin?" Archie was the resident white dudebro that every corporate office was required to hire as part of a secret evil anti-affirmative-action plan to gaslight Black people. And Archie was always at the top of his game.

"Good morning, Archie." Barry quickened his pace as Archie walked with him. The last thing Barry needed was to have his morning hijacked by Archie spending twenty minutes telling him how busy he was. All Barry knew was that Archie didn't have super-powered daughters, one of whom got into a knife fight with a mercenary. At the same time, Barry had been shot at by a sniper while securing a serum that would stop his daughters from dying. So, Barry was busy too.

"Did you see the email with my notes from the last meeting? Are we supposed to be going Agile now? What, are we creating a parkour team or something? Ya feel me on that, right, B-dawg?"

Barry sighed as Archie followed him into his office.

"Yes, I did receive your email with return receipts. Many software companies have already gone Agile. But I… uh, have to prep for this afternoon's meeting, so…"

"About that, B-Dawg, I just sent you another email with some suggestions on the roadmap. You know how leadership is, but don't worry, I got your back, playa."

It took everything Barry had not to roll his eyes. But Barry had more critical concerns, such as getting in contact with David. Barry knew David had taken advantage of the boys who helped them at the meet a couple of months back, and Barry wanted to ensure they were OK. Barry's mother died when he was in eighth grade. His oldest brother dropped out of college, eschewing a promising football career. His second oldest brother never accepted his basketball scholarship. They did that so the two younger Parker boys didn't have to go to a foster home. There was no way Barry could pay back that type of sacrifice. But he could pay it forward.

Three hours later, Barry was slumped in his chair. The meeting had been brutal, with a lot of finger-pointing and no ownership, and Archie was the primary culprit. Typical corporate chicanery, and it was exhausting. To help him unwind, Barry accessed the private server Ana had set up to watch his daughters' sparring matches. One of the dumbest things that Barry had ever done was smuggle some smart virus for his former friend David. He had swallowed the virus to get past airport security, but it leaked and changed his DNA and subsequently the DNA of his daughters. And not a day went by that Barry didn't regret that decision. Now, because of him, his uber-athletic daughters could no longer compete in sports, but that didn't mean their hunger for competition went away. So, he and Michelle allowed them to spar as a somewhat healthy release to channel their competitive energies. Watching them spar quickly turned into his favorite pastime. His daughters were amazing. Every match filled him with pride, which he imagined was not too different from how his brothers felt when their sons scored touchdowns. But it also reminded him that he was the reason the girls couldn't compete in the first place.

Ring ring

Barry hit the speaker button on the office phone. "Yes, Archie?"

"Hey, playa, whatcha doing for lunch?"

"Brought my lunch today. I have a couple more meetings, and I need to complete some slides for a client before I get out of here today."

"OK, B-dawg. Holla back."

Barry winced. He could not tell if Archie thought he was cool or knew that he wasn't and was desperately trying to be cool. But, whatever his motivations, the results were disastrous and cringeworthy. Barry was embarrassed for him.

Halfway through lunch, Barry started experiencing a euphoric high. He was eating the best turkey sandwich he ever had, and the lemonade had his tastebuds dancing the salsa. All his problems became minor inconveniences Barry could fix. He had a clarity of purpose. A surge of optimism allowed him to knock out his work in record time, view his daughters' sparring videos, and then check out a few sports cars online. The Parkers had a minivan and luxury car, but Michelle always drove the luxury car for some reason. They had a three-car garage, so a classic sports car from his father-in-law's shop would fit in perfectly. Barry whistled at the thought before diving back into his work.

Thirty minutes later, Barry had an intense headache and couldn't focus, which made him irritable. Barry thought that if he ever saw David again, he would kill him for what he did to his family. And Barry was putting his foot down tonight. He was driving the luxury car for the rest of the week. Also, he was sick and tired of his spoiled-brat daughters falling asleep in church. It was so disrespectful. Back in the day, if he fell asleep in church, his mother would get the strap. Headache increasing, Barry blocked out his calendar for the rest of the day and decided to head home early. If he was lucky, there might be some more of that lemonade left.

"Woah, look at the part-timer. Must be nice," Archie teased him on the way to the elevator, and it took everything Barry had not to punch him in the face. But violence wasn't the answer, plus there were too many witnesses. Barry ignored him as the elevator doors closed.

It took Barry over an hour just to reach his subdivision. Traffic was heavier than usual, and it seemed to be increasing the closer he got home. It got to the point that Barry found himself in a traffic jam two blocks from his house. Frustrated and craving more lemonade, he parked in a non-parking area, thinking he would figure out what was going on and come back for his car when the traffic died down.

Barry fell in with a group of people, all walking in the same direction. A young college-age kid began talking to him with a

California surfer accent. "Hey, dude, you already got your order in? Listen, I'd be willing to pay twice as much. Just let me know, bro," the surfer guy said, then winked at him.

"I'm sorry, what?"

"Come on, dude, the lemonade. But I see you trying to keep it on the DL. I hear you, bro, can't be too careful. I heard some dude already got stabbed."

"Sorry, I have no idea what you're talking about," Barry said, quickening his pace to put distance between himself and the surfer dude. The surfer guy caught up and then passed him. Annoyed by this, Barry started a slight jog and passed him again. This game proceeded as the surfer guy and Barry took turns passing each other until they were both in a full sprint, followed by close to fifty people chasing them.

Panting and sweating, Barry reached his front yard with his lungs on fire. He took off his glasses, put his hands on his knees while sucking oxygen, and promised going forward he'd start taking the stairs at work. After a few minutes, he gathered himself, leaned back, and was stunned at what he saw. There were two police cars parked in his driveway and two more parked on the street. A news helicopter was flying overheard like it was reporting on a crime scene. People he had never seen before were camped out in his front yard, having a good time drinking lemonade. *My lemonade!*

Scanning for his daughters, he saw Ana behind a folding table with Claire and Jen, filling orders for a line of people that snaked down the block and around the corner. Every neighborhood kid under twelve was running and up and down the line taking orders. Police escorted Gwen out of the garage while she pushed a large barrel of lemonade balanced on Ana's skateboard. Two clowns were walking up and down the line, entertaining people, one making balloon animals, and the other juggling. A local radio station's van was parked across the street playing the latest tunes and interviewing people. The entire scene was surreal. And not normal. Not even close to normal.

"Anastacia, what the heck do you think you're doing?" Barry asked, walking directly to the front of the table.

"Hey, buddy, back in line like everyone else."

"Excuse me? I'm talking with my daughter.," Barry said, challenging the police officer who was eyeing him.

"Officer, this is my father."

"Oh, sorry about that, Ms. Parker. Just trying to be careful. That last fight got pretty scary."

"And you are appreciated. Also, I made a special batch of lemonade for your wife to help with her back pains that she could take with her prenatal vitamins. And I emailed you a study guide for the sergeant exams next month, along with a couple of practice tests. Best of luck with that, but I am confident you will be fine."

"Oh, jeez, Ms. Parker. Thank you. Thank you so much. And if you or your grandmother need anything, anything, you have my card." The officer practically genuflected in deference to Barry's youngest daughter, which did not help his mood.

"Hey, Pops!" Gwen said as she scooped two pitchers of lemonade out of the barrel. "Ana, I think we need to up our price again. I mean, can't we do surge pricing or something? They can't get enough of this stuff. And we probably should order a port-a-potty too. A couple of dudes got arrested for watering the Ramseys' flowers."

Barry took off his glasses and rubbed his temples. This was the opposite of normal. "You two shut it down now! And I mean right now!" Barry said, pointing at Gwen and Ana.

"But Pops, we're killing it!"

Barry glared at Gwen, barely holding onto control, and Gwen took notice as she boomed to the crowd, "Party over. It's been real. You don't have to go home, but you gotta get out of here! And y'all need to stop watering the Ramseys' flowers! There are kids here!"

Two hours later, the cleaning crew that his daughters had contracted were leaving, and you would've never known that, not long ago, there had been people and trash everywhere. They had to call in extra police as people started rioting when they stopped selling lemonade. Which, of course, made the news.

Barry looked at Ana and Gwen sitting innocently on the couch as if they couldn't comprehend what they did wrong. But he had a better handle on things now that his headache had dissipated.

Eve shook her head. "I told them not to do it. I told them you hated clowns," she said as she leaned on the stair railing with an acoustic guitar slung over her shoulder, which she had been torturing the family with. "I told them not to do it. I told them it was a bad idea. I told them…"

"Eve, do you mind? You know what, why don't you just go to your room and let me handle this? Thank you. Thank you, Eve. Bye. Bye!" Barry watched until his oldest disappeared up the stairs. "Now…" Barry continued as he started pacing, "can either of you explain how I got addicted to lemonade along with half the city?"

"Technically, you were not addicted, at least not from a chemical dependency perspective," Ana offered.

"Technically, I had a high and then crashed. How is that not addicted, but more importantly, why would you do this?"

"Well, endorphins provided you a euphoric high, probably because the batch you consumed was more… uh, concentrated than the batch consumed by our customers."

"Yeah, Pops, you drank that uncut lemonade. That pure stuff."

Barry started rubbing his temples. "This is not OK. Low profile, remember? Causing a neighborhood riot and making the news is not low profile. And why the heck would you put endorphins in lemonade?"

"Father, you are hilarious. Your pituitary gland released the endorphins that gave you that euphoric high. The lemonade just induced the pituitary gland to release the endorphins. But no worries. You seem to be stabilized now."

"Child, what is wrong with you? And what do you mean, no worries? Did you have some?"

"Oh heavens, no, Father. That would have been ill-advised."

"I did. It was delicious," Gwen said, smacking her lips.

Barry shook his head. "Girls, I know you're going through a lot, and I know it's not fair, but really? I mean, not causing a riot and staying off the news is not a high bar."

"But Pops, you said we should help Jen and Claire with their lemonade stand? And now their entire fencing team is going to Cali for the tournament!"

"The entire team? How much did your little enterprise make?"

"After expenses, we cleared thirty-five thousand dollars and ninety-seven cents."

"What? From selling lemonade?"

"But Pops, it's really good lemonade."

"I'm home! Where are my hugs?" Michelle yelled from the kitchen.

Barry shook his head. He had been thinking of having his daughters help him locate David. Unfortunately, it was painfully obvious they lacked the maturity and discipline for such a delicate operation. Maybe the lemonade was a sign. His daughters were young girls who needed protection despite their powers. He would go about his task alone.

"Hey babe, is everything OK? And did I see our minivan being towed?"

Chapter Three

"You stay rockin afro puffs," Gwen said as she and Ana sat at the breakfast bar the morning before the first day of school. "And yo, dork, you are like a billionaire, so can't you put a stylist on payroll or something? Because them pants ain't it."

"I acknowledge my hair and sartorial flair are not for everyone; however, they do serve a purpose. I can express my individuality stylistically. Also, being a non-conformist, and I admit being considered different, leads people not to take me seriously, enabling me to hide in plain sight. Something I'm sure you can appreciate. And, these are parachute pants. They were prominent in the eighties."

Gwen shrugged. "They should have stayed in the eighties." Gwen usually would have better one-liners, but she wasn't feeling it this morning. She had stayed up late planning with Ana after sparring Eve. She was glad eating breakfast didn't take up as much time anymore. After they got the cure from David, her appetite spiked again like when her powers first manifested. Except this time, she didn't gain any weight. Her weight stayed right around three hundred and fifty pounds. But she experienced three weeks of intense skin itching that came and went with no predictable pattern. She was also shedding dry skin like a snake. Thankfully, the itching had stopped, and her appetite returned to normal. Or at least normal for her. "Anyways… what it look like today? We good?"

"Yes, all systems are a go. But after David's last correspondence I have not been able to contact him. He appears to have gone analog, leaving no digital footprints or clues, which is impressive considering he's using bitcoin."

"Stay on it, because if the bad dudes get to him first, he's dead. And what up with the company you hacked into last year that tested it on the soldier? It seems they would be involved in all of this?"

"Last week's front-page story in the *Wall Street Journal* detailed that one of their employees gave information about fraudulent activities to the federal government. Their CEO and CIO both got indicted and they're scheduled to go to trial in a few months. They might be too exposed to take any undue risks. Meaning their competitors have positioned themselves to take advantage. But they are actively searching for David and anything that could lead them to him, which includes us as we previously discussed."

Gwen nodded. It was a lot to digest, even for her.

"Hey, the first day of school! Let's go! Let's go!" their father said as he strutted into the kitchen. "Grilling a few chickens this weekend, Gwenny, it's going to be the bomb!"

"Uh, Pops, no one says the bomb!" Gwen laughed. And although her father's grill skills weren't up there with her Uncle Benjamin's, Gwen was looking forward to the weekend because her pops could actually make some bomb chicken.

"Where is that child? She is going to make y'all late," their mother said as she walked into the kitchen, kissed their father on the cheek, and poured herself a cup of coffee.

"Eve! Let's go!" their father shouted before grabbing their mother, dipping, and planting a loud kiss on her lips. "And there's plenty more where that came from," he winked.

"Gross! I just lost my appetite!" Gwen complained.

"Evelyn!" their mother shouted. "Time to go!"

Gwen gathered up her belongings, shaking her head. Eve didn't rush for anybody. She kept her own time, and her parents' shouting wouldn't change that. Her mother looked at her watch as Eve came down the stairs. Eve took her time, like she was Cinderella going to the ball but dressed like she was going to the club. Gwen almost spit out her orange juice as she sat back to watch the show.

"You must be out of your eva-loving mind!" their father said, almost choking on his coffee. Eve was wearing a form-fitting pink blouse and tight black knit skirt that stopped just below her knees, and a pair of her mother's red bottom shoes. The girl had lost it.

"Oh, so you think you are grown now?" her mother said, setting her coffee down and crossing her arms. Gwen wished she had some popcorn.

"What? I couldn't find anything else to wear so I just threw on the blouse and skirt you and Aunt Zora bought me last week."

Point Eve.

"Ahh, so you think you invented slick? Listen, child, these little games you're trying to play, I've already played them at a higher level. So, I'll allow you to wear your clothes, but you will not be wearing my shoes. So, take your tail upstairs and put my shoes back and hurry, child, you're already late." Game over.

Evelyn looked like she would stomp away, but her mother gave her that *You better not even think about it* look, and Eve's posture changed as she quickly went upstairs.

"Yeah! And don't even try to act like you mad about something!" their father shouted after her.

Eve came back down a few minutes later with the same blouse but painted-on jeans and flats, while managing to hold her head up high like she won something.

Their mother made the short drive to school, dropping them off in front of Eve's school, which had eleven minutes before the first bell. Eve's high school and Gwen and Ana's middle school shared the same campus, heavily influenced by Romanesque architecture. The campus more resembled an Ivy League school than a public campus. That was one of the benefits of living in one of the wealthiest zip codes in America and having donors and boosters with unlimited pockets.

"Enjoy your first day, girls, and let's try to get by with no distractions, meaning no fights, no pranks, and no financial shenanigans. OK?"

"No worries, Mom, Eve's jeans are too tight to kick anyone in the face and Ana already stole everyone's money. But I'll keep them both in check and report back at seventeen hundred."

"Bye, Mom." Eve hopped out of the car and rushed up the stairs to her new school, which was funny because Eve didn't like rushing.

"Mother, would it be too much to ask to drive the one hundred yards to our school entrance?"

"Yes, it would be too much to ask, Anastasia. A little walk will do you good. Get the blood flowing before school. Now off you go."

Ana stuck out her lip as she and Gwen got out of the car and watched their mother drive off. Eve's high school started forty minutes before their middle-school classes, giving them plenty of time to get ready. Over the summer, the girls didn't have opportunities to interact with their adversaries of the previous year, Lurch and Elvis, so the first day of school was an opportunity to gather intel on the bad guys. "OK, sis, I guess this is it. Let's synchronize our watches."

Ana nodded while adjusting her watch. "Vande says time is the most valuable and undervalued resource we have."

"Girl, if you don't stop quoting that clown, I'm going to smack you. Dude gave one speech about saving the bees and everyone thinks he can walk on water. He uses child labor like just all of them other gazillionaires. Besides, aren't you worth more than him now? And when do you plan on telling Mom and Dad that you're like a legit billionaire?"

"I am in no hurry. And as you mentioned earlier, the work we do requires a level of anonymity, which we would lose if the world knew my true net worth and technical aptitude. But I am looking forward to the day when I can be publicly acknowledged as the youngest self-made billionaire."

"Bro, you trippen. As smart as you are, and you act like you don't know what privileged means? How are you claiming self-made when you were born on third base? And on top of all that you have an artificially enhanced IQ? You better wake up, my sista," Gwen said, tapping her temple with her index finger for emphasis.

Ana didn't say anything as she pulled on the school door. It was locked.

"We have three minutes before the door opens," Gwen said.

Ana nodded, still staying quiet.

"What's up, dork? Nothing to say?"

Ana opened her mouth to say something, closed it, then opened it again. "I... I am just a bit confused as to why we are doing all of this? What is the endgame?"

"I get it, sis, you scared. I'm scared myself. But, on the real, doing nothing is not an option. I mean they are coming for us regardless, so we got to get ready. And the more info we can get, the more ready we can be, right?"

"Point taken, Gwendolyn, but again, what is our endgame? How do resolve this? How do we bring them to justice while ensuring our safety and anonymity?"

"Not sure, sis. We kind of making up the rules as we go. But we need you on this. We need that big brain, because if this blows up Moms and Pops could end up in jail. And you know how Princess is, she doesn't want anyone to know she has powers, like it might ruin her chance of being Prom Queen one day. She just wants to kick people in the face then disappear in the night and she wants us to schedule it like an AP class." Gwen laughed.

Ana remained quiet.

Gwen rubbed her back. "It's going to be OK, sis. I got you."

Ana nodded. "Just girding myself for what is to come. Napoleon Bonaparte said, 'Take time to deliberate, but when the time for action arrives, stop thinking and go in.' And yes, sister, I am ready to go in."

"You quoting a narcissistic boy billionaire who wants to rule the world and a megalomaniac who died in exile? You need to up your role-model game, for real."

Ana looked at Gwen sideways.

"What? Don't let all these muscles and good looks fool ya. Half of my classes are honors," Gwen said, turning her head when she heard a click. Mr. Jones cracked the door open saying, "Gwendolyn, Anastasia, the school doors are not scheduled to be open for another two minutes." He then closed the doors, folded his massive arms over his barrel chest, and watched from the other side.

Gwen made a note of his rudeness and filed it away for future reference. "Fatneck trippen," Gwen said, loud enough for Mr. Jones to hear. He didn't move, and Gwen looked away, thinking about how the day was going to play out. Her first day in ninth grade, but instead of enjoying it and having fun, she had to execute a plan with Ana to gather more intelligence on their adversaries. The first day of school and Gwen was already exhausted.

"How are you feeling?"

"What? I'm good, bro. You are just gonna have to pay me more for helping you clean up after your Franken-birds. And when those birds gonna start putting in work? We've had drones all over our neighborhood for weeks and your sciency countermeasures have done nada."

"This is your third request for a pay increase. The pay stays as originally negotiated and agreed to by both parties. Unless you care to clean the kitchen on my night? And there have been a few minor setbacks, but the countermeasures should be online in twenty-three days."

"Whatever, bro, but if it doesn't happen, I'm like really throwing you out the window. And you do know Dr. Frankenstein was killed by his monster, right?"

Ana sighed. "To equate a year of consistent breakthroughs in genetic engineering, cybernetic enhancements, and avian intelligence to Mary Shelley's novel is absurd."

"There's a book? I was talking about the movie."

The doors clicked, and Mr. Jones ushered Ana and Gwen in. Other students started arriving, and Gwen and Ana gravitated to separate and unequal social circles.

Five minutes later, Gwen was at her locker when Rebecca ran up to her. "Look! Check it out!" she said, modeling her football jersey. "My dad got it for me yesterday! He's a big fan!" Rebecca was a cute freckled-face girl who frequently covered her mouth to hide her braces. She was rocking the college football jersey of Gwen's cousin Walter. Which was identical to the jersey Gwen was wearing. Awkward.

"Ha! How cool is that!" Gwen replied as she smiled through her teeth. A crowd started gathering, and Gwen became envious of her sisters. Gwen felt trapped in a prison of popularity that she had built. And the popularity monster was insatiable, demanding Gwen say and do things to meet everyone's expectations. Pressures that Gwen didn't know how to refuse. Unlike her sisters. Ana only had a couple of friends, and Eve didn't care if she had friends or not. Gwen eventually relaxed as her classmates badgered her with questions about lemonade and neighborhood riots. Gwen retold the lemonade story. For the next few minutes, she was an average kid embellishing her summer adventures and enjoying the attention. But the truth was, Gwen wasn't normal. People were after her. And, kid or not, she had a job to do today.

Between the second and third periods, Gwen was staring at a toilet in frustration. She had tried to get it to overflow, but the toilet swallowed everything and asked for more. After using all the toilet paper in her stall, Gwen grabbed paper from other stalls, forcefully jamming it into the toilet. That worked. The toilet complained when she flushed it and overran. Gwen quickly scrubbed her hands like a surgeon, clogged the sinks with more toilet paper, turned on the water, and twisted off the faucet handles. Running out of the bathroom, she barely beat the overflowing water that chased her.

"Spider wide banana. The eagle has farted," Gwen whispered, casually leaning up against the lockers across from the bathroom. Gwen smiled as water rushed into the hallway to the terror of some girls who got splashed by a couple of boys unable to resist jumping into a puddle of toilet water.

"Gwen! Stop being a clown! This is serious!" Gwen heard Eve's voice in her earpiece.

"Roger that, Roger!" Gwen replied.

The bell rang as Ana leaned against a locker on the opposite side of the hallway and nodded. Gwen nodded back, smiling at the other students, who were having too much fun to leave for class. The principal ushered them away with help from both the security guards, Elvis and Fatneck. The janitor arrived, went into the bathroom, and returned after a few minutes glaring at Gwen. Ana gave Gwen another nod and slipped away.

When the halls cleared, the principal, Dr. Gupta, strode over to Gwen, flanked by the two security guards. "Gwendolyn, why are you not in class?"

"Hey, Dr. Gupta! How was your summer? Did you do any traveling?"

"Did you not hear my question?"

"Yeah, I hear ya, Dr. Gupta; we didn't do much traveling this summer either. Oh, snap! Did you hear my cousin is the running back at Big State? Peep the jersey!" Gwen said, popping her collar. "And wouldn't it be awesome if we had like a team spirit day? I'd be happy to chair it. Just say the…"

"Gwendolyn, stop talking. Stop talking and tell me why you're not in class. Now!"

Gwen folded her arms, shrugged, and started looking at the water still rushing out from the bathroom.

"Gwendolyn?"

Gwen didn't respond, instead inspecting her fingernails. She was in desperate need of a manicure, but her fingernails required special tools because they were as strong as bone and, of late, had gotten even stronger. Lucky for her, she had a super-genius sister who designed unique nail and toe clippers for her.

"I'm waiting…" Dr. Gupta looked like he was losing his patience. "Why are you not in class, young lady?"

"But, uh, I'm confused. Do you want me to tell you why I'm not in class? Because I thought I was supposed to stop talking. Remember?"

"Gwendolyn, just go to class. Now!"

"But I have to go to the bathroom!"

***

Ana melted into the background as students swarmed Gwen, peppering her sister with questions about Ana's lemonade. Catching herself slouching, Ana stood to her full height but immediately felt self-conscious. She had grown a couple of inches over the summer and was now a six-foot eighth grader. It didn't matter if she slouched or not; Ana was going to get noticed. And she was still skinny, especially when juxtaposed against curvy Eve and muscular Gwen. The summer workouts provided some muscle tone, but it was barely noticeable.

"Ana! Ana! Ana!"

Ana smiled before she turned around, already knowing Stacey was enthusiastically running towards her in ill-fitting clothes. Ana turned, and Stacey's eyes lit up as she barely slowed down before barreling into Ana, almost knocking her over.

"Oh my God! Your sister Gwen is crazy! Did you bring some of her lemonade? Did the cops arrest your father? Was SWAT there? I miss everything! Will your grandmother sign my mom's copy of *Time* magazine with her on it? Is Eve still going out with Tyler? Look, Ana! I'm down a couple of sizes! And since I didn't go to fat camp this summer, I'm taking jumping lessons! Ana, I'm jumping! Look at my horse! Isn't she beautiful? Oh my God, this year is going to be so exciting!"

Ana smiled as Stacey droned on and on. They had been best friends since third grade. Neither fit in—Stacey because she was short, chubby, and talked a mile a minute; Ana because she was tall, skinny, dressed funny, and hardly said anything. With other students not choosing them for group projects, they were almost always paired and quickly became friends and then besties.

Madhuri approached, smiling and acknowledging Ana and Stacey. They had met her in fifth grade. She was new to the area, a gifted musician, and socially awkward. They became the three amigos. But Maddy had changed over the summer. Last year Maddy and Ana were near the same height and body type. While Ana had grown a couple of inches and was still very thin, Maddy had filled out, looking more like a teenager. Ana looked away from Maddy's body, hoping that hers would go through the same changes one day soon.

"Maddy! Maddy, so glad to see you! You barely texted me back or returned my calls over the summer! Oh, look at my horse! Isn't she beautiful? And why do you have that red dot on your head? Oh, my gawd! Did you guys see Javier? His hair grew back, and he is SOOO cute!"

Smiling and laughing, all three friends linked arms and walked down the hall together. Ana enjoyed the moment of being with her two best friends on the first day of school and pushed everything else to the back of her mind.

Between the second and third periods, Ana met Gwen at the designated spot. With a nod, Ana slipped away as the Principal and security guards converged on Gwen. Using a key card she developed, Ana gained access to the janitor's office. She didn't notice any family pictures or personal items as she placed listening devices around the office. The devices were small and transparent, making them practically invisible. She left the office as quickly and quietly as she came and headed for class.

Later that day, Ana glanced around for a spot to sit at lunch that was consistent with her current status and flexible enough to allow upward mobility if her accurate valuation became public. Seeing Gwen, she wondered if it was intentional that the administration scheduled them for the same lunch period. Last year none of the three sisters shared a lunch period, but maybe their strategy this year was to contain the blast area. Gwen was surrounded by an eclectic group of students at the most crowded lunch table in the cafeteria, laughing it up like she did not have a worry in the world. Maddy was sitting with a group of orchestra students, smiling and talking and seemingly oblivious to anything else. But Ana was an expert in body language. She could anticipate before someone punched by the stiffness in the shoulders and tilt of the head. She could anticipate a kick by weight distribution and foot placement. It was a learned survival skill from sparring super-fast and super-strong sisters. She could also tell when she was being ignored like Maddy was doing her now. Maddy made the calculation to sit with students more consistent with her social ambitions.

"Ana! Ana! Ana! Over here!" Ana dropped her head to hide her smile as she turned toward Stacey's voice. Stacey was sitting at a sparsely populated table. But when Ana sat down, they were joined by three of her former candy customers.

Ana smiled as Stacey went in on her beautiful horse, lemonade recipes, and cute boys. While Stacey rambled on, Ana thought about messy birdcages, cybernetic enhancements, and mercenaries. She then shook it off and focused on the moment, detailing her summer of lemonade and neighborhood riots.

***

Eve kept her head up and walked with confidence, still mad at her mother for siding with the patriarchy in policing Black women's bodies and dictating what was appropriate. That battle was not over. Eve fumed then tried relaxing as she searched for some landmark to lead her to her friends. A few students noticed her and stared and whispered. Some even acknowledged her with smiles. Eve ignored them, and the students kept their distance. Eve's larger-than-life persona consisted of a seductive elixir of celebrity, wealth, and violence. Granddaughter of a Civil Rights icon and billionaire, with a track record for hospitalizing people that got in her face, provided Eve a level of notoriety and popularity that she didn't want. But she did appreciate the privacy it afforded her.

Eve steered towards the loudest buzz. It led her to the school courtyard, filled with the stereotypes and school tropes that students swore didn't exist but was always the mainstay of every school Eve attended. Cheerleaders were sitting with football players and other varsity athletes at the center of the courtyard. The next set of tables consisted of student government and drama types. Senior academics and music students followed that. The perimeter tables sat underclassmen, goths, gamers, and skaters. That's where Eve found her friends Amy, Toni, and Lucia, trying to look cool but instead looking out of place.

"Hey, girl!" Toni said, giving Eve an uninvited hug. Lucia followed suit. Eve instinctively tensed up. She was still getting herself acclimated to having friends and the ceremonial hugs that she guessed were required.

Eve forced herself to smile, saying, "Girl, you got your nose and tongue pierced?"

"I know, right! Lady Tremaine hates it!" Toni replied, laughing and sticking out her tongue.

Eve laughed. Lady Tremaine was the nickname Toni gave her stepmother, which was funny and mean because it was the name of Cinderella's evil stepmother. Toni was a trip and acted like she didn't know she was already winning. Being beautiful and rich was not enough for her. Toni had to reinvent herself almost every year. In grade school, she was a tomboy breakdancer. Middle-school, she was goth for a year, then a fashionista diva type. Eve didn't know what she was transitioning to next, but she knew Toni would do so on her own terms regardless of the patriarchy or Lady Tremaine. Or maybe to spite them. But Eve wasn't mad at her. Toni was sporting a mini mini skirt, had legs for days, and looked good. Eve just hoped Toni found whatever she was looking for.

"Whaddup, peeps?" Kang said, joining them with Tyler in tow.

Tyler embraced Eve, and Eve reciprocated. Eve was always receptive to Tyler's attention. But she quickly pushed him away. "Football practice this morning?" she asked, wrinkling her nose.

Tyler nodded. "Yeah, but the seniors stay trippin. They take all the showers and hold court like they royalty." Tyler knotted his brow while looking at the courtyard's center, where the varsity football players were sitting. His low-key slow melodic voice had more tension than usual, and Eve pulled him into her for another kiss on the cheek, forcing a smile that brought his dimples to life. Smelly or not, the boy was still fine. Eve then kissed him again to avoid any confusion from the onlookers.

Kang stopped kissing Toni long enough to offer his commentary. "Preach!" Toni and Kang were going at it like they alone. Eve felt both embarrassed and envious. Toni and Kang had liked each other for over a year, and Toni finally asked him out over the summer because Kang was either too shy or scared to ask her out. They had been inseparable ever since. Eve smiled, hugged Tyler again and kept her arm around his waist, despite the smell.

"But Kang been killing it at practice. Even got a few reps with varsity," Tyler said as he and Kang high-fived each other.

"You know what is," Kang said, dusting the dirt off his shoulder and doing an impromptu dance. Everyone laughed. Kang and Tyler couldn't be any more different outside of their mutual love for hip-hop and sports. Tyler was tall and lean with a colossal afro you could see a mile away and a light brown complexion. He had an easygoing, laidback flow. Kang was shorter, muscular, high-energy charismatic, and seldom stopped moving or stayed quiet. His mohawk haircut matched his personality.

The first bell rang, and the group dispersed, as it seemed everyone had separate classes. As Eve was walking away, Amy touched her elbow. "Hey, Eve."

"Hey, Amy."

"You playing ball this year?" Lucia asked, joining them, and as usual, Lucia couldn't talk without being inches away from Eve. Eve leaned back to give herself some space from Lucia's inquisitive brown face. Eve liked Lucia. She was tall, with broad shoulders and thick arms and legs, and always sported two long ponytails. Lucia also might be the friendliest and most unassuming person Eve knew. And that grounded her in a way that Eve admired. She just needed to be more mindful of Eve's personal space.

"No, uh, but we're good. They're just saying no sports for now." Eve shook her head as she lied. Her parents had told everyone that the sisters had a genetic disorder that precluded them from playing sports as a cover story. But the truth was it had been a long time since Eve thought about playing ball or running track. When their powers first manifested, their parents made them quit sports, and Eve thought it had ruined her life. But now, all she wanted to do was fight bad guys. Getting better at fighting consumed Eve. Eve's last fight, she considered a tie, and it was eating at her. She needed to put something in the win column fast. "But I've been keeping busy. My sisters and I have been working out and doing some light sparring."

"Girl, you look like it.," Amy laughed. "Check out the guns."

Eve laughed and flexed. Her arms did look good.

"We need you back on the court, Eve. Amy and I are making varsity this year and going to state!" Lucia said, getting in Eve's personal space again.

"I don't doubt it," Eve smiled as she took a step back. A pride of senior cheerleaders strolled by, making a point to look Eve up and down without speaking. Eve was a threat to the natural order of things. She was a sophomore with national, if not international, name recognition. That put her in the upper echelon of social strata most students would never reach. So, Eve could understand the cheerleaders' frustration—they spent three years climbing that social ladder only to have some upstart sophomore cut to the front of the line. Eve would allow the stares, but they better not try anything more than staring.

"What was that about?" Amy asked, watching the cheerleaders walk away.

"Eve, girl! They don't know about you! They have no idea, but they better ask somebody!" Lucia laughed, putting her arm around Eve. Eve breathed but didn't tense up like before. Lucia was referring to Eve knocking out Big John last year and sending him to the hospital, and putting Elizabeth's father there too with broken ribs. Eve was embarrassed by both of those fights. Big John was an overgrown boy with no impulse control, and the incident with Elizabeth's dad was Eve's temper getting the best of her. Eve concluded she was a bully. A cute bully with impeccable fashion sense, but a bully nevertheless. When Eve faced a real adversary, the result was less than spectacular. But she wanted another shot at the title.

The warning bell rang, and Lucia felt the need to hug Amy and Eve before she and Toni raced off, leaving Amy and Eve standing awkwardly together. "Really hoping you can play this year, Eve. I met the coach and she's pretty cool. She even asked about you," Amy said.

Eve just nodded and was about to leave before Amy continued, "And, uh, how are your cousins doing? I, um, started following them after your family's barbecue and looks like they enjoyed their summer?"

Eve suddenly saw Amy in a new light. "Girl, they a hot mess and stay in trouble, so, yeah, they really enjoyed their summer if you know what I mean," Eve said, laughing.

Amy laughed as well. "Yeah, girl, I know exactly."

After a brief pause and with Amy avoiding her stare, Eve asked, "You want me to tell them you said hi or something?"

"What? No, just making small talk, girl. Talk to you later," Amy said as she hurried away from Eve and quickly blended in with other students.

Eve watched for a minute before heading down an adjacent hallway. In middle school, Amy was on top of the world. She was one of those beautiful, tall, rich blonde girls that their suburb seemed to mass-produce. But Amy was also more than that. She was super-smart, athletic, funny, and didn't back down from anything. However, in high school, Amy was just an overwhelmed sophomore with acne starting over at the bottom. And, like most high-school girls, she was chasing after someone oblivious to her. But Amy would work everything out. She was resilient.

On the other hand, Eve had no idea what was in store for her or her sisters. Mercenaries, knives, and being exposed worried Eve at night, not acne, basketball or boys. Well, maybe one boy.

Chapter Four

"Exit my room immediately. I have homework I must complete and, as you are aware, I require an after-school nap before I begin my lab work," Ana said, covering her head with a pillow. As usual, Gwen had entered her room uninvited, making empty threats.

"Going with the lab work and homework excuse, huh?" Gwen said as she stood over Ana and repeatedly poked her with a finger. "As if you ever do homework, plus it's the first week of school. And you asked me to help you with your Franken-birds and ballistic testing for our uniforms, remember?"

"Apologies, but now is not a good time. I'll need to reschedule."

"What? My time is just as important as yours, dork!"

"I said I need to reschedule. I stayed up last night. Now please exit my room immediately."

Gwen stomped out of Ana's room without replying. Ana dozed off, only to wake when Gwen picked her up by her pants' seat and the back of her shirt collar. Gwen carried her over to the window as Ana protested.

"Release me at once! Unhand me! I am telling Mother! No! You better not throw me out the windowwww…"

Ana was panicking, and Ana seldom panicked. She felt it was a waste of energy and counterproductive. But she had never been thrown out of a second-story window. Panicking was in order, especially since gravity laughed at her protestations and taunted her by pulling her down faster. Ana saw Eve standing next to the air mattress their father told them not to use again. *Oh, how kind.* Ana closed her eyes and held her arms out, bracing for impact. She promised herself she would garnish Gwen's wages and put vinegar in Eve's makeup case. But gravity decided to toy with her by taking its time and increasing her anxiety. Something wasn't right.

"Oh! My! God! Ana! How are you doing that?!" she heard Eve shout.

"What is happening! I can't see from up here!" She heard Gwen shout from above her. "Oh my God! That's impossible! I'm coming down!" It sounded like Gwen jumped out the window.

Ana slowly opened one eye and looked around. Her arms were still fully extended, but they were about six inches above the air mattress. Confused, Ana opened her other eye. Eve was directly in front of her next to the air mattress with her mouth open and eyes wide. And Ana realized there had been no impact because she was levitating in the air directly above the mattress.

"Eve?" she cried out to her sister, which broke the spell as gravity reasserted its authority, and she continued her descent. "*Oof!*" She was definitely garnishing Gwen's wages.

Her sisters helped her up and bombarded her with questions as their father pulled up. And he had questions of his own.

"Oookay… so let me get this straight, you threw your little sister out the window?" their father asked as he cleaned his glasses on his shirt and appeared to be grappling with conflicting emotions. After being initially as excited as his daughters when he learned Ana could fly, his excitement turned to frustration when he was told how they discovered it.

"But Pops! Ana can fly! I mean like really fly!" Gwen replied, practically stumbling over her words in excitement. And after some brief experimentation, Ana could fly, although a more accurate description would be ballooning, as spiders do to travel long distances. Ana theorized that in her moment of panic, her body tapped into the earth's electrical field like a spider would to prevent her from crashing to the ground. Ana could not wait to practice this some more. And she was thrilled to have a new power that manifested itself physically like her super-fast and super-strong sisters.

"Ana, again, I am just amazed. I mean that is incredible. But I don't know how your mother is going to take this, so let me tell her first. And Gwendolyn, I heard you the first three times you said it. And my point is, Ana wouldn't have to fly if you wouldn't have thrown her out the window."

"But—but we had the air mattress so she wouldn't be hurt, or seriously hurt, or break anything, and you know it's all part of our training and…"

Their father took a breath and held up his hand. "Gwendolyn, stop. Just stop it! She is your younger sister. Your family. You are supposed to look after her. Protect her. At the end of the day when it's all said and done, your sisters are going to be all you have, and you need to act like it…"

"But…"

"Enough. Enough! This is exhausting. It's not funny, it's not cute, and you're much too old to be playing these childish games. You're a young lady. Not a child. No, no, not another word. As a matter of fact, I need you to go to your room until your mother gets home. From now on you are on punishment. And I really shouldn't have to say this out loud, but throwing your little sister out the window is just insane. I mean, what were you thinking?"

Eve raised her hand. "But Dad, if Gwen hadn't done that, Ana would have never known she could fly. I mean, that's the big takeaway, right?"

"No, Eve, the big takeaway is you girls act like this is a game. What if Ana couldn't fly? What if she broke a leg or arm or something? Or what if someone saw and put it up on YouTube? Again. We have to be careful. We all agreed on keeping a low profile, remember? No more high jinks, remember? Or am I talking to myself now?"

"But Pops, Ana can fly!"

Chapter Five

"Hey, Melissa! Today your first day back? You get my text in Europe? I have some wild ideas for us this year! They fell asleep and scheduled us for the same lunch period! You believe that?" Gwen heard herself rambling and forced herself to stop talking. Still smiling, she shifted her weight and waited for a response from her best friend and partner in crime for the last six years. They were standing in a busy hallway during the second week of school, and Gwen couldn't understand why Melissa was looking bored, but maybe she was jet-lagged. Melissa's elite travel soccer team extended their exhibition play in Europe, making Melissa miss the first week of school.

"Europe was good. Had a great time. Got a chance to sightsee between games and stuff. And sorry about not returning your messages, but you know how my dad is with schedules," Melissa responded with a forced smile.

Rebecca and Elizabeth approached as Gwen started to feel irritated but pressed forward. "Yeah, your pops don't play when it comes to schedules. Hey, did you hear about our lemonade stand? It was wild! We even made the news!" Gwen shifted her weight again. She waited for a response while Rebecca and Elizabeth looked like they were watching a bad horror movie. Gwen thought it was more train wreck than horror movie.

Melissa smiled as she waved at a couple of passing students. Gwen noticed she had a manicure and lost a little muscle tone from the last time she saw her. Her usually red curls were straight, making her look more like a wannabe fashionista than the tomboy who used to terrorize the school with Gwen. But her green eyes still had a hint of mischief, so maybe there was hope her old friend was still in there. "Yeah, saw the clips and stuff, it was some funny stuff. Hope you saved me some!" Melissa said with a laugh. "Well, gotta run. Catch you later, girl."

Gwen watched Melissa walk away and felt uneasy in a way she couldn't articulate. It felt like Melissa was leaving her behind. And not only Melissa, but a lot of her so-called friends thought they needed to race forward with grown-up clothes and boy talk. Gwen remained stuck. She couldn't move forward. She didn't know how and wasn't sure she wanted to. Gwen had enough grown-up stuff to deal with, including mercenaries, corrupt businesses, and stopping an arms race of super-killers. At school, she wanted to goof off and have fun with friends.

"Did you see that? Who does she think she is? And I hope she doesn't think that dress is cute," Elizabeth said as she and Rebecca gathered around Gwen in what they assumed was going to be a gossiping gab-fest. But they weren't Gwen's friends, because if they were, they would know Gwen didn't talk about people behind their backs. She was like her big sister and mom in that regard and preferred to address issues directly. And if she were going to gossip, it wouldn't be with someone who had on more makeup than a clown and clothes that were too tight.

Gwen waved her hand and dismissed Elizabeth's comments in a gesture that was out of character for her. Gwen needed to be patient with Elizabeth. Eve beat down her father last year, which led to the eventual separation of her parents. However, Gwen's grandmother did give Elizabeth's mom a job as a paralegal. She was also paying for her to finish law school, so all things considered, Eve probably did Elizabeth's family a favor.

"You OK, Gwen?" Rebecca asked, using her hand to cover her braces.

"I'm good, bro." Gwen smiled. She liked Rebecca. Rebecca could be awkward and inept at times, but her heart was always in the right place, and she never said a mean thing about anybody.

A few hours later, Gwen took her seat at the head of the busiest table in the cafeteria. The table was commonly referred to as the island of misfits because it was a hodge-podge of athletes, academics, creatives, and students who didn't fit comfortably in any space. Gwen started it a couple of years ago when she was in seventh grade and stopped a couple of ninth-grade cheerleaders from clowning some gamers. The gamers started sitting with Gwen and her friends from basketball and track and were soon joined by other students once they understood it was safe. It had been going strong ever since.

Gwen smiled, and as she sat down stuffed her mouth to the enjoyment and laughter of the table. Mid-chew of a bad cafeteria hamburger, Gwen spotted a patch of red hair and a yellow dress. She almost choked. Recovering, she slowly stood, clenched and unclenched her fist, and walked over to the table that Melissa was sitting at with Javier and some of his friends.

"Whaddup, Missy?"

Melissa, still seated, looked up at Gwen as her pale face became pink. "Oh, hey, Gwen," she replied before looking away.

"Yeah, so, uh, what's going on?" Gwen asked through a forced smile, focusing on slowing her breathing.

"Oh, nothing. Saw your table was crowded so Javier invited me to sit with him. No biggie," Melissa responded with that forced smile again. *No biggie?* Melissa had been Gwen's best friend forever. Now she was sitting with the reason Gwen and Melissa put hair remover in the boys' shower soap-dispensers in the first place. Javier, Melissa, and Gwen had all been good friends in grade school, but Javier became a jerk when they got in middle school.

Gwen scratched her head like she was working out a math problem and chuckled. Taking a breath, she said, "No worries, Missy. No worries at all. Enjoy lunch with your new friends. Football team sucks anyway."

"You're being a jerk!" Melissa shouted, jumping up, her green eyes blazing.

"You should talk!" Gwen shouted back, getting nose to nose with her. "At least I know who my friends are!"

"Friends? You don't have any friends; you have followers!" Melissa retorted. They were nose to nose and breathing heavily as their chests rose and fell in unison.

"Hey, it's cool. It's cool. Let's just chill," Javier said, jumping up and trying to get between them.

Gwen pushed him away, sending him flying over the table, drawing gasps from the other students. Javier quickly bounced up. "I'm OK! I'm OK! Just playing around, is all," he said, grinning on wobbly legs while pushing his friends away.

"Just leave, Gwen. Just go and hang out with… with your friends," Melissa said, while checking on a visibly dazed Javier, who couldn't stop grinning.

The cafeteria was quiet, and every student was on their feet. Then the whispering started. Angry, but not sure what she was angry about, Gwen stormed out. The other students gave her a wide berth.

Gwen headed to the locker room because she knew it was empty. Sitting on the bench, she buried her face in her hands. She had so much to deal with and didn't have time to worry about stupid middle-school games. People were trying to kill her. All Melissa worried about was pretty dresses and dumb football players. But it hurt. Her friends were pretending they were adults leaving Gwen behind. But Gwen had saved her sisters' lives, fought bad guys, and developed plans to expose multinational corporations. So, if everyone thought being an adult was so cool, they could have it.

Gwen heard the door open as students entered from the gym. She washed her face in the sink and inspected her red eyes. Gwen had sunglasses in her locker, so she hurried there before the hallways filled with students. She also had to be more careful. She could have seriously hurt Javier. Gwen put on the glasses just as the bell rang and the hallways filled. Her phone started buzzing with texts from so-called friends and Eve. Gwen didn't return any messages because it was nobody's business. But as she went to class, ignoring the stares and whispers, she kept replaying what Melissa said. *You don't have any friends; you have followers.*

Chapter Six

"Evelyn, right?"

Eve slowly and deliberately turned around, leaned against her locker, and folded her arms. "It's Eve. And you are?" She already knew. He was Mike Garoppolo or Mike G or QB1. He had a few names that all referred to the same person. The cocky senior quarterback who didn't have the arm strength to throw an out from the far hash. Eve knew football. She grew up playing it with her cousins. One of whom had a full-ride scholarship to a Big Ten school. Another was one of the top high-school quarterbacks in the state. Eve had mastered throwing a spiral and running a zig route in grade school, and she knew that, despite all his confidence and bravado, Mike G's game was lacking.

Mike G smiled and ran his fingers through his black curly locks so that his too-tight t-shirt could accentuate his biceps. The boy was tired, but she gave him an A for effort. "My bad, Eve. Name is Mike, just wanted to welcome the beautiful Ms. Parker to my school," he replied smoothly, spreading his arms wide and bowing.

Eve almost laughed out loud. The boy was cute with confidence but couldn't stick the landing. She nodded at Tyler, who was approaching from behind Mike G. He put his arm around Eve and kissed her on the lips a bit longer than he should have. Eve tried not to tense up. Two boys with more testosterone than sense were attempting to remove her agency and use her to define their territorial boundaries. She had done something similar last week; however, when Eve did it, it was different.

"Whaddup Mike?" Tyler finally said with his arm still around Eve. His tone put Eve on notice. Tyler and Mike were not friends.

"Whaddup, soph. Just hollering at Eve for a minute before practice. What's good with you?"

Mike G poured condescension all over the word 'soph' then threw it in Tyler's face. Smiling all the while. Eve rolled her eyes. She didn't have time for this. She had been getting texts about Gwen knocking out Javier and then throwing him over a table. Ana finally got back to her and let her know it was nothing as dramatic as the Internet and her texts were making it seem. Gwen still needed to text her back and settle down. Gwen had been all over the place lately, and Eve needed her to stay focused and keep her head in the game.

"I told you about that soph mess. You keep calling me that, we gonna have problems," Tyler spoke softly as he took his arm from around Eve and faced Mike.

"Whoa!" Mike said, laughing out loud. "Look at you! All swoll up like you about to do something. Be nice to see some of that fight on the field."

"Whateva…"

"Whateva? Alright, soph… oh, my bad, Tyyyyler, I'll catch you at practice." Mike didn't wait for a response as he turned and left with as much misplaced confidence and bravado as when he had arrived.

Tyler watched him go, clenching and unclenching his jaw. Eve grabbed his hand and squeezed it. Tyler forced a smile while Eve asked, "What was that about?"

"What? Oh, these suburban cats think they special. Ain't none of 'em half as good as your cousins. And on the real, Kang probably the best quarterback on the team. And I'm not saying that because he my day one, but half of Mike G's passes is straight ducks. But I guess if your daddy is a big-time doctor and booster, the talent thing is not required."

Eve squeezed his hand again. "You OK?"

Tyler shook his head. "My bad, Eve or Evelyn," he said, laughing, showcasing the dimples she loved so much.

Eve punched him in the arm. "Don't play with me," she said, but she was smiling.

"It's all good. Just, you know, with the long train ride, practice, homework it… it can be a bit much at times."

Eve hugged him because she didn't know what else to say. She and Tyler were from two different worlds. She was the pinnacle of Black privilege in America. Tyler was a stowaway. Stowaways used a friend's, teacher's, or coach's address to go to a better school. Tyler used Kang's address while the school looked the other way. It was a transactional relationship with stowaways showing and proving in sports, academics, or the arts. Eve hoped he wasn't checking for the exits. Not because this school was the best shot for him having a better future, but because he was her boyfriend and was super cool, made her laugh, looked good, and she liked the version of herself when she was with him. It might be her best version. However, it was also great that he was getting a quality education and a shot at a better future.

"Girl, you need to ease up on showing me all this attention. You know I got to get practice."

"Whatever ever, boy!" Eve said, laughing. "So what time are you coming over Saturday?"

"Early. Your uncle wants to get a good tailgating spot, and your gramps wants to leave early too. Oh, and, uh, Amy's coming…"

"Ex-squeeze me?"

"Yeah, Kang and I were chopping it up about the game and balling out in your grandmother's luxury box and Amy overheard us and was like, what time should she be there. And we were like stuck, because you know, it's Amy and…"

Eve laughed. "Amy is more than welcome."

Eve's older cousin Walter, the oldest son of her father's oldest brother, was playing in his first home game Saturday for Big State. Eve's grandmother had secured a luxury box for the entire family to watch. It caused some tension because her father's brothers always made a point of not taking any favors from her grandmother. But Aunt Alicia put her foot down, and Eve was excited she could watch her cousin build on their family's athletic legacy. A legacy she couldn't participate in and had to watch from the sidelines. But when all was said and done, her legacy might eclipse anything she could have ever accomplished on the court or the track.

"Eve, you good?" Tyler asked, as they walked down the hall together, arms linked.

"Yeah, I'm just thinking about how lucky you are," Eve teased.

"Girl you a trip," Tyler laughed.

But Eve was the one feeling lucky. The weekend could be special. But before that, Eve was going to speak with her sisters on being more aggressive with their planning. It was past time they took the fight to the bad guys.

Chapter Seven

Gwen fumed as Ana noisily slurped her slushie while she typed on her notepad. It took everything Gwen had not to slap the slushie out of her hand. "What's the deal, dork? People are after us, remember?"

"I am a nerd! And I would appreciate it if you stopped sitting so close to me while yelling in my ear," Ana replied as she scooted away from Gwen. "And thanks for reminding me that there is a high probability of a nefarious plot that seeks to monetize a process of creating super-soldiers that is dependent on us being captured and experimented on. It slipped my mind. Silly me."

"Both of y'all chill. But Ana, what's up with your counter-drone defensive system? Drones have been all over the neighborhood? And how are the uniforms coming? They were supposed to be finished by now?"

"Evelyn, time is finite. I do not have the bandwidth to go to school every day, spar and lift weights at night, do homework, help with the kitchen then do lab work while listening to the bugs in Lurch's office. It is overwhelming."

"Any updates on the bugs?" Gwen asked while unwrapping her hands from the too-intense sparring session she just had with Eve.

"Not really. Lurch and Elvis still want to quit but are terrified. And the fact that Elvis was present when Gwendolyn threw Javier over the table but didn't intervene suggests their new orders are just to observe."

Last year Lurch and Elvis had tried to ambush the girls a few times in clumsy attempts to get blood samples. But they were so inept Gwen was convinced they were just pawns being used or sacrificed to gather intel on the sisters.

"Why did you throw Javier over a table? That's not keeping a low profile. And what's going on with you and Melissa?"

"It was an accident! An accident! I already told you that! And nothing is up with me and Missy so stop asking…"

"Jupiter!"

"Seriously, dork, what is wrong with you?"

"Gwendolyn, as you suggested, I've been checking hospitals and clinics around the nation for anything unusual, and oddly the mercenary that Eve fought was discovered in Northern Virginia, dead."

"In Northern Virginia? How?" Gwen asked.

"By cardiac arrest. Which I would allow could be from an undiagnosed heart condition, but although possible it is not probable."

"Not probable is right. That super-fit muscular dude died of a cardiac arrest? Not buying that."

"See! See, that's why we need to take the fight to them!"

"Yo, Princess, you need to chill with that take the fight to them talk. You're treating this like it's a basketball game. It doesn't work like that."

"What doesn't work like that? Because if you think I'm going to wait around and be someone's victim then y'all got me messed up."

"This isn't about fighting in the street. This is bigger than that! All the sparring in the world can't help us. And Ana, you're going to have to choose! You can't do what needs to be done to get us ready and run all your businesses. That's why you don't have a lot of time."

"I know that! But that is no excuse not to train! Because take it from me, we are not ready!" Eve exclaimed.

"That's what I've been saying! And Ana and I do all the heavy lifting! Since you've become a born-again naturalista you spend more time on your hair than in the lab."

"That lab smells! I'm not going down there with all those stinky birds! And going natural means I must spend more time on my hair. You're just jealous!"

"No one is jealous of you!" Gwen said, jumping up. "And you keep saying you're going to help with planning but all you want to do is fight. And Ana, you're just as bad! You won't be able to spend all the money you're making if we're not ready next time! Maybe we need to go to the authorities or something? I mean, this is a lot to deal with."

"We went to the authorities! Remember when dad called the cops? What happened? Oh yeah, one of them cops tried to kill me. And what happened when we went to the doctor? Oh yeah, he's dead now! So, what we not gonna do is put anyone else's lives at risk because we're too scared and punk out. That's what we not gonna do!" Eve said, standing and facing Gwen. "It's us three! Period! We just need to stay committed so…"

"We couldn't even commit to Kwanzaa!" Gwen shouted.

"It has too many days!" Eve shouted back.

Ana stood and got between them, and for once, Eve backed down. "OK, Gwen, I get it. It's a lot. But we can do this. We can find them, and we can beat them. I know we can. But only if we work together," Eve finished softly.

Gwen exhaled. She still had her doubts, but they didn't have a lot of options. "OK, OK, Ana you spar twice a week cause you still gotta maintain them skills, dork. Princess and I will take turns listening to the bugs, but to be honest, I think whoever Lurch and Elvis work for know they've been compromised. And Ana, you still need to work on your flying every night. That's our secret weapon."

Gwen watched Eve try not to smile. "Sounds good to me. Anything else?"

"Yeah, we are not engaging with any bad guys or super-mercenaries without our suits being finished and the Franken-birds going live. We don't know what we're dealing with and need all the advantages we can get."

Ana and Eve nodded, but Gwen wasn't so sure. Even if they did discover who was after them, there was no guarantee they could expose the bad guys without exposing themselves. But Eve was right; it was riskier not to do anything. The best they could hope for was to find the bad guys and get as much dirt on them as possible. Maybe negotiate a truce or stalemate. Basically, blackmail the bad guys into stopping them from doing bad things. It wasn't heroic, but it was realistic.

Chapter Eight

"Bye, Ana," Danny said as he rushed past Ana, Stacey, and Madhuri as they were leaving orchestra class. The attention caught Ana off guard. Boys usually ignored Ana unless they wanted to tease her. She lacked the beauty and charisma of Eve and the dynamism and bravado of Gwen, so anytime someone outside of her small circle of friends paid her attention, it was of note. Ana was always the tallest student in her class, which, coupled with her penchant for clothes with contrasting colors and patterns, placed her outside of most social circles.

"I told you! Remember when I told you I heard Danny liked you! Remember that? And guess what else?" Stacey droned on and on, not unlike a metronome in a way that Ana found soothing. And as usual, Madhuri quietly slipped away. Maddy had been doing a lot of that lately.

"Ana? Ana! Are you staring at Danny's butt?" Stacey asked, laughing.

Ana felt her face become flushed as she dropped her head, saying, "What? Of course not! I was just lost in thought." Ana did have a lot on her mind. Her businesses had grown exponentially with her wealth. As such, they commanded more and more of her time, leaving her in a quandary. She would have to either scale down everything to focus only on projects related to confronting and finding their adversaries. Or she could cede some responsibility to help her run her businesses.

"I bet Danny is going to ask you out! I bet he is! And Ana, he is almost as tall as you! But you probably shouldn't wear heels. And guess what? Guess? I heard his older brother is in a band! How cool is that?"

Ana nodded. Being in a band was cool, and outside of Maddy, Danny was the most talented musician in their school. Leading one to believe there might be a genetic upside that could balance the right side of Ana's brain. Ana shook it off. Thinking of the potential genetic upside of her and Danny's imaginary progeny was not productive. She needed to stay focused on her lab work and her nightly flying sessions. She had managed to increase her speed and stamina significantly since her first flight. But gravity was vengeful and fought her every step of the way. The last thing she needed was to worry about whether a boy was going to ask her out. Even one as cute as Danny.

Later that evening, Ana headed for the basement after her after-school nap. Eve and Gwen stopped sparring when she came downstairs.

"Headed to the lab?" Eve asked.

Ana nodded. "Indeed."

"I cleaned the birdcages when I got home, and I need that money. And one of them Franken-birds pecked me, so I want hazard pay," Gwen said as she and Eve lifted a section of the mats that exposed the center of the hardwood dance floor.

"I will transfer the funds tonight," Ana said before saying, "Open Sesame." On her command, a small section of the dancefloor descended into a staircase. After Ana got to the bottom of the stairs, she said, "Close Sesame." The stairs lifted into the ceiling. Ana was now in her secret lab beneath the basement, or her Fortress of Smellitude, as Gwen called it. She thought both of her sisters were accurate in their description, given the foul-smelling air that assaulted her nostrils, causing her to cough. She needed to invest in a more robust ventilation system. The current one was not adequate for twenty birds.

"Lights." The entire ceiling gradually became illuminated. The ceiling now bathed the lab in fluorescent light. Ana put on one of the pristine lab coats that were hanging on a wall. The donning of the lab coat was ceremonial. She felt more productive wearing it and found it easier to focus. Ana smiled while surveying her hidden hideaway. The lab's dimension mirrored a large cargo trailer of the type that semi-trucks used to haul goods. It felt a bit cramped as Ana had to maneuver around two stainless steel tables directly in the center of the lab. One of the tables contained four robotic arms, two on each side, which helped Ana operate on the birds and other projects. Birdcages occupied the long wall opposite where she hung her lab coats, contributing to the cramped space.

"Too bright! Too bright!" the birds screamed as the ceiling lights intensified.

"Quiet please," Ana said, raising her voice. The twenty birds mumbled amongst themselves but quieted down. "Thank you," Ana said, grabbing the larger of two boxes on a table. She moved a fencing helmet off to the side to give her more room to open the boxes. The fencing helmet was inspired by her neighbors, who were on a fencing team—they would provide a needed addition to their suits without impairing their vision. Ana just hated that it was Gwen's idea.

Ana removed a Smith and Wesson model 500 handgun from the box and loaded it with armor-piercing rounds she retrieved from the smaller box. The gun was one of the most powerful handguns made. Gwen was adamant that the suits needed to withstand high-caliber rounds at close range and sniper rounds from a distance. The mercenaries had raised the bar.

"Guns are dangerous! Guns are dangerous! Guns are stupid! Guns are dangerous and stupid!" all the birds started shouting. Ana shook her head. She had invested millions to genetically modify birds and equip them with cybernetics enhancements to provide air support, surveillance, and counter-drone measures. She had yet to see a return on her investment. "I am working!" she shouted as frustration set in. It seemed lately the only time Ana raised her voice or lost her cool was when dealing with the birds. They taxed her patience to a level only previously achieved by Gwen.

The birds quieted down again as Ana placed the gun at one end of a three-foot rectangular transparent box. At the other end of the box was the suit material Ana had been working tirelessly on. Snapping the gun in place to a holder, she clamped the lid of the box shut. Pressing a couple of numbers on her phone triggered the gun, which emptied its rounds into the suit material. Most bullets bounced off, but one remained embedded in the material. Ana stomped her foot in frustration as she poked out her lip. *Not good enough.*

She walked past the cages to the other side of the lab. The birds became restless as she passed. Their cages consisted of black metal crates with electronic displays on the front and a water dispenser suspended from the top of each. The water dispenser made it easy to drug the birds when she needed to operate. A pipe attached to the sides facilitated food dispersal. Each floor was slanted back towards the wall, which allowed droppings to slide into the bin Gwen emptied earlier. Ana checked the electronic readings as she headed for her desk.

"Hmm… good weight game, Thirteen and Fourteen," Ana noted. She wasn't surprised by the twins' weight gains. She had spliced their raven DNA with a higher percentage of raptor DNA, specifically that of a ferruginous hawk, which, along with being female, could account for their larger size.

"Teacher's pet! Teacher's pet!" Number Three started saying, and all the other birds joined in. Outside of the twins, Number Three was the de facto leader and, according to tests, the smartest by a wide margin. But unfortunately, also the most mischievous.

Ana held up her phone. "I have a special treat if you can manage to stay quiet." The birds quieted, and Ana punched in some numbers on her phone, filling the trays with food. The sound of the birds eating as their beaks clanked against the trays was almost as loud and annoying as their complaining.

Continuing past the birdcages and tables, Ana plopped down in a plush leather recliner with a keyboard on each arm that faced a wall of nine flatscreen TVs.

"Guns are stupid!" Number Three shouted. Ana sighed and didn't bother to turn around. She interlaced her fingers, stretched her arms, yawned, and went to work. The big TV was at the center with two medium ones below it and three smaller ones on both sides stacked vertically. She started typing on both keyboards. The molecular rendering of her bulletproof cloth appeared on the big screen. Stock quotes from the Tokyo exchange displayed on one of the medium monitors and Ana's businesses' financials on the other. The three screens stacked vertically on the right showed the birds' DNA sequence, projected growth and intelligence charts, and the 3D model of their cybernetic enhancements. The three monitors stacked vertically on the left showed MTV's *Daria* cartoon, *Animaniacs*, and *The Sandlot*.

"Everyone goes out tomorrow. Seven, you have speed work. Thirteen and Fourteen, you have strength training. Three, I need you to work with everyone on else on lock-picking and coordinated attacks," Ana announced after a few minutes of studying the data.

"We're the strongest! We're the strongest!" Thirteen and Fourteen sang in unison.

"Teacher's pets! Teacher's pets!" the other birds complained.

"We'll fight! We'll fight you!" the twins shouted.

The most prominent and most robust birds' threat immediately shut the other birds up, except for Number Three, who replied, "You're bullies! You're bullies!" Ana ignored the noise as she continued her work. Eve texted two hours later, letting her know the basement was clear and it was time for dinner.

Ana ate dinner with her family, helped with the kitchen, went to her bedroom, and did more work on her laptop before going to bed. Her mother opened the door to check on her, and the last thing Ana remembered was her mother's kiss on her forehead before she fell asleep. Her alarm went off at one-thirty AM. Ana stretched, yawned, grabbed her fighting staff from the corner and the black hooded cloak laid across her desk.

Ana exited the house through the sliding glass doors in the kitchen that led to the backyard. The quiet fled back to the house, frightened away by boisterous crickets. She slid her staff into a diagonal sheath in the back of her cloak. Of all the weapons she experimented with, the staff had become her weapon of choice. It kept her sisters at bay, helping her mitigate their strength and speed.

Ana closed her eyes and slowed her breathing and heart rate, feeling the energy that surrounded her. Ana was right in her initial assessment that her flight ability mimicked the ballooning of spiders. This meant her body could establish a connection between the positive charge of the upper reaches of the atmosphere and the negative charge of the earth's surface. Ana opened her eyes and breathed deeply once she had tuned into the invisible negative and positive charges surrounding her. She rose a few feet off the ground, feeling the strain on her core as she held her arms out for balance. Once stable, she focused and rose until she was two hundred feet above her house.

Ana spread her arms and welcomed the cool night wind. She welcomed the solitude. She welcomed freedom. Most of all, she welcomed the challenge of her persistent nemesis, gravity.

Ana reoriented herself west, took a deep breath, and flew as fast as she could. Her cloak's drag limited her speed, so she adjusted horizontally to minimize the resistance. Flying horizontally strained her core as her body fought for balance while maintaining an equilibrium with the earth's electrical field.

She flew eight miles before her stomach muscles fatigued to the point she needed rest. She found herself directly above Eve's high school and landed on the roof without making a sound. Sitting crosslegged, she placed her staff in her lap and rubbed her stomach muscles with one hand while eating cookies with the other. A glitch in her software had her cloak oscillating between the grey gravel of the roof she sat on and its original black color.

Ana resigned herself to the fact that both her sisters were right. It was riskier to do nothing, and they should be the aggressors dictating the battlefield. And Ana was dividing her time between business interests and the prep work her sisters wanted her to do. But there was a shared space between the two. And there was nothing wrong with profiting from the technical achievements derived from said prep work. Two things could be true. Ana could care about doing the right thing and stopping the bad guys while also using it as an opportunity to create new verticals to increase her wealth. The two things were not mutually exclusive.

Ana stood to her full height. But if one took priority, it would be beating the bad guys. Everything else was secondary. Ana checked the digital display on her armband, which looked like an oversized leather wristband inspired by Viking movies. Ana noted she had traveled eight miles in fifteen minutes. A new record. But it still wasn't fast enough. Closing her eyes again, she charged her cells until they were ecstatic with potential. Holding her breath, she released it at once in dual explosions. She pushed against the negative field beneath her while she simultaneously pulled towards the positive field above her. She blasted into the air like a rocket. It was the first time she had succeeded in that maneuver, and it was exhilarating. After one second, her cells depleted. Her momentum kept her moving upward, gradually slowing. Ana clocked her initial burst at ninety-seven miles an hour, and she was beyond excited.

When she reached her apex, her cells had recharged, and she was able to steady herself after a brief but scary descent. She was one mile above the city. The sky was clear, the crescent moon beautiful, and the air unsullied.

Bzzz, Bzzz.

Ana checked her wristband. Three was trying to escape again, which was nonsensical. All the birds got out every day and always chose to return. The fact that Three would willingly return then try to break out was puzzling. She made a mental note to change the locks. The last thing she needed was Three flying around her lab unsupervised.

Staring at the moving lights of cars, Ana lost herself for a minute before refocusing. She unsheathed her staff and practiced. Ana worked on counters, combinations, attacks, evasive maneuvers, and acrobatics. She attempted to meld it all together into a unique flying fighting framework. Her audience was the moon and stars, but they flirted with each other and paid her no mind.

Thirty minutes later, she was exhausted and barely able to stay afloat. She pointed herself towards home and let gravity do its work. Gravity celebrated its win over the non-believer by pulling Ana down faster and faster, headfirst. Ana didn't fight it as the wind stole her breath and made her eyes water. She used enough energy to guide herself towards her backyard. Twenty feet before she hit the ground, she did a forward flip so her feet were first as her cloak opened into a parachute.

She touched down gracefully, smiling at gravity while catching her breath. *Maybe next time.* Tired but rejuvenated, she went to bed thinking about bad guys, software glitches, financial markets, and for some reason, Danny's butt.

Chapter Nine

"Hey! Am I the only one who hears the doorbell?" Barry bellowed from upstairs. Eve ignored her father and continued to read her book. It was early Saturday, and with Ana sparring less, Eve and Gwen had been going extra rounds and she was in no mood to move. Punching and kicking Gwen was akin to striking a brick wall. Eve and Gwen had also incorporated more grappling to mix up the workouts, and Eve hated grappling. Eve hated grappling because she hated people touching her. Besides, with Gwen's strength, once she grabbed Eve, the matches were usually over. But Eve was getting better at her scrambles and managed to take Gwen's back a few times. But she still hated it. Plus, the additional sessions initially gave Eve sore muscles and joints. She embraced this because she knew her muscles and bones were adapting and getting stronger, and the soreness eventually went away. But she still wasn't getting the door.

"Get! The! Door!" Their father yelled again.

Eve and Gwen didn't budge.

"Pitiful!" Ana exclaimed as she hopped down from her barstool and went to answer the door. "It's Grandmother and Tyler!" Ana yelled.

Eve threw her book down and picked up her compact mirror. She surgically inspected each one of her French braids to ensure they were neat and not frayed. She then patted and shaped the afro that the French braids turned into to ensure it was round and perfectly shaped. Gwen could hate all she wanted, but Eve was a proud naturalista.

"Princess, you are killing me!"

"Mind your business before I mind it for you!" Eve snapped while contorting to view her pink football jersey and designer jeans from every angle.

"Child, if you don't get out that mirror…!" her grandmother laughed, walking into the kitchen. "I swear you as bad as your mother. If y'all ain't got y'all's nose in a book, y'all got it in a mirror."

"Grams!" Gwen yelled, jumping down and hugging her grandmother. She was the same height as Gwen, but thin as Ana with a long slender face and majestic close-cropped crown of silver hair.

"Child, please! Not so tight! Feel like you been eating your spinach like Popeye." Their grandmother laughed again at her joke, which was something she always did. She was going to laugh at what she said, whether anyone thought it was funny or not. Eve hugged her grandmother after Gwen.

"Dig my new shoes!" Grams said, nodding at her feet and pointing one of her toes like a ballerina.

"Grams! You got Converse!" Gwen laughed.

"I got to keep up with you young 'uns!" Their grandmother was also sporting Walter's signature red college jersey, as was everyone else in the family except Eve, who went with pink.

"Hey, Tyyyllerrr…" Gwen teased as Tyler stood a few feet back in the hallway, his hands in his khaki shorts.

Eve cut her eyes at Gwen before turning to Tyler. "Hey Tyler," she smiled, noticing he kept shifting his weight from one foot to the other like he had to go to the bathroom. He exuded nervous energy, and Eve's radar went up. "Everything OK?"

"Can you come outside right quick?" he replied, still shifting his weight from foot to foot.

Eve cocked her head to the side and studied him without responding.

"Please?" he added, grabbing her hand and leading her outside. Eve could feel the excitement and enthusiasm through his touch. It forced a smile on her face. When Eve and her sisters got outside, they saw two cars in their driveway. One was their grandfather's 1967 white Eldorado Cadillac, or the El-dawg as the family called it. The other was an early model convertible with Kang in the driver's seat, grinning and profiling like he won the lottery.

Ana walked around the car, kicking the tires in her combat boots. "Hmm, a black 1970 Plymouth 'cuda convertible with tan leather interior. Excellent investment, Gramps," she said, nodding in approval.

"Child, you know all I drive is Cadillacs," their Grandfather replied in his usual gruff voice. He was leaning against his car with arms folded, sporting his ever-present frown. He also had on Walter's jersey over a collared shirt, and his black slacks looked like he spent an hour and a full can of starch on them. And, as always, his Stacey Adams shone like glass. Eve's grandfather didn't play with his shoe game.

"It's mine!" Tyler blurted out, almost giggling. "Check it. I've been working on it for the last three months in my spare time. I rebuilt the engine and everything. Put in a new sound system. Arman helped me with the bodywork. But your grandfather is a trip. He said if I did all the work in my spare time, he split the profits with me when he sold it! But he just straight gave me the keys this morning! I mean it's, it's just..."

"Oh my God! Tyler, this is incredible!" Eve exclaimed.

"Say what? Gramps, where's my new whip?" Gwen asked, jumping in the passenger seat next to Kang.

"But yo, Eve! No more trains! Lucia and I can be at school in like forty minutes. And I can stay late for you know, stuff like dinners or whatever..."

Eve laughed. Her boyfriend had a dope ride, and the possibilities were endless. Not even the drone that buzzed overhead could rob her of her joy.

"Let me get that door for ya," Tyler said, holding the passenger door open while Kang and Gwen climbed in the back. Tyler then ran around to the driver's side so fast he almost slipped. Eve laughed. Tyler had a rep for being cool personified, but this was the most uncool Eve had ever seen him act. It was cute. Tyler jumped in the driver's seat and cranked up the music to an ear-splitting, ground-shaking level.

Eve's grandfather slammed his fist on the back of Tyler's car. "Turn that hickity-hop mess down!" he shouted. Eve's grandfather was old-school and thought rap music was just noise by thugs in oversized clothes. But Eve was aware of her grandfather's rep. In some circles, he would be considered a thug or OG himself. He was a rent collector and driver for Eve's great-grandfather, and his name still rang out in the city for the work he did to collect rents and evict people. But he did like Tyler, and her grandfather did not like a lot of people. Including some family.

Eve's parents came out to admire Tyler's new car as her father's two oldest brothers, Benjamin and Brandon, pulled up. Uncle Benjamin and Uncle Brandon were super-cool, but Uncle Baldwin was the brother who shalt not be named. He was a debt collector himself of sorts, and lent his services out to the highest bidder amongst other hustles. He had spent most of his adult life in and out of jail, but now he was out and had been blowing up the Internet by using his athletic gifts in bare-knuckle street-fighting tournaments.

"What it do, fam? Whose whip?" Emmitt, the youngest son of Uncle Benjamin, asked as he whistled while walking around the car.

"It's Tyler's," Eve said, proudly hopping out of the car and hugging her newly arrived family members.

"Word? T-money, you rolling like that?" Antonio, Uncle Brandon's son, asked.

Tyler smiled and popped his collar.

Ten minutes later, the family was ready to leave when Amy's mother pulled up. Amy hopped out in Big State regalia, including a red-painted face and a big red foam finger. "Go Big State!" she shouted to everyone, drawing laughter and praise from Eve's family. The enthusiasm and face-paint seemed out of character for Amy. But a lot of girls acted out of character around Eve's cousins, the Parker boys. Especially Antonio, who was tall and had the broad shoulders and athletic build of the Parker family with the features of his mother, a beautiful Columbian woman with almond eyes and full lips. The boy was a looker and knew it. But as her grams said, the heart wants what the heart wants, and unfortunately for Amy, many hearts wanted Antonio.

Amy hopped in the car with Tyler, Kang, and Eve, while Eve sent a complaining and pouting Gwen back to ride with their parents and Ana.

It was over a two-hour drive and Kang, Tyler, Amy, and Eve spent most of it shouting over each other and the wind about their favorite plays from Walter's high-school days. Amy surprised everyone with her football knowledge and familiarity with Walter's high-school accomplishments. The girl did her homework. Eve shouted, laughed, and argued for almost two hours at the top of her lungs in her boyfriend's new car with two of her closest friends, and she couldn't have felt more special.

Halftime was approaching, and Eve was dispirited. Her family and friends were being catered to and pampered in a luxury sports box courtesy of her grandmother. They were effusive in their thanks, even her stoic Uncle Benjamin. However, the day wasn't unfolding as Eve had imagined. Tyler and her friends couldn't sit still, shouting and high-fiving each other or yelling at refs after every single play, and Eve felt left out.

"Yo, Princess; you notice our concierge is missing, and our server is on swoll?" Gwen asked, with Ana standing next to her.

"What are you talking about?"

"The concierge was all types of doting on Grams and kissing her butt, now she ghost? What's up with that? And have you peeped our server? Dude is rocked up like he should be playing middle linebacker even though he dresses like he is trying to hide it."

Eve gritted her teeth. She wasn't in the mood for any mess from Gwen. "The more you talk, the less sense you make."

"Listen, you think all the stuff I get away with is by luck? I've been pulling off pranks since before you were a twinkle in your daddy's eye. Or *our* daddy, but regardless, there are levels to this game. I know all the tells, and right now I'm telling you that dude is no minimum-wage server. He moved like a fighter and avoided eye contact. Dude got my spidey-sense going off…"

"What? Did I kick you too hard in the head? Moved like a fighter? You can barely fight yourself, so how would you know what a fighter moves like?"

"Oh, I get it. Tyler playing more attention to the game than you, huh? So, all that big talk about taking it to the bad guys only counts when it's convenient for you? But you do what you do best, Princess, look pretty and pout." Gwen turned her back to Eve. "Come on, Ana. If we hurry, we can be back before halftime is over."

Eve wanted to stomp her feet. As much as she hated to admit it, Gwen was usually right about this kind of stuff. "I'm coming, but you best mind your manners and keep your opinions to yourself," Eve said, shouldering past Ana and Gwen and rushing out the door. She wanted to get this over with and get back to the game and Tyler.

When Gwen and Ana caught up with her, she asked, "OK, where are we going?"

Gwen brushed past her. "Jeez, pay attention. We're going to the kitchen."

The sisters walked past other luxury boxes and an open bar area where the one percent were sipping flutes and munching on pre-cracked crab legs. The one-percenters didn't seem to notice the game was on. That annoyed Eve, but everything was annoying her right now.

Gwen walked through the double two-way doors that led to the kitchen. "Excuse me, sir, we're in suite 987 and we're still waiting on Wendy to bring us our pickles." Gwen stepped in front of a cart on its way out.

The man was barely able to stop the cart hitting Gwen. "What? What are you doing? You shouldn't be back here."

"But our concierge Wendy said she was going to get us pickles."

"Oh, Wendy? Josephine's suite, 987? Yeah, not sure what happened to her, but I just heard you're getting a new concierge. And you kids shouldn't be back here," the man said as he rushed past the girls in his all-white uniform and through the double doors.

Stepping back into the lobby, Eve said, "OK, I'll admit that something is off." And she regretted it immediately when she saw Gwen's smirk.

"Wow, don't hurt yourself, Princess," Gwen replied. "Now we have to get to the garage. That be the best way to get rid of a body."

"Get rid of a body?" Eve asked incredulously.

"Did you forget Dr. Jim? The mercenary? This is serious stuff, Princess. We need to find out what happened to Wendy and who did it and we need to do it as soon as possible."

"Gwendolyn's logic is sound and checking out the garage should only take seven minutes," put in Ana.

Eve stomped her foot. "OK, alright, let's just do it and hurry back."

"This way," Ana said, leading them to a stairwell that came out in the parking garage twenty-one flights down. Eve and Gwen followed Ana to the garage section reserved for employees. They stopped behind a utility truck with a full view of the freight elevator. She watched as two parking garage attendants loaded large barrels into the back of a waiting van. Eve got butterflies, and her palms became sweaty. One of those barrels could have Wendy in it.

Gwen exhaled. "Ana, you already hack the surveillance cameras?"

Ana nodded.

"Cool. In about thirty seconds do the loopy thing that they do in all the caper movies."

"What's the plan?" Eve asked, wiping her sweaty palms on her jeans. She was getting in game mode.

"Ana, can you give us a headcount and positions? Oh, and check if any of them have a unique heat signature."

"I will not be able to discern heat signature as I am using their surveillance cameras and they do not have that capability, but..." Ana talked as she typed on her wristband.

"But what?" Gwen asked.

"It seems someone already clumsily commandeered their camera system. But... there might be another entity. A skilled hacker. Extremely skilled."

Gwen took a breath. "Two hackers? It just got real. But Ana, if you reboot their system that will kick everybody out, right? And if so, how long before it comes back up?"

"Excellent suggestion. A reboot will kick everyone out. And I should be able to delay it coming online for nine minutes."

"OK, give us a headcount and positions and then do it. Eve, when Ana gives us the go, I'm going to draw their attention and you approach from the rear. Ana, you stay hidden, get your back against a wall so no one can approach you from behind, and give me and Eve a heads-up on any surprises. The last thing we need is someone sneaking up on us. And if we find a body, we all agree that we call the cops."

Eve nodded. She was ready. The sisters gave each other a hug and a fist pound and whispered, "For family," in unison.

Eve and Gwen then headed off in opposite directions. Eve maintained her cover while keeping an eye on Gwen, Ana, and the parking lot attendants. Once in position, she waited for Ana's signal. Seventeen seconds later, Eve's phone buzzed with an image of the parking garage layout and five red dots indicating headcount and positions. Gwen texted, *Go time! Ana reboot the system!*

"Here, boy! Come here, boy! Here, boooy!" Gwen whistled as she strolled from around a car toward the van.

"Hey! Hey! What are you doing down here? You are not supposed to be down here!" a parking lot attendant yelled as he approached Gwen. The other parking lot attendant jumped out the back of the van, and the driver got out as well. A small thin man who looked like a chef emerged from the hallway that led to the freight elevators.

Eve's view of the chef became obscured by the van. She had a clear line of sight of Gwen and maneuvered behind the parked cars to get closer. She slowed her breathing and wiped her sweaty palms on her jeans again.

"Hey! What's going on out here! Keep it down and get that little girl out of here!" the cook said, putting his hands on his hips.

"But I'm looking for my dog. Have you seen him? One hundred and fifty pound Rottweiler? Answers to Fluffy?"

"Listen, little girl, you need to…" The attendant stopped in front of Gwen.

Gwen dodged the attendant and kept walking towards the van. "Hey, what's in the barrel? Smells like fish and I love me some fish."

The attendant recovered and grabbed Gwen by the arm while the other attendant and cook blocked her path to the van.

Gwen yanked her arm free. "Let me go! I'm just looking for my dog, Fluffy!"

The cook held up both hands. "OK, calm down. Look, there's no dog down here. And no one down here has seen a dog. So, you have to leave."

"I'm not going anywhere until I find Fluffy!"

"James, we don't have time for this. Escort this little girl out of here so we can get back to work," the cook said.

Game Time. Eve stood from behind the parked car and quickly approached from the rear.

"Hey, there's another one," the attendant closest to Gwen said, pointing at Eve. "Must be a school field trip or something, but I hear ya, boss, I'll escort them back to the game."

The driver was closest to Eve, and as he turned to her, he reached down in his belt for something. Bad move. One step and Eve jumped in the air, and Superman-punched him in his chest. He fell back against the van and slid to the ground.

"What's going on? Why are these little girls attacking us?" the cook shouted.

The other attendant rushed over and Eve dropped to one knee, punching him in the stomach. He collapsed to his hands and knees, coughing and wheezing. Eve checked to see what the first one had reached for and pulled out a walkie-talkie. She stepped on it, crushing it, and then helped the attendant sit back against the van next to the driver so he could catch his breath.

The other attendant grabbed Gwen's wrist and tried to twist her arm behind her back. Gwen reversed it and twisted his arm behind his back but twisted it too far, and he screamed in pain. "Ah, my arm! Let go! You're breaking it! You're breaking my arm!"

Eve shook her head. She was going to have a talk with Gwen about her strength. Again.

"Aww, jeez, sorry about that, maybe you should just have a seat with your homies," Gwen said, leading the attendant over to his friends and sitting him on the ground as he cradled his arm. Eve was proud of herself. She had been able to subdue them without seriously hurting them or breaking any bones, unlike Gwen.

"The barrels?" Eve said, nodding at Gwen.

"Right," Gwen said, taking a deep breath and jumping into the back of the van. She picked up her phone. "Pops—wants to know where we are. He said something happened to the jumbotron and it's not working anymore. Oh, snap, Mom is calling now… Hey, Mom! Met some friends from school and got turned around. This place is huge! Yes, ma'am. Yes, ma'am." Gwen put her phone away. "We better hurry."

"I can't breathe… My chest… I think something is broken…" complained the driver.

"Dude, she broke my arm. My arm is broke," complained one of the attendants.

Eve knelt to examine his arm. "You'll be fine. Elbow is just hyperextended." Eve had learned a lot about minor injuries during the last few months of intense sparring sessions. "Everyone stop crying. I have to call my mom back."

"We're not crying," the driver retorted as he wiped his tears.

Eve gave him a look, and he went silent. "Hey, Mom, yeah, just saw your messages. Yes, we're both with her. Yes, ma'am." After putting the phone away, Eve looked at Gwen, who was still standing in the back of the van. "Can you please hurry?"

"OK, just give me a sec…" Gwen scrunched up her face and puffed out her cheeks like she was holding her breath. Eve was nervous to the point of nausea. She had never seen a dead body before, and her mouth went dry as she rubbed her sweaty palms on her jeans. Gwen made eye contact with Eve, nodded, and snatched off the lid with her eyes shut.

From Eve's vantage point, she couldn't tell what was in the barrel, but she felt guilty. Eve didn't know what type of impact looking at a dead body would have on Gwen and shouldn't have to know. "Do not move!" she told the men.

Jumping into the van, Eve took a breath and looked down.

"Wait!" the cook shouted. "It's not what it looks like!"

"We are so fired…" the attendant with the hyperextended elbow complained.

Eve fumed. She couldn't believe she was missing her cousin's first home game for this. These clowns were criminals, but they weren't killers. Frustrated, she kicked the barrel out of the van. It hit the ground, sending crab legs and prawns flying everywhere.

Gwen opened one eye, looked at Eve and the crab legs and prawns on the ground, then opened the other eye. "How about that…" she said, pulling off the lids from the other two barrels.

The cook turned to run. Eve jumped down, and in a few strides caught him, managing to kick out one of his legs from under him to send him crashing to the ground.

"What's in the rest of those barrels?" Eve asked Gwen.

"Um, more crab legs and prawns, some silverware, oohh, I think this is New York strip. Oh snap, rack of lamb. We should confiscate some of this stuff. You know, for our troubles..."

The cook rolled over and sat up, breathing heavily with an abrasion on his forehead. "Listen, it wasn't our idea!" he pleaded. "It was the new guy!"

"Yeah, it was the new guy!" the driver chimed in.

Eve checked her phone. Ana just texted the system would be online in three minutes.

Gwen jumped out of the van. "Newb guyb?" she asked with a mouth full of crab.

Eve slapped a crab leg out of Gwen's hand.

"Ouch! It was going to waste!"

"Pay attention!"

"I am paying attention! We're missing one." Gwen faced the men. "Can one of you brain surgeons tell us what happened to the fifth musketeer?"

"Hey, aren't you girls Josephine's granddaughters?" asked the cook.

"Oh, snap! You're right! That's the one that started a riot with lemonade! And I think that's the mean one that fights all the time," the driver said.

"No, no, no, that's the one that jumped her bike off the roof and got stuck in the tree. Had to take away my daughter's bike because of that video. But, yeah, the other one is the mean one, for sure," one of the attendants offered.

Gwen clapped her hands. "Hey, stop stalling. Where is the fifth guy? And where is our concierge, Wendy?"

"Oh, yeah," the cook said, snapping his fingers, "Wendy did have your box. She was bragging about it all week. She was psyched. But she had to leave early. Something about a fire at her house."

Eve and Gwen looked at each other. Gwen asked, "And the missing guy?"

"Uh, that's Riggins. He and another guy just started this week. It was Riggins' idea about the crab."

"Yeah, it was Riggins! It was Riggins and Smash!" the driver chimed in.

"Smash?" Gwen asked.

"Yeah, he came from the same temp agency as Riggins. They said we could make some easy money and wouldn't nobody know. Aww, man, my wife is going to kill me if I lose this job," the attendant with the hyperextended elbow said.

"Are you serious? Riggins and Smash? That doesn't ring any bells?"

Everyone looked at Gwen with blank stares.

"*Friday Night Lights?*" Gwen offered.

"The movie or the show?" the driver asked. "They were both great. You know, I played football in high school. And could've got a scholarship but I…"

Gwen clapped her hands again. "You guys are missing the point!"

"Oh, oh! I know!" one of the attendants said, raising a hand. "Riggins and Smash aren't their real names!"

"Bingo! Gentlemen, you got played. They wanted you guys to get caught and get fired. That way their temp agency can replace y'all and make more money. Look around. You don't see Smash or Riggins anywhere, right?" Gwen said with her hand on her chin like she was Sherlock Holmes.

All the men looked at each other, and Eve saw the light go on. "Aww, man, we're screwed! She's right, we got played."

"Yeah, they can replace us all with temp workers, so they don't have to pay any benefits or anything. Same thing happened at my last job," the driver said, shaking his head.

Eve and Gwen both checked their phones at the same time. The systems and camera would be back online in ninety-seven seconds.

"Yo, fam, I got you," Gwen said, holding up both hands. "Put everything back, don't say anything, and we won't say anything.

Hate to see hardworking people get played and taken advantage of. But on the real, this is your get-out-of-jail-free card. I hear any stories about me or my sis, I'm dropping dime and all y'all going to be wearing orange jumpsuits. We good?" Gwen said, gesturing to Eve so they could leave.

"Yes! We are so good! Oh, lord! Thank you! My God, thank you! I will never steal anything ever again!"

"Me neither. And I'm going to stop drinking too…"

Eve and Gwen quickly left, and Eve nudged Gwen with her shoulder. Her little sis was good at this stuff.

"We only have seven seconds to get to the stairwell before the cameras are online," Ana said as they approached her. The sisters maintained their cover between the cars as they rushed to the stairwell. Eve checked her phone. She had seven missed messages from her parents and her friends.

"Yo!" Gwen said. "The jumbotron is back on but it's playing *The Sandlot Gang*! You know anything about that, Ana?"

Ana stopped and started typing on her arm bracelet. "I've been hacked."

Gwen shook her head. "Ana, you stay being hacked. And they played us like they played the workers. They knew Ana would hack the cameras. They put down false clues to get us out the suite. I bet they wanted to see how we operated, too. Ana, can you check our suite for bugs when we get back and…" Gwen checked her phone mid-sentence. "Pops is hot. He thinks we hacked the system and started the movie. We're so dead."

Wake me before you go-go

Don't leave me hanging on like a yo-yo

Wake me up before you go-go

"Ana, answer your phone!" Eve shouted as they ran up the stairs.

"But it's Mother!"

"Yo, Ana, you need to hack the jumbotron and do a *Mr. Robot, V Is for Vendetta* thing and make up a group to take credit for the hack. Mix in something about… oh, do something like the tyranny of capitalism and the exploitation of college athletes," Gwen said between breaths as they continued to sprint up the stairs.

"That is a fabulous idea..." Ana said, typing. "OK... message posted... and the system will back to normal in thirteen seconds."

"And change your ringtone," Eve added as they stepped out of the stairwell onto their floor.

Chapter Ten

"Tyler, Toni, and Kang are here!" Ana yelled from the front door.

Gwen strutted to the front door to meet them. "Ahh, isn't this sweet? Teenage love," she mocked.

Tyler smiled. "Well, if it ain't the Gwenster."

"Hoi!" Kang yelled, getting into a fighting stance. The Parker sisters had been friends with Kang for years. They started the friendship in grade school when they ran for the same summer track club, and the bonds became stronger when they enrolled in Kang's parents' Tae Kwon Do school.

"Boy, you ain't ready!" Gwen countered, getting into the Crane stance from *Karate Kid*. Gwen was still mad that, despite the absence of proof, her parents still punished them for the jumbotron incident a couple of weeks ago. But Princess got early parole for her double date. And Gwen had been right about Smash and Riggins. They or someone else had planted bugs in the luxury suite and on jackets and purses. The Parker sisters were on someone's radar, and they were getting antsy.

Gwen smiled. It was hard to stay focused on anything else with her grade school crush standing in front of her looking and smelling like he did.

"My girl!" Toni said, rushing past Kang and embracing Gwen. Although Toni was in Eve's grade, she and Gwen had always been closer. They clicked. Both liked to test boundaries, albeit in different ways. And both had painted outside the lines for so long that neither appeared able to discern where the line was. With Gwen's powers, that could be dangerous for everyone in her orbit.

"Where you crazy kids off to?" Gwen asked as she linked arms with Toni.

"Dinner and a movie, baby. You know how we do it," Tyler said with his half-smile and dimples. Gwen couldn't hate. Her big sister had game to pull someone that fine.

"Well, someone better check on Princess. She's been upstairs for like two days getting ready and way moodier than normal. The girl needs Jesus."

"I'll go check on her," Toni said, vaulting up the stairs two at a time, which was impressive in her tight jeans and high heels.

"So, Gwen, you look good. Have you been working out? Or are you allowed to do that?"

"Kang, look at you! Toni ain't gone two seconds and you already trying to flirt with me?" Gwen purred, batting her eyes.

Kang laughed. "And it don't stop. But on the real, you good? I mean with your condition and all? My parents and uncle keep asking. They want to know when y'all coming back." Kang avoided Gwen's eyes as he spoke and finished with his head down.

Gwen got serious. "Thanks for asking, but we're good. Don't think we're playing ball this year or going back to Tae Kwon Do, but we're, uh, good. Just taking it day by day." Gwen was tired of lying. She was tired of doing research and planning. She was tired of sparring and lifting weights every day. Gwen wanted a break. She wanted to pretend she was normal for a couple of days, maybe a week. But she couldn't afford to, as Smash and Riggins reminded her.

The silence was smothering. Tyler coughed and moved away, giving Gwen and Kang space. Kang put a hand on Gwen's shoulder. His touch triggered something. Gwen became flushed and paralyzed with conflicting emotions. She forced herself to take a step back while brushing Kang's hand away and smiling. "Stop trying to flirt with me. You know Toni is my girl."

"There you go again!" Kang laughed. The laughter sounded forced, but Gwen was grateful for the distraction.

Tyler whistled, and Gwen looked to see Eve coming down the stairs trailed by her mother and Toni. Eve's hair had Bantu knots like Jada Pinkett in the Matrix. Her one-sleeve, dark orchid blouse was form-fitting and exposed one muscular shoulder. Gwen didn't know how Eve managed to have muscles and look feminine while Gwen felt mannish. It didn't seem fair.

Kang nudged Tyler in the ribs, and Tyler closed his mouth. Gwen sighed as her beautiful sister came down the stairs like a queen. She had knee-high soft brown riding boots, tight designer jeans with big hoop earrings, and looked like she belonged on the cover of *Essence* magazine.

"Hey Tyler," Eve said, giving him a hug and kiss on the cheek.

Tyler grabbed Eve by both hands. "You look beautiful, Eve…"

"Oh God, I think I just threw up in my mouth."

"Gwendolyn, not today," Gwen's mother said.

Gwen melted in the background and conceded she shouldn't step on Eve's moment.

"Hello, Mrs. Parker."

"Hello, Tyler, nice to see you. And I trust my father is not working you too hard at the shop?"

"Naw, not at all. Working at the shop is the best part of my day. And your father knows more about cars than anyone I've ever met. It's cool. Is Mr. Parker around?"

"He's playing pool with his brothers so they can strategize how to open a sports bar and rib joint without going broke. I mean, it's not like he's married to someone in finance," Michelle laughed.

Tyler laughed as well. "No doubt, but I tasted them ribs and please believe I'll be first in line if and when that happens."

"Where did Ana go?" Toni asked.

"She's hovering around here somewhere," Gwen chuckled, drawing sharp stares from her mother and sister.

"Mom, we have to get going," Eve said as she hugged her mother and playfully punched Gwen in the arm. "Me and you when I get home tonight, girl."

Gwen smiled despite herself. "Princess, take the night off for once. I promise to knock you out tomorrow."

Gwen followed them out the door as they loaded into Tyler's car. Gwen lingered in the driveway for a few minutes after they left. She was happy for Eve. Eve never had friends growing up. Having friends and being popular was always Gwen's thing. But it seemed there was a finite amount of happiness and popularity allowed. And the universe took some of Gwen's to give to Eve and did not provide

Gwen any of Eve's beauty or SWAG in return. Gwen shrugged. She did not have time to feel sorry for herself. Ana's intellect and arrogance gave her blindspot, so Gwen was working with her to game out how to set a trap for the person that hacked them. But it would be nice to take a break and go on a double date in a cool car.

Two hours later, Gwen was watching TV with her family. They were all sitting in the plush leather sectional in the basement at the opposite end from the dancefloor workout area. Gwen was sitting next to her mother and Ana. Ana typed on her notepad as usual and ignored everything around her.

Gwen fanned herself with one hand while she reached for the popcorn bowl in her mother's lap with the other. Her mother moved the bowl out of Gwen's reach. "No! You are not putting your sweaty hand in my popcorn. Get a bowl and I'll give you some or pop your own."

"Mom!" Gwen complained. But her mother was right. Gwen had worked out her frustration on the heavy bag and then went extra hard lifting weights before taking a long hot shower. Now she couldn't stop sweating. Her father had dozed off with the remote control in his hand because he was the only one qualified to operate it. Now he pushed his glasses up and reached for his phone. Her mother's phone started buzzing at the same time.

"Eve? Calm down. Calm down, sweetie… Yes… And you're still there? OK, we're leaving now."

Their father was already standing up. "Kang texted me. I'll be in the car."

Gwen didn't know what was going on, but she was going if it involved her sister. She stood up with Ana at her side. "Ana and I will be in the car with Pops."

Their mother frowned, then nodded.

Ninety minutes later, they were all back home from the hospital, with everyone seated around the dining-room table. The house was still, with the only sound being Eve's breathing and an occasional sniffle. Eve's face looked drained, and her eyes bloodshot. Gwen was close to tears herself. She had never seen her big sister so scared. So unsure. So… defeated. Eve was Gwen's first role model. Eve's tenacity and striving for excellence were superhuman before she had powers. And although they fought like cats and dogs, Eve didn't play if someone ever looked at Gwen or Ana sideways. For as long as Gwen could remember, Eve had always been her protector.

Their father cleared his throat after a sip of water. "Can you try again?" he asked. His voice was delicate and unsure, like the tone of someone walking in a minefield knowing the slightest misstep could detonate an emotional explosion.

Eve looked up for a second, and there was a fire in her eyes. That patented Eve's strength and defiance. It didn't last, and Eve dropped her head again and sniffled. Eve, the fighter, the warrior, didn't have any fight in her right now.

"Take your time, dear," their mother coaxed.

Eve took a deep breath and began talking without looking up. "We had just finished eating and were walking across the parking lot to the movie theatre…"

"Go on, sweetheart," Michelle encouraged again.

Taking another deep breath, Eve continued, "Tyler and I were holding hands, walking behind Kang and Toni. Then… then… I… can I have some water please?" Eve asked as she cleared her throat and coughed.

Gwen grabbed Eve's glass without saying a word and returned it filled with water and no ice. Eve didn't like ice in her water. That was important to Gwen right now.

With a trembling hand, Eve gulped the water down and set the empty glass on the table. One of the unique things about Eve's physiology was she seldom ate. According to Ana, Eve's body got the carbohydrates, proteins, and sugars her body required from carbon fixation. The flipside was this process needed large amounts of water and or sunlight to fuel the carbon fixation process. The more sunlight she got, the less water she needed, and vice versa. It was cool and the opposite of Gwen, who consumed between five thousand to seven thousand calories daily.

Eve coughed, wiped her mouth with a napkin, and started again. "Tyler and I were holding hands walking behind Toni and Kang… and, and then I got a tingling inside, like the one I get when my speed power kicks, but this tingling was more ticklish than intense.

So, I stopped walking and then Tyler stopped… I— I'm sorry, can I have some more water, please?"

Gwen grabbed her glass and returned it filled with water and no ice. Eve drained the glass and set it down.

"So, Tyler was looking at me, and I think he wanted to kiss me. He grabbed my hand and the tingling got stronger. And I didn't know what to do. I had the tingling and Tyler was looking at me so I… I kissed him. And the tingling exploded. I tried to pull away but, but I couldn't, at least, not right away. And then…" Eve looked at her hands. "…And then, Tyler… his lips, and both his hands were burned, and he like, seized, and dropped to his knees."

Eve got up and paced behind her chair as she continued, "So, I shouted for Kang and Toni, and we rushed him to the hospital." Eve stopped pacing and put her hands over her face, then clasped them together as she started pacing again. "The doctor said his injuries were consistent with low voltage burns. And I didn't know what to say, so, so I lied and said we were standing in a puddle with a wire running through it." Eve sat down and placed her hands in her lap and didn't look up.

Gwen exhaled. Tyler was going to be OK. He just had first-degree burns, which would heal on their own. And Eve would be OK too. Eventually. It was just a lot to take in for everyone.

After a few minutes of loud silence, Gwen said, "Well, as far as lies go, you could have done worse."

Chapter Eleven

"I'm working late, so your mother will be picking you up," their father said as Ana and her two sisters climbed out of the car Thursday morning.

"Moms takes forever! Can we just walk through the park?"

"No, Gwendolyn, and stop asking."

"OK, Pops!" Gwen said, shutting the car door. Eve was halfway up the stairs when Gwen and Ana started their trek across the parking lot.

"She needs to get over it," Gwen mumbled. "Tyler recovered pretty quick and she has a new super-power. She can like legit electrocute people! Now she's using what happened with Tyler as an excuse to not help with anything. And it was all her idea to take it to the bad guys in the first place! Are you even listening to me, dork?"

Ana yawned; she spent nights rebuilding her system from the circuit board up and incorporating new security protocols. Fortunately, she had an eidetic memory, so data loss was not a concern. Unfortunately, it consumed most of her time. And Ana was still mad at herself. When she hacked the football stadium's security cameras, she used a secure channel that the hacker slipped through. Novice mistake that she would never make again. "Yes, Gwendolyn, I hear you, but I am a bit tired of your constant complaining. Evelyn needs a bit more time and we should allow her that."

"It's not complaining if it's true. And this is serious. We fell into another trap. We're always one or two steps behind, and now we have to worry about Eve being all up in her feels."

Gwen had a point, but Ana refused to dwell on the negative. Her top flying speed had remained stagnant at ninety-seven miles per hour, while her stamina continued to increase. She was now able to maintain her top speed for thirty-four minutes. And the strain and stress flying put on her body sculpted her physique in ways that weight training didn't. She now boasted an impressive abdominal musculature that Gwendolyn referred to as a six-pack. And her burst now maxed out at two hundred and thirty-three miles an hour, but the burst only lasted one second.

"All I'm saying is I'm getting tired of her diva attitude. We don't work for her. And you know I'm pretty sure we've been made. Lurch and Elvis don't even talk anymore in their office."

Ana didn't respond as she yawned again. Rebuilding her system consumed most of her time. But when she manually re-entered all her data, she had identified the bug in her cloaking software, moving her closer to completing the suits. Hopefully, she could finish up Eve's sticks tonight, which would allow Eve to increase her taser range. Eve was consumed last week in mastering her new power. After the first couple of days, she could trigger it at will with a lot of effort and focus. But that wasn't good enough for Eve. She worked nonstop until it became almost effortless. Her new power generated seven times the voltage of police tasers. However, it used the same fuel source as her speed power, so when she used her shock power, she couldn't use her speed power for up to an hour.

"Yo, dork, you listening to me? Did you do a background check on the two new students? Roman and Aaron? Not to sound racist, but two Black students showing up at this school without the administration parading them around and bragging about how inclusive they are is suspect. And I bet they're the two boys from the meet over summer."

"Gwendolyn, enough. I do not have the bandwidth to run background checks on every student! I have been overwhelmed by rebuilding my system and trying to find the hacker!"

"Dork, all you do is complain about how tired and busy you are and all the while I bet you spend most of your time stacking chips!"

"You. Are. Not. The. Boss. Of. Me! And let the record show that all you do is eat and crack unfunny jokes while having flatulence!"

"It was the bean dip! And I'm telling you, those boys might be from the meet!"

"Stop giving me orders! The top priority for the last week was to help Eve understand and control her new power. You know that!"

"OK, sheesh. Maybe we need to get you an intern. See you after school, dork," Gwen said as she left to join her waiting entourage. Ana watched as Gwen seamlessly transitioned to popular mode and moved on with the crowd. At the same time, Ana remained charged from their conversation.

Ana exhaled. She needed a mental break. She had been working around the clock for the last two weeks, and her brain was on overload.

"Ana! Ana! Ana!"

Ana smiled for a minute before turning around.

"Oh my God! Our football team sucks! Did you see the new boys? They look scary, right? Ghetto, right? I bet they're stowaways. No way they live around here."

Ana's radar went up. But she was exhausted. Stacey needed pushback, but not today, and not from Ana. Today all Ana wanted to do was get through the day, go home, and crawl into bed.

"Where's Maddy? She's been acting weird. Oh, and look! I have some more pictures of my horse. Isn't she beautiful? Did I tell you I named her Brittany?"

Stacey's constant opiniated droning might be why Maddy had been scarce. But she was right about the new students. They did stick out. Most of the students at their school had an entitled naivete that was unique to exclusive environments. Not so with the new boys. Their innocence was gone, stolen by something their peers could only ponder.

"Ana, did you hear me? I said Hawaii! How cool is that? Have you heard from Tyler? I saw some pics and the bruises are all gone. Oh my God! Tyler and Kang are so hot! I'm going out for cheerleading next year when we're in ninth grade just like my mom and big sister."

Ring Ring!

The bell for the first period rang, and Ana and Stacey parted ways. Ana was alone again. She found it peculiar that, outside of Stacey and her family, her only social engagement was with birds, who complained about being underpaid and wanted to unionize. Ana sighed and looked forward to orchestra class in a few hours when she could happily ignore Stacey again.

"Bye, Ana," Danny said as he rushed past her while blowing his cowlick out of his eyes. He managed to navigate through a stream of students, slinging his violin case over his shoulder and balancing his book bag. His dirty blond hair went every which way, and Ana could not tell if he intentionally styled it that way or if he woke up like that. Either way, it was cute. She watched him avoid other students like his path was predetermined. Ana mused on whether he did like her.

"Uh, hey, Ana…"

"Yeah, what's up, Ana?" Jeff and Tom said as they stepped in front of her, blocking her view and path.

"Greetings, Jeffrey, and Thomas." It seemed middle schools had to maintain a consistent level of arrogance and tough-guy machismo. With Big John moving on to high school, Jeffrey and Thomas competed to fill the idiot vacuum created in his absence.

"Don't look so surprised, Ana. Just wanted to say that, um, you know it's a new year, so no hard feelings with you or your sisters, right?" Jeff said.

"Yeah, things got kind of wild last year. And we just want to make sure your sisters know we're cool so, uh, they could be cool," Thomas added.

Ana nodded. Jeffrey and Thomas had made the mistake of attempting to stuff one of Gwendolyn's friends in a locker last year. Gwen then humbled and emasculated them in front of their friends. Not long after that, Eve knocked out the resident middle-school tough guy, the biggest kid in school, and sent him to the hospital. The fig leaf they were extending was not altruistic but calculative. They wanted to dispel any residual bad feelings from last year's confrontations. "No explanations required. A new year is symbolic of new beginnings."

Jeffrey and Thomas both exhaled and smiled. Jeffrey said, "Thanks for being cool, Ana. And if… Hey! I'm talking!" Jeffrey pushed one of the Booger twins away as he attempted to say hi to Ana. The Booger Twins were best friends with Gwen. They were referred to as the Booger Twins because they were heavyset identical siblings and had an aversion to soap and water when younger. However, they recently took to bathing regularly and now styled themselves in golf-themed attire with bright contrasting colors. Ana approved.

"Keep your hands off my brother." Sammie stepped to Jeffrey. Or it could have been Dean. Ana had a hard time telling the Booger Twins apart.

"Yeah. Ease up on the little homie," the new kid Roman said, entering the fray.

"Hey, Roman!" the twins said in unison.

Smiling, Roman got directly in Jeff's face saying, "What it do, B?" Roman was one of the boys Gwen wanted her to do a background check on. At five foot eight, he was the same height as Jeffrey and Thomas, but with a stockier build. He had light brown skin and close-cropped black curly hair. His skin tone and hair texture would have made him difficult to identify ethnically if his last name was not Sotomayer.

Roman didn't acknowledge the twins, Ana, or anyone else. He focused on Jeffrey and Thomas with an intensity that took the wind out of their sails. It appeared their status at the top of the middle-school food chain was short-lived. Thomas lost the color in his face and backed away as if he had accidentally stepped on a rattlesnake. Sweat formed on Jeffrey's head as he seemed to shrink by a few inches, and his voice cracked as he said, "I don't think anyone was talking to you."

Thomas pulled Jeffrey's arm, and Jeffrey moved away like he didn't need much convincing.

"What's going on?" Javier asked, walking up as the forming crowd parted to make room then closed behind him like a trap.

"Whaddup?" Roman said, squaring up to Javier and looking him up and down.

"Do I know you, bro?" Javier replied, puffing out his chest and holding his chin up. He was shorter than Roman and with a smaller frame, but he had more fight than his two larger friends Jeffrey and Thomas.

Roman rolled his neck like a boxer, the way Eve did when she was ready to fight; then he laughed. "You wiling, B! Trying to sound all hood." He took a step closer, so he and Javier were nose to nose, and said in a low tone, "But, yo, rich boy, I ain't the one."

Ana found the situation curious. From Roman's stance and weight distribution, he knew how to handle himself. Unlike Javier, who had his feet too close together, his knees locked, and most of his weight on his heels. But this was Javier's school. He paid his dues and waited his time. Now he was top dog, and Jeffrey and Thomas were his friends. And the code dictates you protect your friends. It didn't matter if they were idiots.

The bell rang, and both Jeffrey and Thomas pulled Javier away.

Roman blew him a kiss saying, "I'll catch you later, homie."

The students dissipated with looks of disappointment while Roman turned to Ana. He still had that controlled intensity boiling just beneath the surface, and the hairs on the back of Ana's neck went up as her heart rate increased. She didn't know what would happen, so she readjusted her weight and noted the distance and spacing between them. Then she waited. Roman smiled, and Ana stood to her full height with her chin up, so she looked down on him. Neither moved. They were engaged in a contest of wills. One which would dictate who was predator and who was prey, and Ana was no one's prey. The bell rang, and neither moved.

"Anastasia, Roman, time to head to class." Ana heard the words of Dr. Gupta, but they didn't register. Nothing was more important than not turning away. A predator was sizing her up, and she could not let that go unanswered. Ana felt hands on her shoulder that turned her in the other direction, and just like that, the spell broke. Ana's face became flushed, and her breathing irregular. She didn't know what just happened and she went to her next class flustered and confused.

After school, Ana walked behind Gwen to meet Eve. Checking data on her bracelet, she noted she was behind in testing the latest cybernetic enhancement for the birds. The birds' beaks and claws didn't have the durability to bring down military-grade drones nor the strength to generate the required torque. Ana enhanced their physiology, giving them night vision, and made them physically stronger by bonding lab-developed synthetic muscle and ligaments to their bones. She increased their endurance by allowing their blood to carry more oxygen to fight fatigue poisons that were a by-product of high exertion activities. Ana also bonded her super-light, super-strong magnesium diamond alloy to their skeletons, including their beaks and claws. From her calculations, the enhancements shouldn't compromise their weight-to-thrust ratio, but that was academic until she could perform more field tests. Thanks to the robotic arms in her lab, the last operation only took seventeen minutes per bird, allowing Ana to finish all of them over the weekend. But Ana was having second thoughts on the ethics of her avian experiments so she decided to shelve any future operations for now.

"Can you hurry? Eve says she's in the bleachers."

"Thank you, but I read the text as well so do feel free to hurry without me." Checking other data on her bracelet Ana yawned and realized the status quo was no longer sustainable. She needed assistance. Ana brought up resumes as they made their way across the parking lot to the football field, which was on the other side of Eve's high school. Eve was sitting by herself halfway up the bleachers. A small contingent of parents and students were also in the bleachers, spread out watching football practice.

"Just talked to Mom, she's running late as usual and won't be here for another thirty minutes," Eve said. She had a book opened on the bench next to her with a notepad on top of it. Her energy and body posture let Ana know she was busy, so don't bother her. Ana was cool with that and walked up a few more rows. She yawned, stretched, and using her backpack as a pillow, laid down for a nap.

Eve interrupted her rest. "How fast did you go last night, Ana? I heard you coming in about two in the morning."

Ana opened her eyes and looked at Eve, who was waiting for a response. "Ninety-seven miles per hour. What were you doing up at that hour?"

"Practicing releasing my shocks," Eve replied, putting her head back down and the pencil back in her mouth.

"Translation: I was talking to Tyler!" Gwen laughed.

"Mind your business, Gwen. We just texted a few times."

"So, lover-boy still not calling you back, huh?" Gwen teased.

"I'm not going to tell you again to mind your business," Eve said, closing her laptop and looking at Gwen, who was standing a couple of rows beneath her.

"I'm shocked and amped from your charged response," Gwen laughed.

Eve set her laptop down, stood, and slowly said, "You must think I'm playing with you?"

"Woah, you volted right up there."

Eve took a step and got in Gwen's face. "Everything is funny to you, right? Tyler could have been seriously hurt and you're being a clown and making jokes."

"You and your bad breath better get out of my face, Princess."

"Guys?"

"What!" Gwen and Eve shouted in unison at Ana.

Ana nodded at the onlookers, who had stopped watching practice and started watching Gwen and Eve.

Gwen stomped a couple more rows down and sat with her back to Eve and Ana.

Eve looked at Ana for answers, but Ana shrugged, laid back down, and closed her eyes. Attempting to decipher what was going on with her older sisters at any given moment was a futile exercise.

A whistle that signaled the end of practice woke Ana. Kang waved in their direction and headed over, while the other players headed to the locker room.

"Hey, Eve, hear anything from Tyler?" Kang asked, waving at Gwen and Ana.

Eve stood up. "We texted a few times but haven't talked much. But I'm surprised he's not here. I thought he was cleared to practice?"

It was sunny and warm for the second week of October, and a sweaty Kang still had his shoulder pads on as he set his football helmet down on the bench. "Yeah, that's what Coach said, but he bounced right after school. Probably still embarrassed. I mean his lips still look a little funny, like he kissed a stove, but it's barely noticeable," Kang said as he unwrapped athletic tape from his wrist.

Eve didn't respond.

"I didn't mean that, Eve. I mean he's going to be OK. But you know T. He can be a bit of a diva."

Eve laughed, and Ana exhaled until she saw two more football players approach and noticed Eve's back stiffen.

"Hey, Eve…" said the one with thick black curly hair. His companion stood off to the side.

"Mike," Eve replied with ice in her tone, and Ana sat up. Her nap was over.

"Have you heard from your man? Oh, snap? Whaddup Kang? Didn't recognize you without you carrying all the water bottles." Mike laughed while looking back at his beta for confirmation, who nodded and grinned in approval.

"You need something, Mike?" Kang said, in a tone that Ana had not heard from him before. Ana stretched and yawned. This was not going to end well.

"Just checking on your boy. He has been missing a lot of practice."

"He's not my boy," Kang responded, raising his tone.

"Calm down, scrub, no need to get all kung fu."

The beta laughed.

"Kung fu originated in China, I'm Korean," Kang said slowly. He then leaned closer to Mike. "Time for you to bounce, Mike."

Gwen was now standing next to Kang with her arms crossed, and they were both a row down from Eve and four rows down from Ana. Ana walked down to be in a better position to diffuse anything that might transpire.

Mike's face changed from confidence to surprise to apprehension as Kang glared at him unblinking.

"You heard him. You clowns need to bounce," Gwen said, pointing her finger at Mike and his beta.

Kang pushed her hand down, and Gwen frowned at him.

The tension amongst the group was almost at the point of no return. However, outside of Ana, only Kang seemed to recognize that.

Mike seemed to reassess the situation as well. He put a conciliatory hand on Kang's shoulder pad. He then said, loud enough for everyone to hear, "I'm out, but nice job at practice today, Kang. You were spinning the rock."

The beta looked disappointed, and as Mike turned to leave, he put his hands on his hips and said, "You Parker girls don't look so tough." And it went downhill from there. Literally.

Gwen said, "Just leave already, tough guy," and gave the beta a light push. He tripped over the bench, and while falling back, grabbed Mike by the back of his collar. They tumbled down twelve flights of bleachers together in a mess of arms and legs.

Ana watched with relieved curiosity as they slowly untangled themselves. Mike had a silly embarrassed grin on his face as he avoided eye contact. He then looked at the bone protruding from his forearm and started screaming like Ana's mom at a Prince concert.

Chapter Twelve

"Starting left tackle and blue-chip All-American out for the season with a concussion and torn ACL. Starting quarterback out for the season with a compound fracture to his throwing arm." Gwen's mother's nostrils flared as she looked down on her daughter like a judge from the bench before handing out a life sentence.

Gwen sat shattered on her bed. She looked up at her mother, then back down, unable to look at the disappointment and anger in her mother's eyes. Gwen squeezed her eyes shut and prayed that it was all just a dream. That it never happened. But the vision of Kang yelling at her as he rushed to help his teammates was real. And excruciatingly painful.

"Nothing to say? You're hardly ever quiet. Well, I guess your two-week suspension will give you plenty of time for one of your snappy responses. And thank God the boys said it was an accident, because with your reputation you could have easily been expelled. Expelled!" Gwen's mother took a breath, smoothed her blouse, and readjusted her collar.

Gwen studied the carpet as the tears in her eyes blurred her vision. She wanted to shrink like Ant-Man and get lost in that carpet. Disappear and never have to think about superpowers, broken forearms, or Kang yelling at her.

"What happened! Someone, please explain to me what happened!" Gwen's father said, rushing into her bedroom almost out of breath. He didn't wait for an answer as he started pacing behind his wife. "Gwen, what were you thinking? Is this a joke to you? Do you think this is funny?"

Gwen felt warm tears roll down her face as her nose started running. She used her sleeve to wipe her eyes and nose, but they would not cooperate and kept leaking. She gave up and focused on the carpet again.

"The school said two weeks, but honestly, I don't see you going back there. You are dangerous. Maybe the fault is your mother's and mine. We wanted you girls to have as normal a life as possible, given the circumstances. Looks like we were wrong about that."

"I agree with your father. And we've discussed this repeatedly. Because of our family's profile, you girls will always be targeted. That's the world we live in. You don't think kids tried me when I was in school because of my mother? Teachers and other parents resenting me for who I was? I know your situation is more complicated, but with your powers, with your strength, when you don't turn the other cheek people end up in the hospital. Maybe this is our comeuppance for putting pride over safety. Maybe we've been enabling you instead of helping you."

Gwen's father took off his glasses, cleaned them on his shirt, and put them back on while continuing to pace behind her mother. "Gwen, it's not... Listen, we can't keep doing this. I mean, we're all trying to work through this together. As a family, or at least I thought we were. But the rules don't apply to you Gwen, do they? I mean, it's always something with you."

"Barry?"

"OK, alright. Get some rest and we'll talk about this later..." When Gwen's parents left, she cried uncontrollably. She convulsed with grief and shame. Her head started aching, and the room started spinning. She felt nauseous and curled up in the fetal position. Within a second, her pillow was a wet sticky mess of tears and self-pity. She tried squeezing her eyes shut again, hoping it would make the room stop spinning. She attempted to will herself back in time to when she was a little girl playing ball in her driveway with her sisters. But time denied her request. Time wouldn't allow her to escape the misery of the present. She was trapped and forced to replay broken bones and Kang's yelling over and over. Her visions tormented her until she fell asleep, and then it became her nightmares' turn to taunt her.

The following week, Gwen stumbled through a self-pitying daze. She stayed in her room, leaving only to eat, and only then because her parents demanded she show her face at dinner. Gwen received her homework assignments online. It was one of the only things that got her out of bed. She tore down her Wonder Woman, Serena Williams, and Candace Parker posters so her heroes would stop staring and judging her. Her sisters tried to check on her every day when they got home from school, but Gwen refused to open the door for them. She didn't need nor want their pity.

One evening at dinner during Gwen's second week of suspension, Eve said, "It's wild, but the team has won with Kang starting at quarterback. The entire school is hyped. Teachers have been giving less homework and everything. The school is probably thrilled that it might be known for something other than the academic decathlon."

Gwen listened and chewed. Eve was a good sister. But the Internet connection worked in Gwen's room. She saw what her classmates posted about her. Eve could save the happy talk.

"Does anyone at this table know anything about the birds that have been attacking drones?" their father asked, peering over his glasses at Ana.

"What an interesting question, Father. Why do you ask?"

"Yeah, interesting is one word for it. Another word might be coincidence. Which brings me to why I asked—one, birds attacking and bringing down drones strikes me as abnormal behavior, two, it only seems to be happening near the school and around our neighborhood, and three, you used to be obsessed with birds. Especially ravens."

"Father, I'm not sure I see the correlation. Ravens are territorial, so one could assume that the drones are infringing on their airspace, which happens to include the school and surrounding areas. Also…"

Ding-Ding!

"It's dinner time, for crying out loud!" bellowed their father as he went to answer the door. He came back with Toni, Amy, and Tyler.

"Hello, Mrs. Parker."

"Hello, Tyler. Isn't it a bit late for you?" Michelle responded, sipping her wine.

"I'm crashing at Kang's tonight. He's gone big-time since he's starting and wants me to drill him on the playbook."

"Hey, Tyler."

Tyler studied his shoes. "Hi, Eve."

"Girl, you have to come to see my birthday present!" Toni said, squealing with excitement.

"Mom?"

"Yes, Eve, you're excused."

"Mother?"

"Yes, Ana, you're excused as well. But do not even think about going to bed without doing the kitchen. Gwen, you go as well. I'm tired of watching you mope around the house."

Gwen followed her sisters and friends out of the house. It was the first week of November, the sun had already set, and there was a chill in the air. In the driveway, still running, was a late-model white Range Rover, fully loaded.

"What! What!" Eve laughed, jumping in the driver's seat. "But this was your father's car! He just got it brand new last year!"

"I know, right? Lady Tremaine put her foot down about me getting a brand-new car, so my dad gave me this and got a new Benz!" Toni said, doubling over laughing. Gwen smiled. The cold war and microaggressions between Lady Tremaine and Toni were legendary. However, Toni might find out, like Gwen had, that pushing the envelope to push the envelope only provided Pyrrhic victories. At best.

Toni bumped shoulders with Gwen and linked arms. "Want to go for a ride?"

Gwen was surprised by Toni's touch and took a minute to find her words before she responded, "I, uh, can't. I'm on punishment."

"Where is Kang?" Ana asked.

Tyler looked at Amy and Toni before replying, "He is trying to act all stressed now that he's QB1. He got his nose in the playbook. Just really big-timing everybody," Tyler finished, avoiding eye contact with Gwen. He was a good friend. A lousy liar but a good friend. Gwen shrugged, left her friends and sisters, and went to bed.

Gwen woke with the sun shining on her face. The house was empty, quiet. Her sisters were at school, her parents at work. She logged in to check her latest assignments and do her homework, ignoring messages from her friends. Or her followers, as Melissa put it. She then did her usual routine when she was alone. She unloaded the dishwasher, ate leftovers, and went back to her room.

She was in bed asleep when her parents woke her up. She turned away from them and covered her head, hoping they would go away. They didn't. Her mother sat down on her bed and began rubbing her back. The touch triggered her. She started crying and couldn't stop. She knew what was coming but was too much of a scaredy-cat to face it.

"Hon, you're scheduled to start school Monday. But the administration made it clear that this is it. Any more pranks or accidents and you'll be expelled..."

Gwen didn't respond, but the tears stopped. She was better than this.

Her mother pulled her covers down. "Sit up, hon."

Her father cleared his throat. "Listen, Gwen, let me tell you something you already know— your mother and I have no idea what we're doing. Raising Black girls in America is complicated and always will be. But those challenges become infinitely more complicated when you factor superpowers into the equation. We're alone on an island here. There is no support group or self-help books for raising super-powered Black teenage daughters. And the responsibility should be yours as to how you choose to define yourself and who you want to share your secret with. But, to date, you haven't proven you can handle that responsibility. And as parents, it puts us in a tough spot. We must think about the other kids you've hurt. Intentionally or unintentionally."

"What your father is saying is that we shirked our parental responsibilities because we were scared. And now we are suffering the consequences. We thought that at the end of the day this is your life and you deserve the right to choose how you want to be seen. But we might need to reassess, because part of who you are, or rather what you're capable of, has proven to be dangerous and our silence has put other children at risk."

Gwen didn't respond.

"Think about that, because the path we are currently on is not sustainable. Now, you're back in school on Monday and until we figure this out the most important thing for you to do is realize that your actions not only affect you but affect me, your father, your sisters... they affect everyone."

Gwen didn't respond. Her mother sighed, kissed her on the forehead, and got up to leave with Gwen's father. Before her father closed the door, he turned to say, "Gwen, you are no longer a child. You are a young lady and it's past time you realize that."

The door closed, and Gwen took a breath, staring at her bare walls. She looked at the Tae Kwon Do, basketball, and track trophies smashed in a box in the corner. She glanced at the dirty clothes strewn across her floor. She smelled under her arms, which confirmed she was overdue for a shower. Still uncertain and uneasy about her future, Gwen opened her window and let the cool night air kiss her face. She smiled. She would go to school on Monday. She would be a model citizen. She would prove everyone betting against her wrong. For her family, she would be a normal daughter. She owed them that. She owed herself that.

Gwen left the principal's office Monday morning flanked by her parents. They walked past Dr. Gupta, who had a pained look on his face as if he had lost a bet. After hugs and goodbyes, Gwen watched her parents leave before exhaling and heading to her first class. She looked straight ahead as the other students stared and gave her space.

"Ma'am, we're not going to fall for the banana in the tailpipe," Dean said, running up and grabbing her arm like he was a cop.

"How'd you get fired on your day off?" Sammie said, grabbing her other arm. The Booger twins could transition from one movie's snappy one-liners to the next without missing a beat and sound like the actors they were mimicking. Their skill came honestly, as their mother was a high-school drama teacher and mini-celebrity who once played Meryl Streep's daughter in a movie.

"I have eight different bosses, Bob. Eight!" Dean retorted.

"He doesn't know me like that, Gwen. I'll make him an offer he can't refuse."

"Hey, guys, my first class is upstairs," Gwen said as she stopped walking and pulled both her arms free.

Dean grabbed her hand and kissed it, saying, "I bid you adieu."

Sammie grabbed her other hand and kissed it. "You complete me."

Gwen pulled her arms free again and laughed out loud as she took the stairs two at a time. Outside of Eve, the only fight Gwen ever lost was when she stood up for the Twins. They were being bullied in second grade when Gwen tried playing the hero. It didn't end well, but Gwen and the twins formed a bond and would spend entire weekends laughing, joking, watching old movies, and the Twins' mother's old audition tapes. Now they were on the varsity golf team, sported wild outfits, and had more important things to do than watch movies with Gwen. They were funny, cool, talented, and loyal. And she didn't think of them as the Booger Twins—they were Sammie and Dean, and they were her two oldest friends.

When lunch period came, Gwen headed to the library. A few students were there studying, and Gwen found a secluded corner in the back. Unfortunately, the Librarian spotted her and made a beeline for her.

"Gwendolyn! It's so nice to have you back! And if you ask me, those football players had it coming." She smirked, revealing white fluorescent teeth and rotten breath. "And what did your doctor say? Basketball season is going to be starting soon, and I am hoping you can play."

Gwen's eyes started to water from the toxic fumes. Breath that bad had to mean something. Gwen thought about having Ana do a background check. But that was another life. Another girl. Gwen was just a regular, normal girl now with a big appetite. "Uh, probably not, Ms. Henderson. But thanks for asking. Hey, do you know if we have W.E.B Dubois' *Soul of Black Folk*? I need it for an assignment."

"Let me check! I love soul music! Huge James Brown fan right here!" The Librarian replied as she scurried back to the front of the library and behind the counter.

Gwen then proceeded to eat as fast as she could. She had picked that book on purpose. She knew the Dewey-Decimal-challenged Librarian would be confused, allowing Gwen to finish her lunch and escape.

"My, oh my! Did you finish all that food? Where does it all go?" the Librarian asked, returning quicker than Gwen anticipated and without mentioning the book.

Gwen ignored her while she chewed. She had almost finished her lunch of three turkey sandwiches, two bananas, two apples, and one protein shake. Gwen had lost most of her appetite and was eating light.

But the Librarian was persistent. "You have good muscle tone. Do you work out? You must, eating all that food."

Gwen looked the Librarian up and down and gave her a serious case of side-eye. The Librarian was stout and a couple of inches taller than Gwen, with ghostly pale skin and frizzy black-brownish hair. She had attempted to tie it in a bun, which the students called the struggle bun behind her back.

Oblivious or ignorant of what that side-eye meant, she proceeded to rattle on. "You know, I stay in shape by boxing. My grandad was a huge Rocky Marciano fan, who everyone knows was the greatest boxer of all time."

The Librarian's incessant chatter grated on Gwen's nerves. It was like fingernails on a chalkboard and set her teeth on edge. It seemed like she was bragging. "My grandfather was a boxing champ in the military. And he taught all his grandkids to box. But I was his favorite. I used to whoop up on all my boy cousins and make them cry."

Does this woman ever shut up?

Unfortunately for Gwen, the answer was no. She tried ignoring her for a couple of days, but it was torture. She tapped out and decided to try her luck in the cafeteria, which was the last place she wanted to be.

Gwen entered the cafeteria on eggshells. The roar and talking lowered to whispers and pointing. Gwen held her head high and walked to an empty table in the back. She gave nods to friends, or former friends, or former followers. Melissa still sat with Javier and the want-to-be jocks, while Elizabeth was in Gwen's regular chair at the head of the misfits' table. Everything was confusing, and Gwen just wanted to sit and eat. Her appetite had started to creep back up, and she was starving.

Gwen sat with her back towards everyone and looked at the empty wall as she chewed. Ana joined her, leaned into her, and bumped her shoulder the way sisters did. Gwen smiled and continued to chew. A shadow fell over her tray, and she looked up, to see Melissa smiling down.

"Uh, can a sista get a seat?"

Gwen and Ana slid down to make room for Melissa, who sat down as Javier also sat down across from them. "Kang is da man!" he announced. "Three straight wins! He is ballin' out of control! Now they talking playoffs! Not practice but playoffs." Javier laughed, extending his hand to fist-bump Gwen. Gwen fist-bumped him back, accepting the icebreaker. Javier and Melissa discussed the game and Kang's athletic exploits. Gwen closed her eyes briefly and exhaled. *Different. Not bad, just different.*

The next week the cafeteria became unsettled. Melissa and Javier started sitting with Gwen and an assortment of friends from the jock and misfits table, including Rebecca. The remaining students at the jock and misfits table took turns looking confused and defiant. Ana gravitated back to sit with Stacey and her friends.

"Yo! You missed a great game Friday! They lost and won't make the playoffs, but still! You talk to Kang lately?" Javier asked between bites at a table that had quickly become crowded in seven school days.

Gwen shook her head and lied, "Haven't had the time. Still getting caught up on homework." Somehow Javier didn't get the memo that Kang was mad at Gwen and not speaking to her.

"Cool, cool. Well, next time you holla at him, tell him I said what's up. Be nice to be on a winning team for once. Who am I kidding, it be nice to just win two games," Javier said, shaking his head and laughing. Kang and Tyler were good enough to carry the middle-school team to a four and four record last year. Everyone had hoped the team could build on last year's success, but those hopes faded once the games started.

"You ballin' this year?" Melissa asked as she stood with Gwen to leave.

Gwen shook her head. Tryouts had started last week, so Melissa already knew the answer to her question.

"Too bad. It's not going to be the same without me crossing you up every day in practice."

"Bro, you trippin', you know you ain't never crossed anybody up!" Gwen laughed. "But what the squad look like?"

"Good, not as good as last year, but we should be good. And hate to say it, but Elizabeth looks good. I guess with her father out of the house and her mother working she's doing whatever she wants. Have you guys talked?"

"A little. We have honors math and honors English together," Gwen replied, throwing away her trash in front of an observant Elvis. Gwen had mixed feelings about Elizabeth. She still felt terrible that Eve put her dad in the hospital, which led to her parents' separation. But Gwen's grandmother also gave Elizabeth's mom a job as a paralegal in one of the country's most prestigious law firms. Her grandmother also was paying for her to finish her law degree. Debt paid.

"That girl a trip. She thinks she's big-time now. Look, check her out, I see her looking at us on the sly. She needs to come sit with the playas and quit the hatas." Melissa laughed.

Gwen laughed as well. "Girl, that might have been the corniest thing you've ever said." Ana tapped her on the shoulder, gesturing for them to speak. "S'cuse me for a second, peeps," Gwen said, stepping away. "What's up, sis?"

"I have developed a new weight set for you that I believe you will be pleased with. The concept was inspired by my flying. And you will also be pleased to know that I can now maintain my top flight speed for sixty-one minutes. Wind resistance notwithstanding."

"Why are you telling me this?" Gwen asked, glancing back at Melissa and Javier, who were waiting for her. Javier had somehow managed to tell everyone but Gwen that he liked her and was going to ask her out but he had yet to pull the trigger. Gwen was still figuring out how she felt about Javier but she was anxious to get back to her friends.

"Now that your spirits are up, I assume you will be rejoining training, which will provide me a much-needed reprieve from sparring Eve."

Gwen shook her head. "I'm through with all that, bro. You find out who's after us, cool. I'm all in. As far as all that training? I'm done." Gwen shrugged her shoulders and joined her friends, walking out of the cafeteria laughing and joking like a normal kid without a worry in the world. Gwen was through with the super-hero thing. That was another girl, another life, another time, and Gwen wasn't going back.

Chapter Thirteen

"A first edition print *Their Eyes Are Watching God*? No! Stop it!"
Eve shouted, unwrapping her last birthday gift. The family was
sitting at the dining-room table, already littered with wrapping paper
from Eve's other gifts. Eve cradled her new book. She knew her
parents worried that her aloofness, coupled with her fondness for
books, would stunt her social development and was why she didn't
have friends growing up. But now she had friends, and she never had
to pretend to be something she wasn't.

"Pops, so now that Princess is sixteen, will she be driving us to
school?" Gwen asked, munching on cake with frosting smeared all
over her mouth.

Their father took off his glasses and cleaned them on his shirt.
"Uhh…"

Bzzz Bzzz

Eve pushed the wrapping out of the way to retrieve her phone. "Hey,
Grams! How's Australia? Ha! Really? Oh, thank you, Grams. OK, I
love you too. Hey, Gramps! Arman? Why would… Oh wait, there's
the door."

"Got it," Gwen said, jumping up with a mouth full of cake. "Eve, it's
for you!" The family joined Gwen, and standing in the doorway was
the slender frame of Arman.

Arman was a mechanic in her grandfather's car shop, and he was
grinning from ear to ear with his boyish face and starter-kit beard.
"Happy Birthday, Evelyn Parker!" Arman always called the sisters
by their full names in his Persian accent.

"Hey, Arman. This is a surprise," Eve laughed.

Grabbing her arm, Gwen pulled her outside and pointed to a 1967
dark blue convertible Mustang coupe with a blacktop. It blew Eve
away.

"Oh! My! God! Gramps! Thank you sooo much! Best birthday
present ever!" Eve shouted into the phone. Eve's grandfather had a
car shop in the city specializing in refurbishing classic American

cars. He boasted an elite clientele consisting of professional athletes, actors, and rappers. Eve was in elite company.

Arman shook Eve's father's hand and handed Eve an envelope that contained registration, proof of insurance, and two sets of keys. He waited until Eve started the car before leaving in another car that was waiting for him.

Gwen held up the seat for Ana to get in the back, and she hopped in the passenger seat next to Eve. "Can we get some heat in this piece!" Gwen said, fidgeting with the dials. She then blew her hands and rubbed them together. It was windy and the first week of December, which probably meant it was cold. Eve checked the temperature on her phone to confirm. Eve usually took cues from her sisters on dressing appropriately for the weather, since her body had become desensitized to the cold. Gwen blasted the heat and music, and Eve drove her sisters around the neighborhood, dancing and laughing in her new whip.

Eve woke up early Monday with the hope of getting to school early. But her mother, who had to leave on a business trip, had other plans. She demanded to take pictures of Eve's first day of driving her car to school with her sisters. It was sweet, and her sisters were just as excited, but their mother took close to a thousand pictures, almost making Eve late.

Driving to school, Eve hoped that Gwen's excitement would make her rethink her no sparring or working out stance. Eve had been patient with her, but they had work to do. Gwen needed to get her head back in the game. Besides, Eve missed spending time with her. Gwen had the unique ability to be annoying and fun to hang around at the same time. Gwen was now spending more time hanging out with friends, and Eve felt off-center without her little sister.

Tuesday, Eve got up early to get to school, and not everyone was happy about it. "Evelyn, apologies, but are we not leaving a bit early for your first class?"

"Get in the car, nerd!" Eve snapped.

"Evelyn, we are a bit early, so would it be too much to ask to drop us off in front of school?"

"Get out the car, nerd!" Eve said while studying her face in the mirror. She looked good. Eve had on her favorite jeans, the ones that complimented her curves, and Eve didn't mind showing off her curves. She had paired the jeans with a snug, pink blouse that showcased her toned body and a black cropped leather jacket. Her mother's favorite Italian designer shoes, she borrowed, completed her ensemble. Eve could tell by how her sisters shivered that her outfit might not be appropriate for winter wear, but this was high school and being chic was paramount.

Eve headed for the library. Tyler was there with a couple of students from Eve's advanced math class. Eve had gone to school with the taller one with acne since fourth grade. He was always respectful and kind to Eve. He became exceedingly deferential after Eve knocked out a bully who had been picking on him last year. But like everything connected to the Parker sisters, the telling and retelling of that skirmish became more fantastical with each iteration. When it made its way back to Eve, she almost wished she had been there to see it because it sounded incredible.

Eve sat at a table three tables down but in Tyler's field of vision. She took out her books and stared at the words, waiting for something to happen. She thought she heard Tyler stand, but she kept her head down, trying not to smile.

"Hey, Eve, Happy birthday."

"Oh, hey Tyler. Thanks."

Tyler laughed, shaking his head. "Surprised you, did I?"

Eve smiled, closing her book. It was worth a try, "Have a seat."

Tyler pulled out a chair and sat across from her. "Guess you got your birthday present? Arman and I worked on it all November. We rebuilt the engine and did all the bodywork. Nice, right?"

"You got some skills. You good at anything else?"

Tyler blushed, looked down, and rubbed the back of his neck.

"Your mother leave for her business trip?"

Eve nodded. "How did you know?"

Tyler smiled, his crooked smile showcasing his dimples. "I can tell by them jeans."

Eve smiled back, batting her eyes. "Didn't think you noticed."

"Be hard to miss..." Tyler countered, looking directly at her.

It was Eve's turn to blush. She almost looked away but steadied herself and matched Tyler's stare. "Thanks. I'll take that as a compliment."

"It was."

Eve nodded. "So how you been? I've missed you."

"Miss you too, Eve. A lot. It's just… you know. A bit complicated right now."

Sighing, Eve sat back in her chair. "So we still going with the time constraints, huh?" Eve knew it was more than constraints. Tyler didn't understand what happened the last time they kissed, but he understood enough. He hadn't tried to kiss her since and had barely even touched her. That hurt. Especially for Eve, who had romanticized kisses. To her, kisses should hint at unbridled passions and the possibilities of promises left unsaid. But their last kiss had culminated in a trip to the emergency room for one, whose physical scars had healed but leaving the other with emotional scars that had not.

Tyler sighed and sat back as well. "Don't be like that. I've been grinding. Working at your grandfather's shop, homework, practice, helping with my little sister. And the thing is, I'm going to college. It sounds wild saying it out loud, but, yeah. I'm going. I'm putting my name on that. I just, I just got to stay focused. If I do that, I'll be Tyler Wilson, college graduate, first of my kind." Tyler laughed.

Eve laughed as well. "Check you out. And don't know if you've heard but I'm a pretty good student, and I'd be more than happy to help you with your math. And anything else…" Eve needed to chill. She was acting out of pocket and needed to slow her roll. But at the same time, there was nothing wrong with a girl shooting her shot.

Tyler shook his head, smiling. "So you want to help me with my math, huh? And anything else? And I'm supposed to focus with you looking like you do in them jeans?"

Eve smiled. She had to concede that Tyler was right. If Eve had some alone time with him, they would be studying more anatomy than math. And she was not going to be some Fatale and interfere with Tyler's ambitions. "Friends?"

"Always," Tyler replied as he stood and headed back to his seat with the math nerds, who both had a lower GPA than Eve. Eve tried to shrug it off, but her pain remained constant, and she couldn't balance the equation. She had her electric power under control now. She knew what triggered it and how to control it. But it didn't look like Tyler was going to give her a second chance to prove it.

Later that day, Eve joined Amy and Toni as they sat down for lunch. "Amy! Girl, what happened?" Eve asked.

Amy adjusted her sling and shrugged. "Dislocated my shoulder in practice, last night."

"Pleeeease! Jennifer dislocated her shoulder," Toni said.

Eve looked at Toni then back at Amy. "What?"

"Toni, chill. It was an accident, Eve. I lost my balance going up for a rebound and landed wrong."

"Seriously? You landed wrong because Jennifer pushed you." Toni then looked at Eve. "Jennifer and a couple of the senior girls are mad because Coach has been giving Amy more time. Now her season is over! We should do something, Eve."

"Toni, let it go!" Amy snapped. "Sorry, I just don't want to make more out of it than what it is. I get enough of that at home."

Eve nodded at Amy, and she knew what Toni meant by "do something." Toni wanted to confront the girls and wanted Eve with her in case things escalated. But that was Amy's problem to solve, and if Amy needed or wanted Eve's help, Amy would ask. And Eve knew why they singled Amy out. The school was a shrine to Amy's mother. Her picture and accolades were everywhere. Valedictorian. Prom Queen. State basketball championship. School record holder for points and rebounds. Eve could commiserate with the weight and expectation of legacy that Amy had to deal with, and she didn't envy her.

Amy smiled and changed the subject. "But when we are going out in your new car! I was sworn to secrecy, but that's all Tyler talked about last month. He called it his passion project."

Eve's heart skipped a beat, and she returned the smile. "Girl, you already know! As soon as it gets warmer, we turning some corners with the top down!"

"Your parents are OK with the car? It's World War Three at my house. Lady Tremaine has been on one," Toni said, looking at Eve and Amy before looking away.

"Uh, my parents were pretty cool for the most part. I think my father had to be convinced, but you know how my grandfather is," Eve said while looking at Toni sideways.

"So, I can tell by your shoes your mom left for her business trip," Amy laughed. "But what are y'all doing this weekend? Want to hang out or go shopping or something?"

Toni shook her head. "Already got plans with some friends from the city."

"I might be down. Can I call you?" Eve did want to hang out with Amy, but she had let her sisters slide too much. This weekend they were going to go over everything. Eve seemed to be the only one who had not forgotten that bad guys were still after them.

"Yeah, just let me know," Amy responded, sounding disappointed.

After school, Eve stayed in the library doing homework until it was time to meet Ana and Gwen at her car. Most of the parking lot was empty, and it was already starting to get dark thanks to the overcast sky. The sisters got to the car at the same time. Eve turned the key, and nothing happened. She pumped the gas, turned the key, and again nothing.

Gwen scanned the parking lot. "Weird…"

Her tone made Eve nervous. "Should I pop the hood?" Eve and her sisters had spent more than a few summers at the grandfather's car shop when they were younger and knew enough to troubleshoot cars.

A drone flew overhead, and Gwen shook her head. "This doesn't feel right. We're too exposed and it's going to be dark soon. Let's woof it through the park. We should be home before it gets too dark."

"Perhaps we should go back to school and wait for Father?" Ana offered.

Gwen shook her head again. "Pops isn't expecting to pick us up. And if he is still in the city it would take him over an hour to get here."

Eve made the decision. "Let's go."

A forested park area separated their neighborhood from their school and commercial district. If the sisters cut through it and hurried, they could be home in thirty-seven minutes.

Halfway through and Eve was irritated. "I can't walk in these shoes and Mom is going to kill me."

"Looking cute comes at a cost, Princess," Gwen said before holding up a finger. "Be quiet… You hear that?" she whispered, turning her head sideways.

Eve froze. She learned the hard way to trust Gwen's instincts. Eve focused and did hear something. She closed her eyes, and the sound became more pronounced.

"Ana, what's up with your birds? We could use some eyes right now," Gwen said.

"The birds are gone," Eve offered. "After they started taking down drones, they tried to strong-arm Ana for better pay or something. Negotiations got heated."

Ana nodded. "It happened during your self-imposed exile. I may have been a bit heavy-handed in my last proposal, which Three used as leverage to turn the others against me."

"Check it out…" Gwen said, pointing to a figure popping in and out of view amongst the trees as he ran towards them.

Eve's hands got sweaty, and she wiped them on her pants as she rolled her neck like a boxer.

"Ahh, it's just Babycakes." Gwen exhaled. "I was scared for a minute." Babycakes was the nickname the students gave Mr. Little, the middle-school math teacher and cross-country coach. He always ran in comically too-small shorts. He was sporting a large knitted cap, an oversized Yale sweatshirt (even though he graduated from Iowa), large mittens, a scarf, and patented shorty-shorts.

He met the sisters coming from the opposite direction and continued running in place while blocking their path. "Well, well, if it isn't the Parker sisters. Hello, girls."

"Mr. Little, do you still own the yellow Subaru? I saw some kids messing around with it," Gwen said as she motioned at the janitor and security guard coming from an adjacent trail. The Parker sisters and Mr. Little were in a heavily wooded area, standing on a path that was about three feet wide. That space was about to become very crowded.

"Uh, young Ms. Parker, trying to fool me again, eh? Well, fool me once, shame on me, fool me twice, shame on you," he replied, still running in place while shaking his head and smiling.

"Mr. Little! Mr. Little, we've been looking for you everywhere. You have an emergency call," Elvis, the security guard, said.

Mr. Little continued to run in place, now frowning. "Emergency phone call? And you needed the janitor to tell me that? I'm not sure what is going on here, but I am not an idiot. And... wait, is that Ms. Henderson, the Librarian?"

Gwen nudged Eve and Ana as they took off their backpacks. Behind the Librarian were five more men in school security uniforms whom Eve had never seen before. That was fine because someone was going to pay for her scuffing her mother's shoes.

"Ms. Henderson, strange catching you out here, but I trust you're sleeping well? You look more pale than usual. And... oh, dear God, Ms. Henderson, I have some gum in my desk back at school, please remind me to give it to you..."

For some reason, the Librarian had on black lipstick and heavy black eyeliner, giving her a ghoulish look on her pale skin in the fading light. She smiled at Mr. Little, tilting her head like a curious dog and showing bright uneven teeth. While Mr. Little was still bouncing on his toes, she casually slapped him with the back of her hand. The slap sent him stumbling sideways before he fell into a bank of melting snow. Eve blinked and questioned everything.

Elvis, the security guard, got in the Librarian's face. "He's a civilian! That was uncalled for! We were getting him out of here!"

The Librarian brushed him aside as Lurch pulled him away from her. She turned to Eve, cracked her knuckles, and smiled. "You look more pretty than tough."

Eve studied her as she kicked off her mother's shoes. She was Eve's height, and stocky. One could assume overweight, but that was all muscle. And from the impact of her slap, genetically enhanced or engineered muscle. Like the Parker sisters.

The Librarian looked Eve up and down as they circled each other. She had training. Eve could tell by the way she moved. Never flat-footed. She kept her balance and didn't cross her feet like a boxer. The Librarian stopped, as did Eve. Eve bounced lightly on her toes. The cold ground didn't bother her, but the terrain did. She had to end this quickly. The Librarian had strategically stopped so that Eve's back was to Lurch and Elvis. It didn't matter. But before Eve could attack, Gwen ran towards the Librarian, trying to grab her. Pandemonium ensued.

Ana took off, running through the trees, and two guards chased her. Eve spun in time to see Lurch dive at her. Eve dropped and rolled under him, rolling into a stomach punch that caught Elvis by surprise. She kneed him in the face when he doubled over. He dropped to his butt as Eve turned in time to slip a sloppy right-hand punch from Lurch. She hit him with a spinning elbow that landed on his jaw. She spun the other way and punched him in the sternum with the same hand she used for the spinning elbow. The punch backed him up, allowing her to step into a kick to his jaw that dropped him.

Someone grabbed her elbow, and her speed power kicked in. Eve spun out of it, grabbing the hand that had grabbed her elbow. She twisted it until the arm snapped and then kicked the side of his knee breaking his leg, turning away before he dropped.

Elvis was recovering. Eve kicked him in the chest as he struggled to stand up, sending him flying backward. She had to take a little off her kick because at the speed Eve was moving, her foot could go through his chest. Another guard rushed forward as everything returned to normal speed. Eve dropped to one knee, punched him in the groin then stood into an uppercut to his jaw and a left hook to the side of his face. His eyes rolled back as she grabbed him by his throat, tossing him in the path of the last guard rushing at her. The rushing guard tripped as Eve kicked him in his head. Both guards dropped.

It was almost dark. Eve saw the Librarian holding Gwen with one hand against the tree and punching her repeatedly with the other. Eve charged, hitting the Librarian in the back with her knee, sending the Librarian stumbling as Gwen fell to the ground.

"Gwen!" Eve screamed before the Librarian recovered and rushed her. Eve dipped beneath the Librarian's jab and hit her with a left hook to the body, then a left hook up top to her jaw. She finished with an overhand right that should have dropped her. The Librarian shook it off. She was strong. Not as strong as Gwen but more than twice as strong as Eve. Eve's speed power had her close to exhaustion. She had to be careful. She jabbed the Librarian twice, snapping her head back. The Librarian spit, grinned, and came forward. Eve hit her with another jab, overhand right, and a kick to the chest, forcing her back. Before the Librarian could reset, Eve stepped into a kick to her face, dropping her. Eve grabbed a handful of the Librarian's hair, snatched her head back, and punched her face two, three, four times. The Librarian slumped against her leg and fell to the ground.

Eve took a step back to catch her breath. The Librarian slowly stood on unsteady legs, and when she took a step forward, Eve dropped her again with a spinning back kick to the head. The Librarian had OK skills. Good movement, decent technique, was super-strong, but her best asset was how fast she recovered. Eve sparred against strength and knew how to mitigate it. However, the Librarian's ability to heal was taxing her. Eve decided breaking both her legs would neutralize her. While catching her breath, a hit to the back of her head dropped Eve to her knees.

"No!" Gwen screamed as someone twisted Eve's arm behind her while pushing her face in the dirt and snow. She struggled to raise her head while spitting out dirt and snow. Eve watched as the Librarian tackled Gwen and rained down punches on her before the hand forced her face back down. She heard a crack. A security guard fell next to her; at the same time, strong hands helped her sit up.

The new boy, Roman, tackled the Librarian off Gwen and rolled away before the Librarian could grab him. Ana dropped out of the sky, landing on a security guard's head as he struggled to his feet. He was out again. Lurch turned to Ana and Eve and the two boys before he backed away to help Elvis to his feet. They both then stood their ground on shaky legs. The Librarian stood up, looked at Eve, Ana, and the two boys as she swayed back and forth. Eve took a breath as she stepped forward. Ana stepped forward too, as did the boys. The Librarian looked like she remembered something, turned, and fled, leaving her fallen comrades behind.

"Gwen!" Eve rushed to her sister, getting there at the same time as Ana.

"Anyone got the number of that truck?" Gwen asked, standing. Her face was a bloody mess and almost unrecognizable with multiple contusions and scratches.

Now that she wasn't fighting, Eve heard screams and shouts for help from somewhere in the forest. She looked at Ana.

Ana shrugged. "They will be fine. They are just handcuffed together to a tree."

It was now dark. The clouds had moved on, leaving a full moon and stars to provide limited light. Gwen put her hands on her knees, coughed, and spit up blood.

"How you feel, sis?" Eve asked.

"Like I got ran over by a train, after falling off a cliff, after getting a paper-cut," Gwen replied through gritted teeth. Eve's watery vision blurred Gwen's face, but she could hear the pain in her voice. Eve wasn't in great shape herself. Her favorite jeans ruined, one knee bleeding, her feet battered, bruised, and bleeding, they needed to get home.

"We better get y'all home," Roman said as he and the other new boy, Aaron, approached.

"We don't need you to get us anywhere," Eve said, facing him.

"Wasn't asking."

Aaron retrieved the sisters' backpacks, giving one to Roman to carry.

Eve opened her mouth, but Gwen cut her off. "Can we just go home? Please?"

Eve acquiesced and scanned the ground for her mother's shoes but didn't see them. She sighed. They couldn't wait. She had to get her sisters home. Ana and Eve sandwiched and supported Gwen as they walked through and stepped over the security guards still on the ground. Lurch and Elvis gave them a wide berth as the two boys trailed them. The walk was long and tortuous. It became a test of willpower as every step became more painful than the last. Eve's pride would not allow her to show any pain or weakness. She focused on counting bad guys and how she allowed herself to get taken from behind. There was a guard that stayed hidden. She hadn't accounted for him, and it cost her. She gritted her teeth. She wasn't good enough. She wasn't even close to being good enough.

When they came out of the trees and saw house lights, Eve temporarily broke, and a single tear escaped her eye. She then held her head up and stiffened her spine, pretending her feet weren't on fire and the back of her head wasn't still throbbing with pain.

They crossed the street, and the last twenty-five yards were the worst. Eve felt like she was on a treadmill of nails. She kept walking, but their house never got closer, and the pain in her feet became more excruciating. Eve mustered her strength to avoid limping. She couldn't let her sisters know how badly she was hurt.

Bzzz Bzzz

Eve checked her phone. "Dad says order pizza. There was an accident and he's stuck in traffic." No one responded.

They reached the front door, and Eve almost collapsed from exhaustion and pain. She opened the door to let Ana and Gwen in and then blocked the path facing the boys. "You can go now."

Roman shook his head like he felt sorry for her before turning to his friend. "Let's roll."

They set the backpacks down at Eve's feet and set off on a quick jog back across the street. Eve soon lost sight of them in the dark.

Eve grabbed the backpacks, went inside, and shut the door. She could hear her sisters upstairs as she slowly slid down with her back against the door until she was sitting, hugged her knees, and started crying. The pain was more emotional than physical. Something inside her chest hurt so bad she could barely breathe. She recovered and went to the powder room just off the foyer. Her reflection angered her. She had dried blood beneath her nose and a blister on her lower lip. She washed and dried her face and tried to brush the dirt and grime out of her hair. Running hot water over another washcloth, she cleaned her feet. The bleeding had stopped, and after cleaning away the blood, grime, and dirt, they weren't as bad as she thought. The washcloth was now red, muddy brown, and black. She threw it away and grabbed some paper towels to dry off her feet. Taking a breath, she rewashed her face and practiced her smile before she went upstairs.

Gwen was under the covers with Ana sitting next to her as Eve quietly entered. "She going to be OK?" Eve asked, getting emotional again but fighting it.

Ana opened her mouth, shut it, and wiped away a few tears. She coughed to clear her throat. "Some contusions, bruising, and scratches but no serious damage. She's already starting to heal given her accelerated metabolism and rapid healing rate. I expect her to make a full recovery in no time." Ana's voice quivered. And she looked down, avoiding Eve's eyes.

Eve understood. She rubbed Ana's shoulder, and Ana started sobbing and shaking. It was too much for all of them. "Gwen?"

"Leave me alone, Princess! Please, just leave me alone!"

Eve was unsure. She thought about leaving. But guilt and regret kept her rooted in place. Ana stood up, and Eve grabbed her, hugged her, and Ana started sobbing again. Eve held onto until she stopped, but now the crying was coming from beneath the covers. Ana and Eve laid down and hugged Gwen and each other like they were at the end of a rope dangling over an abyss. An abyss filled with sociopathic librarians and knife-wielding mercenaries.

When they were spent and couldn't cry anymore, Gwen pushed them away. "I have to get some sleep." In minutes Gwen was asleep as Eve and Ana stayed to watch before quietly leaving. Eve ran a hot bath water and filled it with bubbles like when she was a little girl. She put some Epsom salt to help with the soreness because that's what her grandmother did. The bath helped her relax and focus. She went to bed exhausted but with a better idea of the challenges they faced. And she was going to make them pay for hurting her little sister.

Game time.

Chapter Fourteen

"OK, before we start, Toni is giving us a ride to school. I didn't want to worry Pops. And Eve, Tyler is going to meet us at your car to look at it. We need to get it back today so Ana can start the security upgrades," Gwen said, looking at her sisters as they stood in the sparring area of the basement. She woke up that morning with a new sense of purpose. Yesterday's beatdown reminded her that pretending she was normal was dangerous. And it could be fatal. But after twelve hours of uninterrupted sleep, she had a breakfast of a dozen eggs, five protein shakes, five bananas, and eight pieces of toast. She was ready to face her reality.

Eve and Ana nodded in agreement, but Gwen saw the smirk on Eve's face, and she felt embarrassed. Eve was right. Training fighting, fighting training, was the new normal for the Parker sisters. Gwen was ashamed that it took the Librarian to make her realize it. The Librarian who had been hiding in plain sight. As good as Gwen claimed to be in subterfuge and deception, she had missed her. Right in front of her face every day, grinning with bad breath. Gwen shook her head. She was supposed to be good at this stuff. It was her contribution to complement Eve's fighting and Ana's gadgets. It won't happen again. "Ana, we need a file on the Librarian, and I mean like yesterday. She's strong, like super-strong, but…"

"But not as strong as Gwen and she can recover fast. I mean like really fast," Eve interrupted her.

Ana nodded. "I'm on it."

"Now, how does this new improved weight bench work?" Gwen asked. She needed to get stronger, but more than that, she needed to get better. Strength wasn't everything, as the Librarian proved, and as Eve proved every time they sparred. The Librarian was almost as strong as her but had better fighting skills. Gwen needed to improve before they fought again. And Gwen had no doubt they would fight again. The thought of it scared her, but she needed to use that fear as motivation.

"The bench and floor are now reinforced to handle heavier loads. Father was on board so there was no need to sneak in a crew to do the work this time," Ana said. The bench was on the carpeted area just outside the sparring area, and still looked like a regular bench to Gwen. "The weights are more for balance and show, as the bar works in concert with electronic magnets in the floor and ceiling to add or remove weight."

Gwen nodded, lay down on the bench, and started pressing the weight, stopping after ten repetitions. "Wow, you're a genius. You made two hundred and twenty-five pounds feel exactly like two hundred and twenty-five pounds," Gwen said sarcastically.

Ana smiled and held up one finger. "John Henry, add eight hundred. Now give it a try."

Gwen laid back down and started benching again, with noticeably more effort. After ten repetitions, she sat up. "Um, wow! I mean, wow! That is incredible! You are a genius!"

Ana's smile widened. "That is an accurate assessment. And to engage, you say John Henry, followed by the weight you want to lift."

Gwen nodded and lay back down. "John Henry, add one thousand." She struggled through ten more repetitions.

Gwen took a breath and lay back down. "John Henry, add two thousand."

"Oh, wait! To disengage or release the weight, say John Henry release. I had to put that safety measure in because Father kept getting stuck."

Gwen nodded. "John Henry, add two thousand." Gwen barely managed three repetitions. She got up and paced back and forth like a caged animal, glaring at the bench. "I got this! I got this!" she said to herself, slapping her biceps and thighs. "John Henry, three thousand!" she said, lying back down. She squeezed the bar with anger and frustration.

"Uh, Gwen…"

"Save it, Princess! I just got my butt handed to me by a librarian!" Gwen snatched the bar and tried to steady the weight as her arms shook. She slowly lowered the bar but couldn't budge it off her chest. "John… John Henry…" she cried.

"John Henry release!" Eve shouted as she helped Gwen rack the weight. Gwen slowly sat up and pushed Eve's hand away when she tried to console her. After a few minutes, Gwen took a deep breath, coughed, and said, "Princess, me and you are doing two-a-days. Lifting before school and sparring after. Ana, you need to lift two times a week and spar two times, so pick times that work best for your schedule. We'll do most of our planning and research on weekends."

Eve and Ana nodded.

"Cool, and I wouldn't be surprised if the Librarian has a unique heat signature like from the pharmacy building last year, so let me know what you find. I'm going to reach out to Aaron and Roman today. They are the boys from the meet and probably got some pieces to the puzzle that could lead us to whoever Lurch, Elvis, and the Librarian work for. Too many moving pieces now for everyone to leave a clean trail."

Ana sighed. "Whatever…"

Eve gave her a fist bump. "Let's do this."

Gwen scarfed down a second breakfast after she showered. Her appetite had returned big time. Ana explained that her body needed to replace the calories it used to help her heal overnight. Gwen just knew she was starving when she woke up and barely had any visible signs from the savage beating she took.

Toni arrived a few minutes late, looking like a hot mess. Her car didn't look much better. It was littered with clothes, empty fast-food boxes, and had newly acquired cigarette burns. Gwen didn't ask, and Toni didn't offer.

Lucia and Tyler were parked next to Eve's car and got out when they pulled up. Tyler grabbed his jumper cables, and as tall he was, he had managed to wear a black coat too big for him, making him look like a malnourished black bear. "Hey, Eve, want to pop the hood?" he said, shivering.

Eve popped the hood.

"What? Your battery cable has been cut, fam. Y'all Parker sisters got mad haters up in here. I'll replace it over lunch. And bring it down to the shop this weekend, Eve, so I can put an alarm on it for you," he said, closing the hood.

Eve blushed, saying, "Thanks, Tyler, but Ana is going to take care of that."

Tyler put the jumper cables in his trunk. "Word? Ana got it like that? I mean, I thought she was just like a super-hacker, but she a mechanic too?"

Gwen laughed. "Please, when we were little Gramps tried to teach us everything about cars, but Ana was the only one that paid attention. She rebuilt a carburetor when she was in kindergarten."

"Mannn, you Parker sisters never cease to amaze me," Tyler said, smiling and shaking his head. "But on the real, fam, it's too cold for Black folk out here, so let's head in."

"Uh, I'll catch you guys later. I have to talk to a teacher about a recommendation," Eve said as she started walking with Gwen and Ana towards their middle school.

"Word? You already stacking recommendations as a sophomore? You Parkers really do be playing chess when everyone else playing checkers. But I know you in a hurry cause I've never seen you in sneaks outside of playing ball or running track, so I'm going to leave y'all to it," Tyler laughed before rushing inside with Lucia and Toni.

Gwen and her sisters crossed the parking lot quickly. Thankfully the front door wasn't locked. As middle-school classes didn't start for another forty minutes, the hallways were empty, and they headed for the library unimpeded. The door was closed, but Gwen could hear voices. Ana handed her sisters an earpiece and attached a small black cone the size of a golf ball to the door. Gwen could now listen to what the voices were saying.

"Will you stop saying she disappeared and tell us what happened? I mean, how did you let her get your handcuffs?"

"He's right. And we don't know how she got our cuffs. She ran behind this big tree and we thought she was hiding. But then she wasn't there. Next thing I know, she came out of nowhere and had us handcuffed to the tree before we even knew what happened. And then she disappeared. Leaving us in the in cold, freezing. It's not funny. We could've died."

"Yeah, been thinking about it all night. Still can't figure out what happened or how."

"All I know is I found these two idiots freezing, screaming for help. They were handcuffed together to a tree like they had a crush on it. I thought they were going to take it to dinner and a movie."

Loud laughter from multiple voices, then a voice Gwen recognized. "So, the skinny, nerdy one beat you?" the Librarian laughed.

"What about you? The cute one took you down like it was nothing. Never thought I ever see someone do that to you. Swear to God, I have never seen anyone move or fight like that."

"Agreed, that was ninja-type stuff. I read the reports but it's different seeing it up close. We are going to need more money for this. Upfront. Half my team is incapacitated and…"

"The job is the job! We told you these girls were good. Now, if you have a problem, we can settle it right here!" the Librarian shouted.

"Good? My seven-year-old son who plays soccer is good. These girls ain't human!"

"I got to get to class…" Eve said, taking out her earpiece and opening the door. Gwen and Ana followed.

Lurch and Elvis were leaning against a table across from three men dressed like school security who were sitting with the Librarian. One of the men had on a neck brace. Both Lurch and Elvis had bandages on their face. Outside of some light discoloring around her jaw and eye, the Librarian looked normal.

"We have company!" the Librarian smiled, jumping up. One of the three men rushed the girls, and before Gwen could react, Eve kicked him in the chest, sending him flying back into the arms of his friends. All three fell to the ground as the Librarian jumped out of the way. It was impressive that Eve could react that fast without her speed power. But Eve was almost always in fight mode

The Librarian turned to Eve, but Elvis got between them, holding up both arms. "Please! Please, we are in school!"

Gwen pulled Eve by the arm. Eve snatched her arm away and pointed past Elvis at the Librarian, "You come near my family again, I will kill you!"

"Kill me now!" the Librarian shouted before Lurch held up both his arms like Elvis, blocking her path to Eve.

The group was interrupted when the second security guard, Fatneck, opened the door. "What is going on in here? What is all that shouting and who are these men?"

"Just some old friends," Elvis said. "They work in the area and wanted to drop in and say hello."

"Well, they didn't sign in and they need to leave. Immediately. If they're not off campus in two minutes, I'm calling the police."

The security guards exited, with the one Eve kicked in the chest still out of it and supported by his two friends. He kept saying, "She just disappeared," over and over again.

"Is he drunk? At this hour? That's another write-up," Fatneck said.

After they left, Fatneck turned to Eve. "Do you have a visitor's pass, Ms. Parker?"

Eve pointed at the Librarian again. "Remember what I said," she warned, before storming out, followed by Gwen and Ana.

"I'm going to break that woman's neck!" Eve said, more to herself than to her sisters.

Ana and Gwen exchanged looks.

"That's it, you two are not staying in this school! It's too dangerous here."

"Eve, I don't think staying at home is going to make us safer," Gwen said. "And I think yesterday was not really about us. I mean, not directly anyway."

Eve and Ana stared at Gwen, and Gwen continued, "My guess? We were bait to flush out and test the boys."

"Aaron and Roman?" Eve asked.

"Yeah, I still think all roads lead back to Dad's old friend David, and the bad guys think Aaron and Roman are the keys to that."

Eve shook her head. "Still…"

"We're good, Eve. I don't think we're the ones they want. At least, not if they can use Roman and Aaron as a trap for David."

Eve shifted her weight from one foot to the other while looking at both Ana and Gwen. "I can't leave you guys here alone!" she said, almost crying.

"Evelyn, we will be fine. Our adversaries appear to be working with rules of engagement that prioritize secrecy. That translates to a low probability of anything happening during regular school hours," Ana offered.

"Yeah, what the nerd said. Now go! You're already late for class!"

Eve shifted her weight again and looked at her sisters. "OK, OK, but y'all better let me know if something happens. Immediately! And I mean it."

"Jeez, we will, Princess," Gwen said, but there was a lump in her throat. "Now go!"

After Eve left, Ana turned to Gwen. "Do you believe we will be OK? Or was that just a ruse to pacify our hot-tempered sister?"

Gwen shrugged. "Little bit of both."

The rest of Gwen's morning proceeded without incident. Babycakes had a substitute. Ana's discovery revealed that he had checked himself into a hospital, saying he fell down some stairs.

He was going to miss three weeks of school, but his fragile ego would not allow him to report that the Librarian pimp-slapped him into a snowbank. As Gwen was leaving the cafeteria with friends, she passed Roman and Aaron. They strolled in on schedule as if nothing happened. Gwen excused herself to speak with them. Ana had done a background on them too, so Gwen knew they enrolled in school over the summer using the address of a multimillion-dollar home that showed up in the register but didn't exist. Hacker type stuff.

"Something I can help you with, shorty?" Roman asked as she approached.

"Thanks for the assist yesterday, and we like to return the favor, so come over after school. We need to start working together."

"Word? Work together, huh? Shorty got jokes, but we good."

"You might be good for now, bro, but after yesterday's audition, and please believe that's all that was, you just put a target on your back."

Roman laughed. "So I guess you got it all figured out? You here to rescue us? Like you rescued us yesterday? Like I said, shorty, we good."

Gwen hesitated, but as she went to turn away, Aaron grabbed Roman by the arm and whispered in his ear. Roman smiled and shook his head. He looked Gwen up and down dismissively but said, "Aiight, we might be there."

Gwen nodded and turned. If the boys knew what was good for them, they'd show up. Their only saving grace was that, if they did disappear, David would never show. But now they had the Parker sisters if they were willing to accept the help. Because it didn't matter how tough or unique they were, they were going to need it.

Eve was waiting for Gwen and Ana in her car outside of the front door right after school. They drove home without speaking, but Gwen could see how hard Eve was gripping the steering wheel. Gwen was not looking forward to their sparring session.

An hour later, they were in the basement doing warm-ups when the doorbell rang. "I got it," Gwen said, running upstairs and returning with Roman and Aaron.

Eve stopped jumping rope. "What are they doing here?" she asked, nostrils flaring.

"I invited them. They're probably targets now because they helped us. And now we're going to help them."

"We didn't ask for or need their help," Eve said, throwing down the jump rope.

"Eve, you need to chill, because what we not going to do is turn our back on the people that helped us. Besides, we're stronger together and now the rabbit has the gun."

"What? What are you even saying?" Eve asked.

Roman was strolling around the basement. "What y'all got going on here? This s'posed to be a mini-dojo or something?"

"Put those down," Eve said through gritted teeth when Roman picked up a pair of bag gloves.

"Listen, y'all invited us here so…"

"I didn't invite you," Eve said, putting her hands on her hips.

"Enough!" Gwen said. "I already said I invited them and they're staying." She exhaled slowly. "Now, we're running out of time, so let's cut to the chase—what can you and Aaron do?"

"What?" Roman asked.

"Powers, bro, what powers do you have? My sisters and I have, uh, well, unique gifts, but I bet you already know that. And I bet you and Aaron have gifts too."

"Word? You don't know anything about us," Roman retorted.

"Ana?" Gwen said.

"Your name is Roman Sotomayor. Your parents were born in Puerto Rico and both joined the military. Your father, who was an Army Ranger, was killed overseas in an IED explosion eight years ago. Your mother moved to New York and is currently teaching history at New York College. Her book on colonization in Latin America made the *New York Times* bestseller list and was made into a documentary. She remarried four years ago. After multiple suspensions from your private school, you were expelled. You enrolled in the public school that Aaron went to. But the suspensions continued, and you eventually were expelled from public school about the same time someone shot up your home, injuring your younger brother…"

"Shut up! You read a few files and hacked my juvie record and now you think you know me?"

"We know your middle-class butt need to stop pretending you all hood, ese," Eve replied.

"Yo, shorty, I'm Puerto Rican and proud. Not Mexican so you can squash the ese. And you snobby rich girls think y'all special? Think y'all got unique talents or skills or whatever? But check it, me and Aaron saved your butts twice…"

Gwen said, "We know! We're just…"

"Save it! We out!" Roman said, stomping up the stairs.

Aaron looked around the basement and at the sisters without speaking. It was hard to read his eyes and body language. He didn't carry himself like a tough guy. He was about an inch taller than Roman, with a wiry thin frame and boyish face. His sizeable unkempt afro sprung to life whenever he took off the hoody he always wore. But there was something about him. He looked ordinary. Unexceptional. But he was special. Gwen could tell after closer examination. Not because he showed it, but the opposite. He hid it. Or tried to.

He knelt, unzipped his backpack, and took out the Italian shoes Eve had left behind. They were buffed and polished to near perfection. He left without speaking.

The sisters worked out and sparred after the boys left, with Eve and Gwen going extra rounds. Gwen needed it. Her combinations were rusty, her timing was off, and Eve made her pay at every turn. Gwen then worked herself to exhaustion, punching and kicking the bag until her arm and legs shook. She rested, then went again until Eve made her stop and go to bed. But Gwen had a hard time sleeping. She thought the Librarian might be hiding in her closet. Or under her bed. Every noise scared her. Every shadow was out to get her. Morning found her stressed and exhausted.

The next day the boys were not at school, but later that evening, as the sisters were warming up, the doorbell rang. Ana went to answer it and returned with Roman and Aaron.

Roman walked around the basement while Gwen gestured at Eve to cool it. Eve nodded her consent. Aaron leaned up against the wall with his arms folded and watched.

Roman stopped in front of a jump rope. He took off his backpack and coat and started jumping rope and talking, "Y'all had the facts right but were missing the details. Details matter. My mother married another teacher. Some white dude. And we moved into his crib. His spot. His space. All my dad's stuff was put in storage. No room for it. I had a problem with that. How was my little brother going to remember his father if everything was in storage?"

Roman jumped and talked in rhythm. "After I got expelled from that rich white private school, they put me in public school. Like I was supposed to be scared straight. And the kids tried me, but my knuckle game has always been nice. Pops was a serious Felix Trinidad fan. Taught me and my brother to box as soon as we could walk. And I thought I had earned my respect. But at that school, it didn't matter how tough you were. You needed to be... affiliated."

Roman talked with an emotional detachment, like he was narrating someone else's life. "But I've always had a hard time making friends. Never been my style and it caught up with me. They were giving it to me when Aaron jumped in. Dude can't fight to save his life. I mean, his knuckle game needs serious work, but he got mad heart. He did enough and I did the rest. I got suspended but now Aaron was guilty by association. So, I thought I was doing him a solid when I put a few of them dudes in the hospital. Then things got complicated. They shot up my spot. My little brother got sprayed with broken glass. And my mother was six months' pregnant at the time. And that was the last straw. Never even got to see my little sister being born."

Gwen looked at Aaron, who kept his hood up and was unreadable.

"Aaron invited me to stay with him, his mom, and grandmom in their two-bedroom spot. They treated me like family. It was cool. I talked to my family in Puerto Rico, but I couldn't leave Aaron after what he did for me. The plan was to make sure everything was cool, then head to Puerto Rico. I would finish school there, then join the military like my pops. But it didn't work out that way. Aaron was catching hands every day for helping me out. Like I said, dude got mad heart and don't know how to back down. His mother had to make him stop going to school while she tried getting him in a new one. He started working with her and his grandmoms to clean offices at some lab that was a two-hour train and bus ride away. I wasn't with that, so I stayed in the city.

"Is that the lab that blew up?" Ana asked.

"Yeah, killed his mom and grandmother. Basically, his entire family. And I didn't think he was going to make it. He was in a coma for ten days. I stayed in the hospital with him. Didn't really have any place else to go. That's when I met David. He worked at the lab and said he could help, but needed me to create a distraction. Easy enough, and David gave him something, and bam. Overnight Aaron fully recovered so we slipped out. Whatever made him better was valued at more than a billion dollars and it was stolen. Strange thing though, for three days after he got better, he became highly radioactive. Just for those three days. Both David and I got radiation sickness. David recovered with the help of some pills. But Aaron and I were around each other all the time, so I had it worse. I guess I almost died, but David used the last of what he gave to Aaron on me. Almost wished I was dead because he had to inject in my spine. And we didn't really have a lot of pain meds or anything. Never want to feel pain like that again…"

Gwen nodded. "Appreciate you sharing, but why are you here?"

"David says he owes your father and we should protect you guys until he can make it right."

"And how exactly is he going to make things right?" Gwen asked.

"I don't know. But since he saved Aaron's life, and then mine, we owe him. Besides, neither of us have a place to go. So that's why we're here."

Gwen nodded again. "And your abilities? Talents?"

"Since the injection, I heal instantly, takes forever for me to get tired. And drugs and poisons don't affect me."

"And Aaron?" Gwen asked.

"Aaron is a special dude. Special in a way that has nothing to do with powers. He jumped in and helped me without even knowing who I was. Asking around, it seems that's who he is. He helps people. Don't get me wrong, his knuckle game is tired, but he took me in like I was family. But yeah, after he got better, David said he became radioactive while his body figuring out what it was becoming and how to handle the changes. Now he's strong, real strong. And smart like super-smart. And he can make his skin hot. I'm talking two hundred and twelve degrees hot."

"Interesting. That is the temperature of boiling water," Ana noted.

"It's getting late. Let's get on with it," Eve said.

Gwen coughed. "Yeah, let's get started. We'll start with the bench, and then check your fighting skills, your healing powers, Aaron's IQ, and his ability to raise his temperature."

Roman struggled to bench one eight-five pounds once. Although impressive for a middle-school kid, it was not exceptional or unique. But after Ana retrieved a knife from the kitchen, Roman made a small cut on his forearm. They watched it heal instantly. It was amazing. His healing power was faster than Gwen's, who had the sisters' most rapid healing power.

Eve was unimpressed. Roman handed Ana back the knife and turned to Eve. "Can you do better?"

Eve smiled. "John Henry, add five hundred." With a lot of effort, she managed to bench it twice. She stood back up, saying, "Gwen?"

Gwen nodded. "John Henry, bar three thousand." Gwen struggled to bench it once, but she felt she got her point across. She stood back up and said, "Ana?"

Ana stifled a yawn. "Actually, that will be a no for me. But thank you for asking."

Roman laughed. "Is that supposed to impress me? I took down plenty of chotas who thought big meant bad."

Gwen nodded. "Agreed. Let's lace 'em up." Eve helped Gwen gear up, not taking her eyes off Roman and Aaron.

Ana helped Roman while showing Aaron how to do it. "Appreciate that, mami," Roman told her.

"It's a school night!" Eve complained as she gave Gwen a couple of slaps on her headgear as part of their pre-sparring routine. Gwen bounced on her toes like back when she was in Tae Kwon Do and then switched to a more conventional bouncing stance. All summer, Gwen searched for a fighting style that was comfortable yet effective for her. And she thought it might have been boxing mixed in with some Tae Kwon Do kicks and Muay Thai knees and elbows. But it was hard trying to combine all that, and it made her hesitant. The Librarian made her pay for her that hesitation. But she had to get better, so maybe focusing on boxing for now before adding new skills would help.

Roman dapped Aaron up and joined Gwen in the sparring area. Roman studied Gwen, then started a series of hand and arm movements and head feints that confused Gwen for a few seconds. Then she realized he was a practitioner of fifty-two blocks. A fighting system that Gwen's uncle used in street-fighting tournaments. Gwen was thinking how to attack when Roman unexpectantly, feinted left then jumped right, hitting her on the side of her head with a fist then elbow before tripping her and pushing her down when she was off balance.

"Da Bronx, baby!" he shouted, taking out his mouthpiece and pounding his chest, before helping Gwen up.

Gwen was embarrassed. Roman had some skill. He attacked with precision and quickness but no way should she have let him take her down. "Let's go again," she said, taking out her mouthpiece.

"I'm up," Eve said, stepping in front of Gwen to face Roman.

Gwen shrugged and walked off the fighting area, still mad at herself.

Roman started his rapid arm movements again, and Eve took a quick sidestep. When Roman pivoted to face her, she shot a front snap kick through his hands, landed on his chin, and dropped him. She then stood over him. "The suburbs, baby!"

Roman popped up and paced back and forth, glaring at Eve. "Run it back! Run it back!"

She pushed him out her face when he got close and nodded at Ana to reset the timer. "We can run it back."

Roman started his movements again, and Eve took a step back. When Roman took a step forward to close the distance, Eve exploded into him with a vicious flying knee to his stomach that dropped him again. The flying knee was Eve's signature move, and she executed it every chance she got. And her big legs and explosive athleticism made the move lethal. The one she unleashed on Roman was especially violent, making Gwen wince. Eve was not playing.

Roman rolled on the floor, groaning, and Aaron took a step closer to him. Roman held up his hand to freeze Aaron as he got on all fours, catching his breath. He recovered quicker than Gwen anticipated, demanding they go again. And they did. Again, and again. The timing of their matches changed, but the result was constant. Roman rolling on the floor as Eve stood over him. When the sisters' father got home an hour later, Eve and Roman were drenched in sweat and breathing heavily, but neither would back down.

"Time for your friends to leave," their father announced from the foot of the stairs.

After the boys left and the girls went upstairs, he asked, "Girls, what's going on? Are you telling people about your powers now? And you know I don't like your friends over without me and your mother having met them, or at least their parents. But for now, get cleaned up, dinner should be ready in about fifteen. I'm going to try my hand at this pasta primavera dish… What?" their father said, stirring a pot with a large wooden spoon.

"Pops, those were the boys that helped us last summer. At the meet with your friend David," Gwen said.

Their father slowly stopped stirring, turned the fire off, and moved the pot to another eye. He then turned around, folded his arms, and looked at his three daughters before asking, "Can you repeat that?"

Gwen retold the story Roman had told her, with help from her sisters. Their father took off his glasses, cleaned them on his shirt, and squeezed his eyes shut while pinching the bridge of his nose before putting his glasses back on. "Invite the boys over tomorrow. I want to speak with them."

The sisters looked at each other, and Gwen nodded. "Sure, Pops."

The next day the boys came over, and their father spoke with them in private. They didn't talk for more than fifteen minutes, and afterward, they didn't mention what they discussed, and neither did their father. Their mother got home late Friday night, and things got interesting that Saturday morning when Aaron and Roman came over. Their mother was usually discreet, but discretion went out of the window whenever their father's old friend David was the topic of conversation. She hated him for ruining their lives, and everything associated with him. But whatever they argued about, it was something their father refused to budge on.

All the sisters knew was that the boys didn't ask for this. They were victims of circumstance. Not unlike the girls. Gwen stayed in the garage with Ana and Aaron as her parents argued in the house, while Eve and Roman tried to kill each other in the basement.

"So, uh, this is like some type of green renewable technology like your corporate crush Vande Bader is always bragging about?" Gwen asked Ana. Gwen was helping Ana and Aaron upgrade Eve's car and make it tamper-proof. Gwen provided muscle for the heavy lifting like pulling out the engine, transmission, and other parts.

Gwen looked over at Aaron, who, as usual, had his hoody up with his earbuds in. He was typing on one of Ana's notepads. After testing, the Parker sisters determined Aaron was exceptional. His max bench of three hundred and fifty pounds was borderline extraordinary. His ability to increase his external body temperature to two hundred and twelve degrees for three seconds qualified him as unique. His IQ registering in the lower range of genius identified him as exceptional. But he was the worst fighter of the group. A decent grappler, thanks to his strength, but a limited striker who could not bring himself to punch anyone in the face. Gwen had to remind herself how she struggled with punching and kicking people in the face when she started sparring years ago. Now it was second nature to her and her sisters. But Aaron's inability to fight could make him a liability, so they had to get him up to speed quickly.

"Aaron! Aaron! Who are you listening to?" Gwen shouted at him.

He slowly turned and took out one of his earbuds. "Black Thought."

Gwen nodded. "Now that's real hip-hop." And she felt like a dork right after she said it. For the last few days, she'd been trying to figure Aaron out, but the dude was a closed book. Unlike his friend Roman, who didn't know how to be quiet and acted like he was the baddest dude in the room, no matter what room he was in.

On Sunday, Gwen was in the garage again helping Ana and Aaron. "Yo, dork, you said we'd be finished by now—what's up? I would not want to be you if Princess can't drive her car to school tomorrow," Gwen said, looking at a car without an engine and their garage littered with car parts.

"The materials I need arrived later than I anticipated, but the car will be serviceable tomorrow. However, we are a long way from completion. Unfortunately, the family garage is not equipped for…"

"Tony Stark was able to build his suit in a cave! With a box of scraps!" Gwen shouted, cutting Ana off and laughing to herself.

Ana sighed, briefly looking up before continuing to type on her laptop. "It is curious that you repeat the same tired phrase every day. It is beyond annoying."

Still chuckling, Gwen asked, "Without the engine and other stuff, what are we gonna do with all this extra space?"

"Storage, perhaps?" Ana replied without looking up.

Gwen nodded. She couldn't follow Ana's and Aaron's conversations about tabletop fusion, cold fusion, and pyroelectric fusion, but she understood storage. And if done right, they should be able to add a mini-fridge and microwave. "Good call, dork, and what are we supposed to do with all these parts? If Mom sees this, we're dead."

"I'm selling them back to Grandfather's shop through a third party at cost."

"So, what are y'all going to do with the money from the parts?" Aaron asked, and the unsolicited comment surprised Gwen. Aaron never initiated conversation unless he was talking to Roman.

Even Ana appeared surprised as she looked up from her notepad. "Why?" she asked.

Aaron pulled his hood back, and his short angry afro sprang to life. He swallowed and looked around the three-car garage that was stocked with the latest tools. He eyed the six-figure luxury sedan next to the classic American convertible they had been working tirelessly on. "Don't look like the Parkers hurtin' for change," he observed.

Gwen nodded. Aaron made sense. He had been working side by side with Ana, helping her troubleshoot and calibrate the system while also helping Gwen with the heavy lifting. "Yeah, I hear ya, we'll share what we get for the parts."

"I did not agree with that. You and Evelyn are always taking my largesse for granted. I am investing over two hundred million dollars of my technology into this car, so if we are discussing pay equity I would like to be compensated for my contributions."

"Dork, you're made of money and you're doing this because Princess is your sister and that's what families do…"

"You know what? Y'all can squash that. But remember, y'all asked us here. Saying how we need to stay together. Saying how y'all could help us. Looks to me like we ain't doing nothing but helping the rich get richer. Tell Roman I'll be outside." Aaron pulled his hood back up, opened the garage door, and stood outside in the cold with his back to the house.

Chapter Fifteen

"Ana, those boys are trouble! They're thugs and you should stay away from them," Stacey droned on Wednesday morning as they walked down the hallway together. They had just passed Roman and Aaron, who both gave Ana the universal Black person nod. Ana nodded back, and Stacey was scandalized. But Stacey was nothing if not consistent. "Hey, check out my ribbons."

Ana stifled a yawn while looking at Stacey's ribbons. "Lovely, Stacey. What does pink indicate?" Ana blinked a couple of times and rubbed her eyes to bring the ribbons back in focus. She needed to sleep. She finished ninety-nine percent of Eve's car late last night with help from Aaron and Gwen. Now Ana wanted to get back to her nightly flying sessions, which had been sporadic at best thanks to her workload. She didn't realize the cathartic effect those nightly sessions had on her psyche, and for self-care, she needed to start them again.

"Uh, it's like a participation trophy, but my dad and coach say I'm getting more competitive every day, and…" Ana zoned out. She was feeling betrayed. She had conceded to the birds' demands, but they still refused to come back. Even the twins. For months the birds had been her closest companions outside of her sisters and Stacey. And that they could so unceremoniously sever that bond was painful.

Later that day, as Ana was leaving the cafeteria with Stacey at her side, Roman and Aaron were coming in. Roman motioned for Ana to speak with him. She left Stacey with her mouth open so she could talk privately with Roman.

"Hey, mami, you good? You sure you don't need me to run interference for that library and bug thang?"

"Thank you for asking, but I do not believe this is a task that will require your assistance." Ana was discovering there were two distinct Romans. The version students saw in the daytime and who fought Eve every night as if his life depended on it. That was the Roman who carried himself with so much confidence and swagger he put the world on notice. Then there was the other Roman. The one who told corny jokes and quietly called her 'mami' so no one else could hear. The one who protected and looked after Aaron like it was all that mattered. She was fonder of that version.

Roman nodded. "Cool, cool. Aiight then, mami, peep you at your spot tonight. And tell your big sis I'm coming for the belt."

Ana nodded and excused herself to rejoin Stacey. Roman's strength had increased exponentially in the last six weeks. The aspects of Roman's physiology that allowed him to heal super-fast also allowed his body to respond exceptionally fast to the muscle breakdown that was a by-product of resistance training. His strength was now comparable to Eve's, which was near the pinnacle of human achievement and on par with Olympic weightlifters. And his hand-to-hand combat skills had improved significantly as well. Although he was still losing nightly to Eve, their matches lasted longer. And the longer Eve fought, the more vulnerable she became to an opponent who never got tired. Roman's body was extremely efficient at dealing with fatigue poisons. He could spar for hours with little to no drop-off in reflexes or strength, unlike Eve.

"Ana! Ana! He is a thug! You need to stay away from him. Oh, look, there's Javier. Isn't he gorgeous? Are him and Gwen dating now?"

Ana stopped and turned to Stacey, who stopped as well. "Stacey, can you please refrain from referring to our classmates as thugs and gangsters? Not only is it widely inaccurate and ignorant, it feeds into negative stereotypes of a demographic that has already been historically demonized. Do better, my friend. We need to build bridges, not walls."

Stacey opened her mouth and then closed it before turning away and hurrying to class. Ana sighed. Stacey wasn't alone in the labeling and stereotyping of Roman and Aaron. Ana just wasn't in the mood for it today. Especially not from someone she considered a friend.

Between her last two classes of the day, Ana met Gwen in front of the library. With Eve's car and their suits near completion, Gwen felt it was time to press the issue. But Ana and Gwen had to make Eve promise to stop showing up at school randomly looking for the Librarian, because a confrontation could put everything at risk.

Gwen gave her a fist-pound, and they entered the library together. Everyone had settled into an uneasy truce since their last dustup, meaning Ana must have guessed right about the rules of engagement. Their adversaries appeared to be under strict orders to avoid all confrontations in school. And Gwen had been on a roll with ideas lately. She convinced Ana to create spyware embedded in malware that infected any devices searching for the Parker sisters together with the Icarus Project, and other unique combinations. Gwen also wanted Ana to discreetly purchase or create a company that could remove said malware. She explained it as breaking into someone's house then having them hire you to fix the door. Gwen was sneaky good.

"The Parker sisters! How nice. Can I help you find a book?"

"As if you could," Gwen sneered.

"Temper, temp—"

"What it do?" Roman said, strolling in with Aaron.

"Are we having a party? I love parties!" The Librarian said, pulling a phone out of her dingy jeans and starting to text. Her maniacal smile showcased blindingly white teeth, and she seemed to be enjoying this. Ana was having second thoughts about Gwen's strategy.

Gwen didn't respond to the Librarian but instead nodded at Ana. Ana nodded back and proceeded to place bugs all around the library in full view of the Librarian. These were the latest iteration of Ana's bugs. They were near invisible to the naked eye, but more durable than before, and had a camera and sound-filtering functionality. It would take high-tech tools to locate and remove them all. Which was the point, Gwen explained. Gwen didn't think the Librarian, the janitor, or the security guard had said tools or skills. She explained that, once the bugs started being removed, an attack could be imminent. Ana couldn't argue with her logic.

Once finished, Ana activated the bugs on her black leather bracelet, checked the readings, and joined Gwen at the front of the library. Ana's latest bracelet had a satellite link, and all communications were encrypted. She could see the POVs of her birds, and it would notify her if anyone approached Eve's car or their house. But Ana used it mostly for stock quotes and to watch cartoons.

"We good?" Gwen asked.

Ana nodded, and as they turned to leave, the janitor and the security guard rushed in, practically out of breath.

"Now let's have that party!" the Librarian sneered.

The air became electric and charged with danger. Ana grabbed Gwen's arm to lead her away before it got to the point of no return. The security guard placed himself between the Librarian and Gwen.

The Librarian pushed him aside, shouting, "You're not in charge here! I am! I am in charge!" Which was frightening to Ana.

"We should leave," Ana whispered to Gwen.

Gwen nodded, turned to leave, and then turned back to face the Librarian, "Oh, almost forgot..." she said, tossing a shiny object high into the air towards the Librarian while putting her fingers in both ears and closing one eye.

"Get down!" the security guard said, tackling the janitor and covering him with his body like the secret service. Roman did the same thing with Aaron. Ana checked stock quotes on her wrist while the Librarian froze.

The tin landed at the Librarian's feet, sending breath mints flying in every direction.

The Librarian looked furious as she glared at Gwen, her chest rising and falling rapidly.

"Not cool. Not cool at all," Roman said, getting up and brushing himself off while staring down students coming in who dared to look directly at him.

Gwen shrugged as she walked out of the library, followed by Ana, Roman, and Aaron. "Please. I just did everyone a favor. Have you ever smelled her breath? I should get extra credit for that."

The next day at school, as Ana left orchestra class, Danny sidled up next to her. "Hey, Ana... Oh, didn't mean to surprise you, just wanted to ask if you were going to the Spring Dance?"

"Oh, hello, Danny, I... uh, the Spring Dance? Correct me if I'm wrong, but that is in May, right?" Ana was a bit startled. With it being the final week of January, the last thing on her mind was the Spring Dance in May. She was conflicted. A tech expo was scheduled that weekend with all the thought leaders in IT slated to speak, including Vande Bader.

"Uh, yeah, I realize it's a bit early, but I just found out last night that my brother's band is going to be playing it. So, I have to be there because, you know, he pays for me like doing roadie stuff. Sometimes they let me do background vocals. Sometimes."

"We're going! Right, Ana?" Stacey asked from out of nowhere, which was the first time Ana heard Stacey speak since yesterday.

Ana nodded, still trying to compute what exactly was happening.

"And I can't believe you're in an actual band! That is so cool!"

Danny laughed. "I'm not actually in the band. I'm more of a mascot than anything. But my brother does let me do background vocals and play bass guitar sometimes. Bye." Danny flipped his mop of hair out his eyes and hurried away, trying to balance his violin case, as he avoided students while putting sheet music in his backpack.

"Oh, my gawwwd! That is the coolest thing I've ever heard! Ana, we have to go! We have to!" Stacey pleaded.

"Stacey, the school dance is over one hundred days away and I cannot in good conscience commit to something so far in advance without…"

"But we have a ride! My sister is home from college! And she won't be going back this semester. Something about her sorority and hazing. My mother is not happy. She's called your grandmother's law company because she wants to sue, and she's still waiting for a callback. She said the school is making an example of my sister and it's not like hair can't grow back. But the dance is going to be soooo much fun!"

Ana laughed, which drew stares. Ana seldom laughed out loud, but Ana was relieved that Stacey was chattering non-stop again. That Danny kind of asked her to the dance, and the upgrades to Eve's car were ninety-nine percent complete. And her birds were coming back. Some were as far off as Florida and California, but it seemed they missed taking down the drones and yelling at Ana. They thought both were fun. The twins had made it back last night and had already taken down two drones flying over the school's airspace by the third period.

The rest of the school day passed without incident, and, on schedule, the boys showed up an hour after school for training. Ana had one of her more intense sparring sessions. Ana didn't participate in the grappling sessions because sweaty people touching her was gross. Still, she bested everyone but Eve in the sparring sessions. Ana used her staff to keep everyone at bay and then tripped them or flipped them when they rushed in. She had been secretly experimenting with her flight powers to move laterally and back and forth, and she was starting to figure out the timing and angles. And although Ana was not a fan of fisticuffs or physical exertion, the sessions became more tolerable if she wasn't getting pummeled.

"Nice job tonight Mami," Roman whispered to her. "You're getting sick with that staff."

Ana found her face getting hot and her heart rate increasing for some inexplicable reason. "Thanks. Thank you, Roman. I appreciate that."

Their mother met them at the top of the stairs. Ana froze. Their abode had been experiencing a cold war the last six weeks, with their parents ignoring each other while using their daughters as intermediaries. It was juvenile and put the sisters in an awkward position.

"Evelyn, hon, can you give your friends a ride home tonight? It's a bit late. Also, I made a couple of plates for them to go."

Ana was taken aback. Her mother's tone and offer intimated warming of relations between her parents and a possible concession on her part, which was a first.

"I'm going too!" Gwen shouted, running past Ana and racing to the closet to grab her coat.

Ana stuck out her lip. "Well, surely there is no reason I must stay home," she complained, still surprised by her mother's concession. Their mother was not personable. That, coupled with her intense dislike of David and anything associated with him, dictated she kept the boys at arm's length. But clearly, that was not sustainable for an adult. Especially a parent.

"The kitchen will be waiting for you when you get back!" their father shouted as Gwen and Roman rushed through the kitchen to the garage.

"Hey, dork, start on the kitchen, and Eve and I will finish up when we get back."

"I will not be left home attending to dishes while you and Eve go gallivanting about."

"Gallivanting? Let that nerd flag fly, bro. But come on then, hurry up!"

"Shotgun!" Roman yelled, muscling past Gwen.

"Hurry up, nerd!" Eve said, heading for the garage door.

"Stop touching me!" Gwen yelled in the backseat. Gwen sat next to Ana, who sat next to Aaron.

"In this confined space how would you suggest I stop touching you? I'll wait."

"My gawd, stop talking!"

"Both of you shut up!" Eve shouted from the front seat. "You're not supposed to be yelling when I'm driving!"

"She started it!" Gwen retorted.

"Will you Parker girls chill? Seriously!" Roman complained.

"Wasn't nobody talking to you, Romana!" Gwen shouted back at him.

"I swear I'm about to stop this car and smack everybody in here!"

Eve's threat settled everyone down. Everyone knew Eve would stop the car and smack everybody. After a few minutes of silence, Ana suddenly remembered something significant. "Jupiter!"

"I said what I said! Stop shouting while I'm driving!"

"Apologies, Evelyn. Gwendolyn, remember you asked me to check back on those crab-leg smugglers from the game?"

"Oh, snap! Forgot about that! What you find?"

"They. Are. Dead. All of them," Ana said slowly.

"What? How?" Gwen asked.

"Three were killed in an accident while riding to work together. One in a carjacking and the last from respiratory failure, which, I might add, is consistent with ricin poisoning."

"Word? Killed for smuggling crab legs? That's dangerous business. Must have been snow crab," Roman mused.

"What about the last two musketeers, Smash and Riggins?" Gwen asked.

"No record. The temp agency they worked for no longer exists. It's like they never worked there."

"This is wild! The musketeers must be the gang that runs these suburban streets, right? Listen, I know you Parker girls are set on the paperwork with your grams ballin' out of control, but Aaron and I could use a side hustle so hook me up with the connect."

"You think they were killed because of us?" Eve asked, looking through the rearview mirror. "Like the doctor from last year?"

"Whuuuut? A doctor in on this? A real doctor or is that like a street name like Doctor Dre? Don't matter, once y'all hook me and Aaron up with the connect we'll take it from there."

"Maybe, Eve. Maybe not. The thing is, we didn't show our powers to those guys. I mean Doctor Jim examined us, but those guys just got busted for stealing food. You know, what if it was more about Smash and Riggins covering their tracks?" Gwen replied.

"Wait a minute... Smash and Riggins? From like *Friday Night Lights*?" Roman asked.

"Good looking out, Ana, and with the mercenary being dead it's really hard to know if all this is connected or coordinated or if it's different parties jockeying for position. I mean..." Gwen tailed off, sounding frustrated.

"It's cool, sis. We'll figure it out. It's cool," Eve said to console her.

"Y'all need to stop ignoring me! I want in on that crab hustle!" Roman complained.

"Sheesh, Romana. Chill. There is no crab hustle. We just trying to piece together who's the man behind the curtain."

"Wow, that clears everything up. Thanks," Roman grumbled.

"Uh, you guys stay here?" Gwen asked as Eve pulled into the parking lot of a motel that looked haunted.

"Yeah, will be here for a few more days, but David says we shouldn't stay in one place longer than two weeks."

"But this is like nine miles from school," Eve added. "Do you guys ride-share or something?"

"Y'all know we don't use phones or credit cards. Sometimes we have the manager call a cab, sometimes we run. I mean, yesterday morning we made it to school in forty-five minutes, which was a new record. That's averaging like a five-minute mile. Hope to beat that time tomorrow, right, Aaron?"

Aaron just nodded and turned his head away. He did not want to participate in Roman's ruse.

"So, might I ask how you communicate with David?" Ana queried.

"We don't communicate. We're supposed to stay close to y'all and David's going to reach out once he finishes whatever it is he's working on."

"Apologies for the multiple inquiries, but you are minors. Legally you cannot secure a room in this state without an adult signature."

"I thought you were supposed to be the smart one? This is America. Money talks and everything is negotiable," Roman said, pulling out a large money clip from his oversized pants.

Roman was accurate in stating one truism of America being that with money, everything is negotiable. But there was something depraved about Roman and Aaron living in these conditions. At the same time, their so-called friends, the Parker sisters, slept in a six-thousand-square-foot house. Ana felt guilty. She had just lectured Stacey about doing better, with a smugness and moral authority she had no claim to. She would be wise to heed her own advice and do better.

The girls stayed and watched as the boys climbed the stairs to the second level of their two-level horror motel. It was L-shaped, with parts of the railing bent or missing on the second story. If someone ran out of one of the rooms with a hockey mask and chainsaw Ana wouldn't be surprised. The parking lot had a few cars, with one sitting on bricks and no tires or rims. The motel shared the block with a pawn shop, and across the street at one corner was a dimly lit liquor store. It had menacing flashing lights as if it was coercing patrons to spend their money. At the far end of the block was a church, which was nothing if not convenient. One could get lost in the bottle and walk down the block to find Jesus.

They waited until the boys' door closed and a light came on before they pulled off. "Yo, dork, check your Viking wristband to see if any of the bugs have been found or destroyed."

Ana shook her head. "They have not been compromised."

"Cool. And you have an alert or alarm or whatever, so you know immediately if something happens to them, right?"

Ana nodded again. "That is correct."

"What are you thinking about, sis?" Eve asked.

"I think the boys are safe. At least for now."

"But we just got attacked! And you said that happened to flush the boys out," Eve responded.

"True dat, true dat. But I think that was just a scrimmage. The collecting tape so they can be ready for the game. And now they got data on the boys. They're making calibrations on how to neutralize us when David shows. Then it's on. They'll snatch up David and one or both of the boys because their DNA is probably worth millions."

"But why? If they got David why would they need us or even the boys?"

"You kidding me? How long you think they been trying to stabilize this thing? And you got two success stories without families walking around ready to be experimented on? The boys are low-hanging fruit, why wouldn't they snatch 'em up? Have you ever seen someone that looked like Roman and Aaron on an Amber Alert? They could disappear tomorrow, and it wouldn't even make the news. On the real, fam, Black boys in this country are treated like orphans and expendable, whether they have parents or not. We all know this. And you said it before, Eve, as special and exceptional as we think we are, the only reason they probably won't snatch us is we're too high profile. Too visible. Aaron and Roman are invisible, or at the very least disposable."

Eve nodded. "What do you suggest?"

"I suggest we protect the boys. We owe them that, but we can't protect them forever, so we need to find the big players. 'Cause if we don't, this will never end. We'll be hamsters on a wheel. And we can't live like that."

"I still say we snatch up the Librarian and make her talk."

"Princess, let it go. We are not kidnapping the Librarian. She's just a pawn. No way any multimillion or multibillion-dollar company would trust her, Lurch, or Elvis with anything that could compromise them. They probably don't even know who they work for. Whoever's behind the curtain gives them orders though a handler and then takes notes. I think Elvis and the gang that can't shoot straight really think they are doing something. They probably really think they're important. Newsflash: they're not. They're expendable."

"But what else?" Eve asked.

"There is supposed to be another player in the game, right? What if they are laying low, letting Lurch and team do all the work. Then once David shows up and Elvis grabs him, they grab him from Elvis. Let someone else do the homework and then steal their paper."

The car remained quiet until Eve turned into their driveway. "Sis, I know you. There's still something you're not saying. What is it?"

Gwen exhaled. "Whoever Lurch and them work for, they spent a lot of time and money trying to get to David. They're patient. Like super patient. But if and when that day ever comes, and someone tries to flip the script and snatch David from them? I don't see that happening without a fight. A big fight…"

"And…" Eve prodded.

"Well, we just better get ready and stay ready, because if we get caught in the crossfire when it goes down, we could be collateral damage. Billionaire grandmother or not."

Chapter Sixteen

Eve saw Gwen shift her weight to her back foot. It was subtle. Anyone else would have missed it. But Gwen wasn't sparring with anyone else. *Thump!* Eve kicked Gwen in the face before Gwen could kick her.

"Stop kicking me in the face! I have a dance tonight!" Gwen shouted, taking out her mouthpiece.

"Stop telegraphing every move!"

Gwen put her mouthpiece back in. "Wab evba!"

Eve bounced on her toes and circled away. Gwen pivoted towards her and tensed her shoulders. Eve pivoted to get out of the range of Gwen's overhand right, which she threw every time she tensed her shoulders. Gwen followed Eve, but crossed her feet like a rookie. Eve kicked Gwen in the chest while she was off balance. Eve then pushed Gwen while simultaneously kicking her lead foot out from under her. Gwen's feet went up in the air, and she landed on her back. Eve had gotten better at that sweep kick. It was one of the safest techniques she used on her sparring partners to win a match without hurting them, except for Roman. Eve didn't mind hurting Roman.

Gwen stayed on her back for a minute, and Eve shouted at her, "Get your lazy butt up and get your head in the game! You're telegraphing every move! Every single move! You're practically sending me a text message before you do it! Let's go! Get up!"

Gwen rolled to her feet. "Everybody can't be like you, Princess. This stuff is hard for some of us."

Eve nodded for her to reset. Eve was thinking about dialing it back and taking it easy. But then she had images of the Librarian smashing her little sister, and she raised the intensity. Plus, she was getting antsy. It was May, and nothing had happened. No moves by the Librarian or her team. No contact from David. No hints of what was to come next. So, Eve trained. And trained. And thought about

Tyler. She missed him. Seeing him at school every day and not being able to touch him was a challenge. Maybe after all this was over, they could revisit their relationship, which motivated Eve to bring all this mess to an end. As soon as possible.

Eve started bouncing on her toes as Gwen came forward. "Listen, you tense your shoulder right before you punch. Which is fine, because you can use that as a trap. So, tense your shoulders and then throw a kick. Or tense your shoulder and then pivot away. Mix it up. It will mess with your opponent's timing."

Gwen nodded, and she and Eve circled each other. "Watch your footwork, watch your balance… there, better. Remember, be water. Don't be so rigid, just relax. There you go."

Gwen nodded, stopped bouncing, and set her feet. Eve noticed the heel come up on her back foot, and she snapped Gwen's head back with two jabs, then hit her in the chest with a spinning back kick that sent her feet high in the air and dropped her on her back again.

Gwen got up and threw her mouthpiece at Eve. "I told you to stop hitting me in the face! You know I have a dance tonight!"

"They were just jabs! And I told you to stop telegraphing everything! You need to relax. Be…"

"Stop saying be water! How 'bout you be nicer and stop being a jerk!"

Gwen took off her gloves and headgear, throwing them down, then stomped up the stairs. "I'm going to get ready, so you can be water by yourself."

Eve felt bad. She had to find another way to make Gwen better, because beating her down every day wasn't working, which is why Eve was glad to have Roman to spar with now. He was the only one that could match her intensity, and his super-fast healing power allowed her almost to go all out.

Eve took off her headgear, tossed it in the corner, and retrieved the sticks that Ana had designed for her. The dimensions mirrored the bamboo sticks she picked up when she started researching and practicing Filipino Kali. But the sticks were heavier, retractable, and could act as a conduit for her electrical charges, which she had gotten better at controlling.

Bzz, Bzz!

Eve picked up her phone. It was her mother, saying that they just made it downtown to Eve's grandparents' penthouse. Her mother texted she couldn't talk but told Eve not to wait for the last minute to get Gwen ready. Eve texted back OK.

Eve's mother and father had had to leave after they received a call from Eve's grandmother. Sometimes Eve's grandfather would drink too much and become too much for her grandmother to handle. Eve's parents would have to go and help, as Eve's mother was the only one he listened to when he got like that. For a family whose every move was captured and portrayed in the media, it was their best-kept secret. And their grandmother wanted to keep it that way. She didn't want the public to know that, outside of all the commas in their bank account, their family was just as messy as everyone else's.

Eve set the phone down, wondering why she was such a bad big sister. She let her little sister get beat down right in front of her and couldn't stop it. She had to rely on help from strangers. Granted, those strangers were friends now. At least Roman was. Eve didn't know what was up with Aaron. He had never actually talked to her. They had spent almost every day together for the past six months, and she couldn't remember him even saying hi.

Shaking her head, Eve went to work on the bag. She had to up her game. It was the only way Eve could keep her family safe and she was obsessed with getting better. She spent nights and weekends immersed in researching fighting styles, when she wasn't sparring. She watched boxing footage with her father, attempting to mimic Sugar Robinson's footwork, Mike Tyson's power, and Pernell Whitaker's elusiveness. She drilled everything Muay Thai. The 'art of eight limbs' gave her more options to hurt people. The functional strength and balance developed from judo, jiu-jitsu, and Olympic wrestling were better than weight training. She loved it. And Bruce Lee tied it all together. His philosophy on martial arts and fighting spoke to her on another level and inspired her. 'Be water' was her workout mantra. The freedom of not being confined to one style resonated with her. She focused on fluidity of motion, with no restrictions or limitations.

After a few minutes of hitting the bag, she got into a rhythm. She increased the speed of her strikes while working at different angles.

Her arms and legs started shaking from exhaustion. She clenched her teeth and picked up the tempo, like a drummer wailing away on a solo, oblivious to the world. Eve listened to the slapping of her strikes, and it became her music. She closed her eyes and let the music carry her away. Eyes closed, the sound of her strikes became her radar. She breathed in. She had a runner's high. Endorphins fueled her. She couldn't get tired. She went faster. She missed, lost her balance, and fell. She was dripping sweat as her body shook from exhaustion. Leaning back on her knees, she breathed, coughed, and breathed. She was nowhere near good enough. But it was time to head up and get Gwen ready. Her one job tonight was to make sure this was a special night for her little sister. And for one night, that was all that mattered.

Chapter Seventeen

"Hold still!"

"Why do I need makeup anyway?" Gwen complained while sitting on Eve's bed. Eve had been getting on her last nerve with her micro-focus on every detail. But Gwen was feeling slightly better after a long hot shower that helped her relax. Especially after the grueling sparring session she just had. But all the sparring sessions had been grueling with Eve of late. She broke Roman's nose and arm two days ago. His nose healed in an hour after Ana reset it. Ana also reset his broken arm, which healed overnight. The day before that, Eve had practically decapitated Aaron with a right hook and left uppercut that sent him reeling off the walls. Which was incredibly mean. Because although Aaron was now able to bench over a thousand pounds and was the third-best grappler, he still couldn't bring himself to punch anyone in the face. And that lack of aggression might be OK for English class, but in sparring, not so much.

"Will you stop squirming? And it's not makeup, it's blush."

"Technically, blush is makeup," Ana offered from the doorway.

"Hey, nerd, make yourself useful and get them special clippers and files you made for Gwen."

Ana left, returning in a few minutes and handing Eve a bag of files and clippers.

"Why do I need blush anyway?"

Eve put a finger under Gwen's chin to lift her head while looking down at her like she was a sculpture. She pursed her lips, turning Gwen's head one way and then the other. "Because it highlights your cheekbones," she said softly, applying blush to both sides of Gwen's face.

Gwen closed her eyes and acquiesced. Growing up, Eve was always the pretty one, who liked clothes and excelled at everything. Ana was the genius and child prodigy who was going to change the world. Leaving no space for Gwen. So, Gwen defined herself as a popular prankster. Not an identity she was always comfortable with, but one that drew clear lines of distinction between her and her two exceptional sisters. However, tonight Gwen wanted more. Tonight, she wanted boys to notice her. Tonight, she wanted to be beautiful.

Eyes still closed, Gwen got butterflies. Their mother had had to leave unexpectedly, so Eve took over and spent two hours braiding and styling Gwen's hair. Now she brushed Gwen's cheeks as though she was caring for a priceless piece of art. The tenderness and compassion Eve showed was in stark contrast to the intensity she displayed five hours ago when they sparred. Gwen couldn't remember the last time her big sister was so affectionate towards her, nor the last time she let her.

"Oook! Excellent!" Eve said, stepping back and admiring her handiwork. "Those boys are going to be in trouble tonight! Now let's do your feet and nails." Eve knelt at Gwen's feet and began filing and scraping. She treated Gwen's feet like they were the most important objects in the world, and only she could be trusted with their care.

Once Eve finished scraping, she wiped both feet down with a warm rag and started applying polish to the toenails. Gwen didn't feel worthy. She got butterflies again when Eve blew on her toes after applying the polish. Gwen dreamed that Eve was magically infusing them with her confidence, her beauty, her SWAG. They were now magic toenails on magic feet.

"Hmm," Eve said as she examined Gwen's feet. Satisfied, she started on Gwen's hands next. She massaged and rubbed them, turning them over and back, giving each finger individual and special attention before she started to file.

"What are you doing?" Gwen asked under her breath. She didn't want to speak too loudly and break the magic spell. She wanted to stay in this fantasy where she was the Prettiest Girl in the Land. A land where Snow White and Rapunzel texted her constantly for relationship tips and what they should wear to the ball. Where Cinderella asked for a ride to the after-party while Prince Charming begged her to come on his podcast. It was a good fantasy and made her smile. She just needed to hold onto it a bit longer.

Eve looked up and smiled at her. "I'm filing down your callouses and making your hands soft. They're rough from all that weightlifting. I'm expecting some hand-holding at the very least, and maybe a little more," Eve said, winking at her.

Gwen giggled. *Oh, my God! I'm losing it! I can't believe I just giggled!*

Eve shook her head and laughed out loud as she finished with the callouses. She then filed, shaped, and buffed Gwen's nails with the dedication of an attendant assigned to royalty. Eve's pampering had Gwen thinking that maybe she was beautiful. Maybe this night could be special.

Eve blew on Gwen's nails and stepped back. "Not bad. I'll get your dress while your nails dry."

Thirty minutes later, Gwen looked at herself in a full-length mirror while Eve paced behind her like a nervous parent. Ana nodded her approval while sitting on Eve's bed eating cookies.

"Girl, you get any crumbs on my bed, and it's going to be me and you," Eve snapped.

Ana responded by shoving three cookies in her mouth and ended up spewing cookie bits everywhere while coughing and choking.

Eve snatched her up by her arm. "Go get the vacuum! And hurry up!" she hissed, pushing Ana out the door.

Gwen laughed. The girl was a lightweight. Gwen had just beat her father yesterday by chewing five cookies all at once while he only managed four. Now Ana just embarrassed herself with three.

"What do you think?" Eve asked, looking Gwen up and down, forcing Gwen to refocus.

Gwen studied herself. The image in the mirror looked so adult. So grownup. So beautiful. She was having a hard time reconciling that it could be her. She reached out to touch the mirror to make sure it was real and not a beautiful evil doppelganger from another dimension. The image was real, and Gwen turned side to side to get a view from every angle. "Thanks, sis. I mean, I look... I..."

"You look beautiful, Gwen."

Gwen turned side to side again. "Do you think my shoulders and arms are too big?" Gwen, like her cousins, the Parker boys, was born with broad shoulders and big arms, which had only gotten broader and bigger due to her training. She usually didn't think much about it and always wore oversized sweaters and jerseys. But now, she was wearing a light orange, sleeveless, back-exposing, plunging neckline dress, leaving her feeling self-conscious.

"Girl, please. You got the Serena Williams thing happening. You're gorgeous, with boobies and muscles. And I'm let you know, right, don't underestimate the power of boobies."

Gwen smiled. She did have boobies. She usually covered them, but this dress did the opposite. They were now front and center. Gwen turned to get a better view of her butt. Not as big as Eve's, but round and shapely. She faced the mirror putting her hands on her hips. She felt like a young lady. And she liked the way that felt.

"Ana!" Eve shouted. "Get your butt back in here! And you know what to bring!"

Ana appeared like she was just waiting outside the door. "You rang?"

Eve laughed. "Girl, you got 'em?"

Ana handed Eve a thin blue square box. "Turn around, Gwen," Eve said, taking a string of pearls out of the box.

"Did you borrow Mom's pearls again? She's gonna kill you."

"They are not Mother's pearls, Gwendolyn. These are your pearls."

Eve nodded. "These are you for you, sis."

Gwen's eyes grew wide. She opened her mouth and then closed it as she turned around so Eve could place the pearls around her neck. Conflicting emotions confused her. "These are mine? Really?" Gwen said, touching the pearls while looking at herself in the mirror.

"Yes, sis, these are yours," Eve said.

Ding-Ding!

"Ana, get the door. Tell him Gwen is coming down. Alright, little sis, your chariot awaits."

Gwen took a breath and stared one more time at the more mature, more beautiful version of herself before closing her eyes and saying a silent prayer to her Fairy Godmother. She walked down the stairs, trying to look graceful. Gwen took her time and held onto the railing while hoping she didn't stumble or trip. Walking down the stairs with heels was hard, and if she tripped, she would break the spell.

Halfway down, she saw Javier and caught her breath. The boy knew how to wear a suit. His thick head of curly black hair was combed back, except for the single Superman curl that touched his brown forehead.

Gwen watched as his Adam's apple moved up and down. Eve had told her to look for that, because it could mean an involuntary sign of attraction. As well as dry lips, Gwen noted, as Javier licked his lips. Gwen smiled again. Her big sister knew a little somethin' somethin'.

"Don't you look handsome," Gwen teased.

Javier visibly blushed while looking down at his feet and smoothing out his suit. "Thanks. Thank you. My mother picked out the suit. She says you can't go wrong with the classic three-button. Oh, and, uh, you look handsome too. I mean... I didn't mean that. I mean you look really good. No, beautiful. Yeah, you look beautiful."

Gwen laughed, and Javier looked away, embarrassed.

Ding-Ding!

Kang walked in after ringing the doorbell, without waiting for a response. Kang had been doing that since grade school. He did it so much that Gwen's father joked about getting him a key back in the day.

"Kang!" Javier exclaimed before looking around and getting back in cool mode. "What's up, man?"

Gwen suppressed a laugh. The boys at her school worshipped the ground Kang walked on. Especially the football players. But their adoration was not without merit. Kang only played half the season but made honorable mention by being considered one of the top ten high-school quarterbacks in the state. He was also once a former Junior Olympics national sparring champion in Tae Kwon Do.

"Whaddup?" Kang replied.

"Oh, you know how it is, man. School's having a little dance tonight. Mom and Dad are chaperoning, so I figured I might as well check it out."

"Cool, cool. Hey, bro, mind if I steal Gwen for a minute?" Kang didn't wait for a response as he grabbed Gwen's hand and led her toward the music room.

"No problem, bro! I'm going to tell my mom and dad it's going to be a few more minutes," Javier shouted after them before running outside.

In the music room, Kang let Gwen's hand go and faced her. "My eyes are up here," Gwen teased. Eve was right; boobies had power.

Kang coughed and looked away. "Sorry about that. Just… it's just that I never seen you dress like this before."

"And?" Gwen asked, putting her hand on her hip and holding her head up.

"Javier was right; you look handsome," Kang laughed.

"Boy! And what were you eavesdropping?" Gwen said, punching him in the arm.

"Chill. Chill. I just waited outside to give you and your boyfriend a minute," Kang said, still laughing and rubbing his arm before he got serious. He stopped smiling and looked directly at Gwen, saying, "Gwendolyn Parker, you are stunning."

Gwen swallowed involuntarily and licked her dry lips. She didn't know what to say or how to respond, so she punched Kang in the arm again. "See that wasn't so bad. Was it?"

"Girl, chill! I am not your punching bag. But hey, on the real, I just stopped by for a minute to say something…" Kang put both hands behind his back and intentionally or unintentionally flexed his biceps as his chest strained against a t-shirt that was too tight. And Gwen noticed his mohawk was glistening like he just got out of the shower, while he could exercise a bit more restraint with the cologne. She assumed he was going out with his boys since she knew he and Toni were no longer a thing.

"I'm waiting…"

"Yeah, you know I've been a bit of a jerk to you the last few months. And…"

"No worries, Kang; I was out of pocket. I mean, I apologize for what happened, for what I did to your friends…"

"They're not my friends, Gwen. But here's the thing—you are. You and your sisters have always been my friends. And… and y'all got that medical thing happening and I wasn't there. I was ghost. Too worried about football and other stuff. And I'm sorry for that." Kang dropped his head and looked to the side.

Gwen realized her face was warm, and her mouth was dry. She knew Kang was talking, but her heart beating drowned out his words. Probably due to Kang's Adam's apple moving up and down as he licked his dry lips. She coughed to clear her throat and repeated, "No worries."

Gwen heard the front door open and close and knew it was time to go. She just had to make her feet move.

"Oh, my bad. You got your little dance thing happening. I'll get up out of here. Don't want to make you and your date late."

"We're just friends," Gwen blurted out for some reason and wanted to kick herself for it.

"Gotcha…" Kang said, nodding his head in a way that confused Gwen. He then grabbed Gwen's hand, squeezed it, and kissed her on the cheek. The kiss, and the handhold, lingered long enough to wonder. Long enough to suggest. Long enough to make her legs unsteady, and the butterflies in her stomach fight each other. Then he let go. But the butterflies and shaky legs remained.

Gwen slowly walked to the front door where Javier was waiting. Ana and Eve sat on the steps. They looked at Gwen like she had her hand in the cookie jar. She blushed and looked away.

Kang said his goodbyes and left as Javier followed him out the door before rushing back in and escorting his date to his parents' car.

Head still buzzing and legs still unsteady, Gwen fingered her necklace as she said hello to Javier's parents as they pulled out the driveway. No glass slipper, no magical hair, no poison apple, but Gwen was in a fairytale. She didn't think she would make Prince Charming's podcast because another Prince just kissed her, and it wouldn't be right. She wanted to scream but settled for a small fist pump. *Yeah, that just happened.*

Chapter Eighteen

"Oh my God! Who are you wearing?" Sammie asked as Gwen and Javier walked into the dance with arms linked.

"The hair, the pearls, the dress. Three words, child: Fab. U. Lous!" Dean added, snapping his fingers in a Z formation.

"Will you two stop it? You're supposed to be my dates, remember?" Melissa laughed.

"Melissa, let me just say without hope or agenda, to me, you are perfect," Sammie deadpanned in a British accent while taking Melissa's hand and kissing it.

"You had me at hello," Dean countered, kissing her other hand.

Melissa snatched her hands back and laughed. "I just can't with you two. I need a break! I'm taking your girl, Javier!" Melissa grabbed Gwen, and for the second time in less than an hour, someone led her away from her date.

"Seriously! It's nonstop with those two. My stomach hurts from laughing." Gwen knew how Melissa felt. Gwen was there through the years when Sammie and Dean worked on crafting their rapid-fire back-and-forth. She gave them feedback on what lines were funny, what accents worked, and what jokes were off limits. That was during another, less complicated era in their parents' basement, when it was just the three of them. Gwen smiled thinking about it.

The dance was in the dimly lit school gym, a band at one end on a raised dais, and tables and chairs on the outskirts, leaving space in the middle for dancing. "Whew! Feels good to sit. Hey, where's Eve and Ana? I thought they were coming?" Melissa asked, sitting down at an empty table with Gwen.

"They are. They just had to pick up Roman and Aaron first."

"Ooh, y'all been hanging out a lot lately. What's their story? I think the quiet one is cute."

Gwen laughed at Melissa. "No story. They just needed a ride to the dance."

"Got you and Missy some punch," Javier said, setting cups down in front of Gwen and Melissa. Elizabeth, Rebecca, and some other classmates joined them.

"Kang was over your house!" Elizabeth squealed, which was about the most words she had spoken to Gwen all year.

"What did he say? What did he want? Did he have on a tank top?" Rebecca rambled on and, for once, didn't hold her hand over her mouth, probably because she had gotten her braces off last month and had a cute smile.

"Hey, there go your sisters with those two weirdos," another boy said, puffing out his chest as Eve, Ana, Roman, and Aaron walked in.

Gwen ignored him, because everyone knew he would change his tune if Roman confronted him.

Roman and Aaron grabbed an empty table by themselves towards the back. Stacey and Madhuri dragged Ana to a crowd of students dancing directly in front of the band. Eve strolled the perimeter, looking bored but ready.

"What the heck are the Booger Twins doing?" Elizabeth said, in a tone that was more an indictment than a question. Sammie and Dean were doing a lousy job of breakdancing to claps and cheers as other students joined in.

"Their names are Sammie and Dean. Come on Javier, let's dance," Gwen said as she grabbed Javier's hand and headed for the dance floor without looking back. Middle school was not for the faint of heart. Students jockeyed for attention and respect. They were balancing trying to fit in and stand out, all with the weighted expectation of family, teachers, and coaches. And no one escaped unscathed. Gwen was not mad at Elizabeth for playing the game. She had played it herself. But Sammie and Dean were two of her best friends, and she was not going to co-sign jokes at their expense by remaining silent.

"Wait! I'm coming! I have to keep an eye on my dates!" Melissa said as she joined Gwen, Javier, Sammie, and Dean on the dance floor.

Gwen and her friends sang loudly off-key, danced confidently off-beat, and laughed until their stomachs hurt. Sammie and Dean's antics had her and Melissa in tears. She couldn't remember when she last had such a good time. It was going down on record as the best night of her life. Then Ana touched her elbow, with Eve at her side.

"Some of the listening devices are going out," Ana whispered.

Gwen's heart sank. She knew her fairytale couldn't last. She also knew there would be no prince coming to save her. Gwen and her sister had to do the saving. The bugs going out meant either David was in town, or they already had him and were tying up loose ends, which could mean the boys.

"She said the bugs are going out," Eve repeated over the noise.

"I heard…" Gwen began to say but the alarm interrupted her. It was going down tonight. The fire alarm was a tactic to get everyone out while isolating the girls or separating them from Roman and Aaron. But after last summer's meet when they got the antidote from David, for which they went in unprepared, the Parker sisters vowed never to let that happen again. Eve and Ana had on their gear beneath their clothes, while Eve had Gwen's rolled up in her tote bag. The Parker sisters stayed ready.

"Let's go. My parents said I can have people over," Javier said, pulling Gwen's hand.

Gwen pulled her hand back. "My parents said I have to leave with Eve. But I'll call you tomorrow."

Javier looked confused as the students headed for the exits. "But…"

Gwen kissed him on the cheek. "Go. I'll call you tomorrow," she said with a forced smile.

"OK, OK, great! What time, because we have church tomorrow? Hey, maybe just text me before or…"

Gwen laughed and pushed Javier away. "Will you go!"

Javier beamed as he poked out his chest and left with his friends while shouting, "We'll talk tomorrow!" so everyone could hear.

Gwen watched as teachers and chaperones ushered students to the exits. The students were probably headed to restaurants, movies, and after-parties while Gwen was getting ready to fight for her future and maybe her life. And fight for the life and the future of Roman and Aaron. That was part of who she was. That was part of her identity. And now it was the only part that mattered.

Two police officers entered and ushered the teachers and chaperones out, but not the Parker sisters or Aaron or Roman. The Librarian strolled in, trailed by Lurch and Elvis. More police entered from the four other doors, closing them and staying in place to guard the exits. The Parker sisters and the boys moved to the center of the dance floor. Gwen counted ten police officers. Two more men entered the gym, dressed casually in dark clothes. The shorter, bald, more muscular one looked around, and the officers watched his every move. The taller one with the long blonde ponytail glared at the Librarian. Him and the muscular one had an air of authority and they moved with a confidence bordering on arrogance similar to Eve.

The muscular one pulled out his phone and talked while continuing to look around as if he was assessing the situation. The Librarian looked at him like she was a child waiting for a parent to say she could open her birthday gifts. Gwen instantly realized they were Smash and Riggins and appeared to be running things.

The big one put his phone away and nodded at the Librarian, who grinned from ear to ear. "Can I have this dance?" she asked, stepping to Eve.

Gwen put out her arm to stop Eve. "I got this, sis. Keep an eye on the boys. Ana, get your birds with night vision in the air and give us eyes for what's outside."

"Done," Ana said, typing on her leather bracelet.

"Let's bum-rush 'em," Roman said.

Gwen shook her head. "No, we have no idea what we would be rushing into. Ana, while I'm taking out the Librarian, get us a headcount and position of everyone inside and outside. They probably got something planned so we might need an escape path. And see if you can hack Smash's phone. I'll try to drag the fight out as long as I can, but whoever Smash talked to might be the key to ending this. And if everything goes south and something unexpected happens, your bird's number-one priority is to follow Smash and Riggins."

"But we need to get out of here. We're supposed to meet David tonight," Roman complained.

"David is here?" Eve asked.

"Well, not at the school, but he's in town. He left a message with the track coach. Said he signed the permission slip for us to join the team. That was our signal."

The sisters looked at each other with Gwen saying, "They probably already have David." Gwen watched as Aaron and Roman's faces changed with the realization that David being the super-mastermind they had made him out to be still didn't prevent him from being captured. And for the first time, Gwen saw fear in Roman's eyes. But she didn't have time to console either of them. She had work to do.

"Eve?" Gwen said, turning around so that Eve could take off her necklace. She trusted Eve to protect it at all costs. Gwen then handed Eve her earrings as she kicked off her shoes. She hugged her sisters, gave them a pound, and turned to face the Librarian. She didn't have to win. She just had to stall until Ana got the logistical information and hacked the phone.

"For family," Eve whispered in her ear. Gwen's sisters knew she had to do this alone. They knew she had to face the monster and exorcise her demons while buying her sisters time.

Gwen stepped away from her sisters towards the Librarian. The Librarian looked at Eve, then at Gwen. Gwen shook her head. If she were able to get past Gwen, Eve would be waiting for her.

The gym was quiet as the Librarian and Gwen stood about fifteen feet apart. The Librarian turned away from Gwen, exposing her back, and started shadow boxing. Gwen did the same, ripping both sides of her dress. She bounced on her toes while throwing punches, kicks, and knees. Gwen tried a few combinations. When her body felt warm, she turned to face the Librarian, who was waiting for her.

Gwen and the Librarian slowly circled each other, with the circle gradually getting smaller until they were in striking distance. Gwen stopped and set her feet while the Librarian lightly bounced on her toes. No one else moved. No one else made a sound. Gwen clenched and unclenched her fingers as she inched toward the Librarian. The Librarian smiled, loudly cracked her knuckles, and continued to bounce.

Kaw Kaw!

Everyone looked up to see two enormous and scary-looking birds sitting on the windowsill at the top of the gym. They were Ana's birds, and they looked down as if they could bestow life or death on anyone or everyone in the gym if they chose. It made the hair on Gwen's neck rise.

"What the…" one of the policemen said as he pointed his gun at the birds.

"No!" the bald muscled man said, glaring at him.

The police officer hesitated as if weighing whether he was more scared of the man or the birds. The man won, as the officer slowly holstered his gun.

Gwen refocused on the Librarian. She started inching forward, while the Librarian began bouncing on her toes again. Gwen stopped when she felt she was close enough and gritted her teeth. The Librarian stopped bouncing as well. It was quiet enough for Gwen to hear the fire engines outside. She waited. The Librarian waited.

Kaw!

Gwen attacked with a lunging right hand that grazed the top of the Librarian's head and sent her stumbling back. Gwen chased and put everything she had into a left hook. The Librarian ducked, and Gwen missed badly, losing her balance. The Librarian sneered, snapped Gwen's head back with a jab and straight right hand before she circled out of range. Gwen reset and followed her. The Librarian moved with confidence and skill. But she had a weakness. Gwen just needed to find it and exploit it, or suffer another savage beatdown. The Librarian pivoted one way, then the other, sneered and dropped Gwen with a jab, straight right, and thunderous left hook.

On her hands and knees, a dazed Gwen saw red droplets appear beneath her. She slapped the ground and jumped up. She had to get locked in. She had to do better. Blood trickled into her mouth, but she ignored it as she reset. The Librarian approached. Gwen threw a jab that connected but, the Librarian slipped Gwen's right hand and countered with a left hook to the body, then lifted Gwen off her feet with a right uppercut.

Gwen scrambled to her knees and looked at the Librarian, who grinned, continuing to bounce on her toes. Everyone was counting on her, and she was blowing it. Lives were on the line, and she was getting beat down by a freakin' librarian. And all she could hear was Eve's voice in her head. *Be water.* Gwen didn't even know what that meant. But she knew she had to be different, because the boxing thing was not working.

The Librarian smiled at her while Gwen slowly stood up. Gwen started bouncing on her toes with her arms hanging relaxed at her side. Gwen was a first-degree black belt in Tae Kwon Do and had sparred full contact for over seven years. She was more comfortable with the angles and the spacing of Tae Kwon Do than boxing. And she was hoping it confused the Librarian.

The Librarian stopped bouncing on her toes, looked at Gwen sideways then started bouncing again, but not with the same rhythm or confidence. Gwen spat the blood that was still dripping in her mouth and smiled. She was on to something.

After a few seconds of no action, the Librarian advanced, and Gwen pivoted away. The Librarian frowned, paused, reset, and advanced again. Gwen did two rapid kicks, Tae Kwon Do style. The Librarian blocked the kick to her face, but the second kick to her ribs sent her stumbling sideways.

Gwen smiled. The Librarian smiled and nodded, and they reset. Gwen continued to bounce on her toes Tae Kwon Do style with her arms relaxed at her sides. The Librarian advanced, and Gwen switched feet to southpaw. The Librarian paused, sneered, and Gwen pivoted away. The sneer was the tell. Gwen smiled while feinting a kick to one side, and quickly kicked her opponent on the other side of her face. Gwen's kick was blocked, but its force caused the Librarian to stumble, lose her balance, and fall before quickly jumping up.

The action paused as two firemen entered and nodded at the bald muscled black dude. Gwen needed to end this. Gwen stopped bouncing and set her feet, and the Librarian closed the distance quickly. Gwen didn't move. She knew the tell; she just had to be patient and capitalize on it. Then it happened. The Librarian sneered, and Gwen spun into a back-fist that landed flush on the jaw while avoiding the Librarian's jab.

The Librarian spat blood and rushed Gwen on shaky legs. Gwen exploded into her with a flying knee to the stomach. It felt good to finally hit the move after Eve had caught her with it every week for a year. The Librarian folded over. Gwen kicked her face, snapping her head up. The Librarian stumbled back, and Gwen shadowed her, waiting for an opening. Eve had taught her that timing was more important than speed. The Librarian took a breath, and while she reset, Gwen stepped into an overhand right hand that dropped her. The Librarian struggled to her hands and knees as Gwen kicked her in the ribs. The kick lifted the Librarian three feet in the air and spun her one hundred eighty degrees, dropping her on her back as her head bounced off the hardwood floor.

Gwen gave a subtle nod to Ana that it was almost time to go as she mounted the Librarian, sitting on her chest and raining down punches. Once she started, she couldn't stop. The punches came faster and faster. The Librarian's face became caked in blood.

Kaw!

Gwen stopped. Her hands were bloody and trembling. The Librarian turned her head to the side and coughed blood. Gwen stood and took a couple of steps. She tried to make her hands stop shaking. They didn't listen. She breathed in deeply and wiped her tears. It was time to go. Whether Ana had finished her tasks or not, they were leaving. Gwen took another deep breath, clenched and unclenched her fist as Eve and Ana turned towards the exit. In Roman's words, it was time for the bum-rush. Gwen heard the Librarian get up. She had forgotten how quickly she recovered. Gwen turned to face her and found herself staring down the barrel of a gun. The Librarian sneered, blew a kiss, and she heard Ana scream.

Blam!

Chapter Nineteen

"Gwen! Gwen!" Eve screamed in her sister's face as she cradled her head in her lap.

"Aaron's gone!" Roman shouted.

"Shut up! Gwen! Come on little sis, open your eyes! Please, Gwen! Please open your eyes." Eve was frantic. She had just seen her sister get shot in the head at point-blank range. Eve heard Ana's scream and turned in time to see the muzzle flash. Her speed kicked in, and she moved faster than she had ever moved in her life. Eve's body had changed physiologically, so she could not only handle the stress of moving super-fast without injury, but maximize it. Her tendons, ligaments, and joints contained an abnormally high elasticity level, allowing for longer strides while reducing the risk of tears or sprains. Her bones had a high degree of pliability, along with being exceptionally strong and dense enough to absorb the impact of her foot striking the ground at twenty times her body weight without breaking and rebound like a coiled spring. These adaptations allowed Eve to cover thirty feet, kick the Librarian's gun hand, punch her in the jaw, and catch Gwen before she hit the ground in less than half a second.

The Librarian slid across the floor from the impact of Eve's punch, and the lights went out. When they came back on, the gym was empty except for the sisters and Roman. Aaron was gone, leaving a single shoe where he had been standing.

Ana knelt and examined Gwen closely. "She is breathing, and the bleeding has stopped, but I cannot find an entry wound," she said softly after wiping blood away from the side of Gwen's face where she was shot. Ana picked something up that looked like a mangled piece of metal. "Interesting…" she said, looking at it closely while Eve cradled Gwen's head in her lap.

Gwen's eyes fluttered open.

"Her eyes are open!" Eve shouted. "Can you hear me? Are you OK?"

Gwen shook her head and pointed to her ear. "I can't hear you!" she shouted, sitting up. "What happened?"

Eve hugged her. "Don't ever scare me like that again!"

"Gwendolyn, I was terrified," Ana said, hugging her next.

Gwen pointed to her ear, shouting, "I can barely hear you!"

Ana and Eve nodded while they helped Gwen stand with Ana whispering to Eve, "The proximity of the gun might have adversely affected her hearing. I do hope it is not long-term."

"I heard that, dork!" Gwen said, shaking her head like she had water in her ear.

"How you feel?" Eve asked, still holding onto Gwen.

"Some ringing in my ears, but it's starting to go away. Got a killer headache though. Get me up to speed," Gwen said, wiping the side of her face and then pausing to look at the blood that was now on her hand.

"You sure you OK, sis?" Eve asked, still holding on to her.

Gwen pushed her away. "I'm fine! Now get me up to speed!"

"They have abducted Aaron. And Roman is outside attempting to break into Eve's car, no doubt to go after them. And as you predicted, things did go awry but the birds are following Smash and Riggins, who I assume have Aaron."

"Eve, let me get my suit. We don't have a lot of time," Gwen said, running for the exits with her sisters. Eve handed Gwen her full body unitard, which was packed down to the size of rolled-up jeans. Gwen carried it like a football as they sprinted outside. There was one fire truck, two police cars, and some faculty still milling around, but most of the cars were gone. Eve's car was by itself at the far end of the parking lot, where Roman was trying to smash a window with a brick. Eve shook her head. Ana had designed the glass and told her it was virtually unbreakable, but Eve recognized desperation, and Roman was desperate. Like Eve just had been.

"Don't trip! I'm going after Aaron!" he shouted as they approached. He was in tears and turned like he was ready to fight all of them.

Ana handed Gwen her shoes back that she had kicked off in the gym and placed a hand on Roman's shoulder. "We are with you, my friend. We are all going after Aaron and I promise you that we will do our best to ensure no harm comes to him." She then handed him an earpiece. "Take this so we can communicate. My friends are tracking them as we speak. I will scout ahead to provide intel."

Roman looked confused. "You mean it?" he asked hesitantly. Ana nodded as she took off her pants, shirt, and jacket, placing them in Eve's trunk, and retrieved her hooded cloak, staff, ballistic vest, and helmet. The helmet's latest iteration resembled a slimmer, sleeker, black fencer's helmet with an all-glass front. When Ana donned the helmet, ballistic vest, and cloak while holding her staff, Eve couldn't believe how cool she looked. The black full-body unitard with extra grey padding around the shoulders, elbows, and knees, her modified army paratrooper boots, the ballistic vest... it was lit. It had Ana looking like a superhero with her cloak blowing in the slight breeze. It was the coolest thing Eve had ever seen and gave her hope.

Ana took a couple of steps away from the car, slowly rose off the ground, steadied herself, then shot away in the night sky like a black rocket.

"Did you see that?" Roman asked, turning toward Gwen and Eve. "Did you see that? Ana just flew away. Ana can fly! Is the cloak antigravity or something?"

"Turn around, Romana!" Gwen shouted as she changed into her leotard. Eve retrieved her helmet, vest, fighting sticks, and boots. At Eve's request, Ana created a pair of split-toe ninja-style tabi boots. They were light and allowed Eve a fuller range of motion when running as well as providing a better grip when fighting. And, like all the other gear, they were bulletproof, with Ana's cloaking software.

"Ain't nobody trying to look at you!" Roman shouted as he turned away from Gwen. "We're wasting time—we have to go!"

"Ready!" Gwen shouted, throwing her clothes in the trunk and grabbing her boots, modified ballistic vest, utility belt, and helmet. She then held up the seat, and Roman jumped in the back.

The car had a continuous power source, and Eve didn't need to start it. When Gwen shut her door, they sped away.

"Ana, what's up?" Gwen asked.

"Headed north, approaching city limits, and I have already charted your course. Do not tarry," Ana said over the car's speaker system.

"Yo, fam, really appreciate this. I mean, you know y'all Parker girls doing this, it… it means a lot."

Eve nodded, "We got you," while looking at Roman in the rearview mirror.

"But, uh, what's up with the magic cloak? Or can Ana fly? Either way, I mean, y'all should have told us."

"That's on me," Gwen said, turning to look at Roman. "Didn't want you unintentionally revealing stuff and tipping our hand. I mean, y'all come through for us and all, so it wasn't about trust."

"Naw, I get it. But I mean, just looking at Ana in that all black gear and flying away in the night… Ain't never seen anything like that. Still trippin' over it. And shorty, you got shot point-blank. And you… you like, bulletproof?"

"Just found out about that myself," Gwen responded. "After all this is over, I'll have Ana look into it for some answers. But I still have a headache."

Twenty minutes later, they were outside city limits, following directions Ana had sent. "We should go stealth now," Gwen said.

Eve nodded. "John Henry, go stealth." The car's exterior turned black, the engine went completely quiet, even the license plate faded to black.

"John Henry, show Ana," Gwen said, and a middle section of the windshield displayed what Ana saw as she flew. Eve saw the headlights of two cars driving down what looked like a dirt road. "Ana, what's up?"

"I believe they are headed for the old Lincoln hangar. I'll re-chart your course so you can approach undetected."

They drove for a few minutes, then turned down a narrow dirt road as corn stalks flew past on both sides. Eve clenched her jaw and sped up. "John Henry, go dark." All the windows turned black, the headlights and taillights went off, and the windshield displayed a three-dimensional image of the road and surrounding area, with a red line for them to follow. Eve increased her speed again to one hundred and eighty miles an hour.

"Yo, you Parker girls know ride or die is just a metaphor, right? I mean, Aaron been my day one, but we can't save him if we crash. I'm just saying…" Roman said, his voice raising an octave.

"Chill, with Ana's tech and Eve's reflexes, we good."

"We not good! We are not good! Slow down!"

Eve slowed down as she started sweating. She was a mix of nervous energy, fear, and anticipation. She had to dial it back, because Roman had a point. She had driven in dark mode a few times but not at this speed, and if they crashed, they weren't saving anyone.

"There it is," Gwen said as an image of a building with lights on came into view on the left. "Let's get off the road and walk from here."

Eve nodded as she slowed down and turned off the road, stopping parallel to a wall of cornstalks. It was dark. No stars, no moon, just blackness interrupted by the distant lights of their destination. *Game Time.*

"John Henry, secure and cloak!" Gwen said after she and Roman got out. The car lowered like it was on hydraulics and seemed to disappear, but it was Ana's cloaking software using reflecting technology. It still amazed Eve.

"Dope…" Roman whispered. "Aaron didn't tell me about this."

Eve didn't respond, but the truth was they had kept almost everything from Roman and Aaron. Eve was starting to feel guilty about that. Aaron and Roman had risked it all to save girls they barely knew. When this was all over, Eve and her sisters would reevaluate their relationship. Because up to this point, it had been one-sided.

Gwen handed a ballistic vest and night-vision goggles to Roman, saying "Put in the ear-piece Ana gave so you can communicate with us." Gwen then strapped on her vest and helmet. She looked intimidating. Even scary. Gwen's boots had hidden lifts, making her three inches taller. Her vest also differentiated from Ana's and Eve's. It had padding that covered her deltoids, making her shoulders look broader and more muscled. Her unitard also had more padding around the elbows, knees, and biceps. She looked like a super-strong villain. Not like a ninth-grade girl. Ana designed the uniforms to make them look like men, because if stories got out about three super-powered girls running around fighting bad guys, they would be grounded until they graduated from college.

"Yo, shorty, this doesn't feel right?"

"You have the vest on backwards, bro... Here let me, dude, seriously... you need to take off your goggles first... Aiiight, fam, there you go. You straight. OK, I got point so stay on my heels and keep your voice down. Eve brings up the rear."

"Gotcha," Eve replied while stretching. Her unitard was also unique to her body type. It contained extra padding on her shoulders to help offset her hips and big legs. Unlike her sisters, her ballistic vest had an extension in the back to cover her butt, which would otherwise be a dead giveaway that she was a woman. A Black woman. Eve moved around, noting that her utility belt containing grenades and other tools was bulkier than she preferred. She strapped on her small backpack, then her helmet, experiencing sensory overload. The amplified noises were deafening, and her eyes became overwhelmed by her sisters' visors' views. The helmet self-adjusted, decreasing the volume and shrinking and dimming the images of her sisters' POVs, placing them on the upper right side of her display. Eve grabbed her fighting sticks, and twirled them in each hand to get a feel. They felt good. She sheathed them in the pockets on the side of her left thigh. She was ready.

After walking over two hundred yards, they crawled to the cornfield's edge that was the beginning of the old Lincoln airport. It was small. Two runways that ran side by side were lit by ground lights and twelve dated lampposts. On the far side of the runways was a three-story building that looked abandoned. Some armed men wearing police uniforms stood outside the building next to three cars and a van.

"What you got, Ana?" Gwen asked.

"Smash and Riggins are en route. I believe they have Aaron. A private jet is tracking to land in seven minutes."

"You got a count?" Eve asked. She could tell from Ana's POV that she was sitting atop the building.

"Eighteen. I'm tagging them now."

Eighteen dots appeared on Eve's visor. She licked her lips.

"Van is pulling up now," Ana said.

A white van pulled up, and the muscleman and his tall skinny friend got out. They opened the back and dragged out a hooded Aaron with his hands cuffed or zip-tied behind him, and another hooded dude who was probably David. A few seconds later another car drove up, and Lurch, Elvis, and the Librarian got out. Eve gritted her teeth.

"Plane is approaching now," Ana said as a luxury jet landed and slowed to a stop in front of the hangar. Eve, Gwen, and Roman had to move to get a better view.

"Aiiiright, I don't think bullets can stop me, and Gwen, you definitely bulletproof, so we attack together and grab Aaron and David. Eve, you're super-fast and mad nice with your sticks so when Gwen and I make it back here you take out whoever follows us. We straight?"

It took everything Eve had not to pop Roman upside his head. His plan was comical. It was a miracle he and Aaron had managed to stay alive this long. "Uh, Gwen, any thoughts on this?" Eve asked.

"Yeah, I have a few thoughts. Ana, is the building empty?"

"Um, I believe so?"

"Yes or no, Ana!" Eve shouted but regretted it. She needed to chill. Eve wasn't worried about anyone hearing her because their helmets were soundproof. Still, she needed to be more patient and remember who the enemy was.

"Chill, Eve. What do you mean, Ana?"

"Yes, I do believe it's empty at this point. During my initial sweep, I thought I detected an anomaly, but couldn't verify on my second and third sweeps."

"That's going to have to be good enough. Roman, take this. Ana designed it and it's super-sharp so be careful," Gwen said, handing Roman a small knife with a pointed end.

"Um, yeah, thanks. I always wanted one of these..."

"It's to puncture the tires, genius. Now it's going down like this: on my go, Ana blast one of Aaron's favorite songs to give him a heads-up, kill all the lights for eight seconds—it needs to be pitch black—then do the strobe thing for thirteen seconds. I want them blind and then disoriented. Eve, you and Ana with the darkness and strobe light have twenty-one seconds to take out eighteen dudes. Eve, you built for this, sis, don't play. Roman, on Ana's signal dash and slash at least one tire on every car, then let these go and get back here."

"What the… what the heck are these?"

"They're CS grenades used for crowd dispersal. Slash the tires, then Ana will signal you a second before the strobe starts, so stop and keep your eyes shut until she signals you to open them. After you hit every car, release your canisters and get the heck out of there. You don't want to be caught in this stuff."

"Yo, but what about y'all? Are y'all immune to this gas or something?"

"Hardly. The helmets are sealed and contain forty-eight hours of oxygen, depending on exertion. In short, do not worry about us. As Gwendolyn said, slash the tires, release the canisters, and retreat."

"Right. Ana, have your birds attack Smash and Riggins, and whoever else might be guarding David and Aaron so I can snatch them up and meet y'all at the car. Now, fam, I want to overwhelm them. Their eyes will be adjusted to the darkness when the strobing starts and then after strobing their eyes will need to readjust to the dark again. So, hit 'em hard and fast, get in and out before they know what happened. Everyone meets at the car. Ana, keep their lights out all night if you can. Darkness, strobe, darkness, smoke, got it?"

"Darkness, strobe, darkness, smoke. Got it," Eve said.

Roman coughed. "Uh, yeah, it might work. I'm cool with it."

"Let's do this," Eve said as she activated the camouflage feature on her uniform. Gwen did the same.

"Which of Aaron's songs should I play?"

"It doesn't matter. The song just needs to do two things; give Aaron the heads-up, and be so loud they can't communicate or hear each other shouting. I don't want them to be able to hear themselves scream, so blast it," Gwen said.

"Understood. I am ready," Ana replied.

"OK, on my count. Five, four, three, two, and one!"

It went dark as Eve heard a loud blaring in her ears. She sprinted toward the closest red dot on her visor. The helmet lowered the volume as she approached. Ana had already dropped one from above with her staff and flown away. Eve sprinted past her first, breaking one leg and arm with her sticks. She was through playing nice, and Gwen was right; she was built for this.

Eve did the same to the next one. The following two were standing by each other when it started strobing. Her visor adjusted automatically. One busted kneecap, one broken hand, one broken arm, and one broken leg, and she was on to the fifth. She heard shouts and screams of pain over the music, as did the other man, who she dropped with two broken legs as he had his gun drawn. She ran faster and got lucky again because two more men were close together. She broke both their hands and one kneecap and one femur. Ana dropped down on two more standing close together, which made six for her. Not that Eve was keeping score.

Her next two victims were so scared they almost shot each other. She did them a favor by breaking their gun hands and a leg on each. The next guy heard their screams and fired in Eve's direction, emptying his clip. Reckless—he could have killed his friends if they weren't already on the ground screaming in pain. Two of his bullets clipped Eve. One bounced off her arm, almost making her drop one of her sticks. The other glanced off the top of the helmet, making her slow down. She regained momentum and broke both his arms and legs for being careless as she raced past him.

"I have Aaron and David," Gwen said.

Eve could see from Ana's POV that Gwen had David draped over her shoulder while she and Aaron raced for the cornfields. Eve gritted her teeth, took out the last two guys standing, released her gas canisters as it went dark, and sprinted for the cornfields. Eve wasn't counting, but that was eleven for her, seven for Ana.

"Ana, we need eyes on Roman. I didn't see any of his canisters go off."

"I'm on it," Ana said.

Ana's bird's-eye view showed Roman on his knees with Smash and Riggins standing over him. They both had night-vision goggles and had the discipline to keep their guns drawn on Roman with one hand while fighting off attacking birds. It was impressive and spoke to why they were in charge. Ana couldn't risk attacking them from above because their guns might go off. And as fast as Roman healed, Eve didn't think he could survive a gunshot to the head.

Eve saw Gwen cut Aaron and David's ties and stash them in the cornfields before racing back to join her. They gave each other a fist bump as they ran toward Smash and Riggins. They were not leaving Roman behind. Without warning, the lights came back on. They were in the middle of the runway, right in front of the jet.

"What's up, Ana?" Gwen asked, sounding irritated.

"It was not me. But I will look into it."

"Don't bother," Gwen responded. "Stay hidden and get backgrounds on everybody, especially Smash and Riggins and whoever is on that plane. We play it by ear from here."

Eve twirled her fighting sticks. They were now partially visible to their adversaries. Ana's cloaking and camouflage software were best at night and against objects. In direct light, they looked like shimmering black ghosts. They stood and waited as the smoke from Eve's canisters dispersed into the night wind.

Smash and Riggins took off their night-vision glasses, coughed, and spit blood while wiping more blood off their faces from the scratches of Ana's birds. The Librarian slowly got up from the ground, looking tentatively at the sky. Lurch and Elvis got out of a car. They had tangled with the Parker sisters before and probably didn't want to take any chances. Six of the seven men Ana had knocked out struggled to their feet. The seventh stayed down, but coughed as the gas dispersed. None of the men who had the misfortune of being in Eve's path were in any position to stand. There was a lesson in that, and Ana would hear about it when they got home.

The Librarian squinted at Eve and Gwen, looking hesitant while wiping her eyes and coughing.

"What it look like, Ana?" Gwen asked.

"Using facial recognition to run backgrounds, but the uplink is slow. I'll need a couple of minutes."

"I'll buy you your minutes," Gwen said, turning off her camouflage feature and taking off her helmet. The gas from Eve's canisters was mostly gone now, with only vestiges remaining. Gwen handed her helmet to Eve, who turned off her camouflage as well but kept her helmet on.

The Librarian smiled. Her bruises were almost gone from an hour ago. She was strong, but her super-fast healing power was what made her dangerous. She started for Gwen. The tall blond guy they referred to as Riggins grabbed her by the arm. She snatched her arm away, and he countered by pointing a gun at her. The musclebound guy, Smash, put his hand on top of Riggins's gun, and Riggins lowered it. The Librarian spat at his feet, and Eve thought he might shoot her, but his better angels prevailed. Or maybe it was his bank account.

Gwen had stepped forward to meet her when a short, plump man in a dark business suit hurried down the stairs of the plane. "Stop! This is not necessary! Not necessary!" he shouted as he wiped his sweaty face with what looked like a silk handkerchief. He moved as fast as his short, stubby legs would carry him, intercepting the Librarian. "David! We must secure David! And one or both boys. The girls are off-limits."

The Librarian brushed past him.

"How much time, Ana?" Eve asked while studying the men standing and holding guns. All of them were the men Ana had knocked out. None of the men Eve encountered were able to stand or hold guns, which was intentional from Eve. Lurch and Elvis moved to the rear and were now standing behind the men with guns.

"Another couple of minutes. I'm aggregating and formatting."

Gwen and the Librarian were feet away from each other. "Stop her! Stop!" the businessman yelled, but before the gunmen could move, the Librarian rushed forward and threw a punch. It spectacularly went downhill for her after that. Gwen moved like she expected the punch, and slipped inside, grabbing the Librarian by the throat and crotch area. She lifted the Librarian over her head, held her a second, then pile-drove her headfirst into the ground. It was an amazing move, and Eve couldn't have been prouder. She used anticipation, timing, and, most notably, her strength. Eve could feel the force of the impact through her feet, and she smiled. *Might be hope for that girl after all.*

No one moved as Gwen took a step back. The Librarian staggered to her feet, stumbling towards Gwen and throwing an off-balance punch. Again, Gwen slipped it and lifted her opponent high into the air, slamming her headfirst into the concrete. Eve didn't care how strong or resilient the Librarian was, she wasn't getting up from that. The Librarian didn't move. Eve thought she might even be dead until she heard her moan.

"Go!" Smash said as the gunmen surrounded Eve and Gwen. Eve calmly handed Gwen back her helmet.

The businessman approached, stepping in front of the gunmen. "You Parker sisters are truly remarkable. Remarkable. You demonstrate a tactical and fighting brilliance that rivals the Special Forces. Truly remarkable, and the reports do not do you justice. But where is the other one? Watching everything remotely in your special car, I imagine? But that is of no consequence, because all we are here for is David. Provide us David and you can have your little friend."

"Sending report now," Ana said, and Eve's visor displayed the biography of the man standing before her. Gwen's visor would be showing the same thing.

"Can't do that, Mr. Belov, or would it be OK if I called you Mikhail?" Gwen's voice sounded different when using the helmet's external speakers, but the snarkiness was still there. "Listen…" Gwen continued. "This is how we are doing this. You shut down the Icarus Project, and I mean like yesterday. Or my sisters and I will visit you and—what is it now— your third wife? Each one is more expensive than the last. But it doesn't matter. Shut it down, or my sisters and I will visit you, and there is no house that Ana can't get into, and if you read the reports you know how Eve likes to break things. Decision is yours, but choose wrong and your employer Massive Dynamic won't be able to hire enough lawyers to handle all the investigations we will unleash. I'm talking kidnapping, espionage, fraud, embezzlement, murder, but on the real, Mikhail, how are you going to embezzle money that your company embezzled from the government? That's just next-level shady. Oh, Roman and Aaron leave with us tonight, and from here on out, they're off-limits. Period. As is David."

Mr. Belov tried to smile while wiping his sweaty face, and Eve could see the wheels turning. "My, you are smart girls. Maybe too smart. But you should know that not everything is negotiable. I will allow you to have the boys, and your privacy, so you can return to your normal lives, but David comes with us. There is no room for negotiating there."

Everyone turned as the Librarian struggled to her feet, and Eve felt sick. The entire left side of her face was smashed, bloody, and showing bone. Her nose was unrecognizable, one eye hung loosely from the socket, and she had teeth missing. "Kill her!" the Librarian managed to say. Everyone just stared at her.

She snatched a gun from the closest man and pointed it at Gwen. Eve wasn't worried. Gwen was bulletproof, on top of wearing the most advanced bulletproof tech ever designed. Eve didn't move and didn't need to.

"Enough! Enough! I knew you were a liability! That's it, you're out!" The businessman grabbed the Librarian by the arm.

"You monster!" the Librarian said, facing him. "You don't own me! You don't own me anymore!" She pointed the gun and fired.

Fear and horror triggered Eve's speed power, but she didn't know what to do and could only watch as the businessman fell in slow motion. It didn't seem real. It didn't seem possible that life could be ended so carelessly. It wasn't right, and Eve felt sick to her stomach. The businessman crumpled to the ground and twitched once as his life, and the Parker girls' last chance at normalcy, leaked out. Their plan was as dead as the businessman on the ground. No one to blackmail. No one they could threaten to leave them alone.

A murder of crows suddenly appeared and attacked the Librarian. They surrounded her, pecking and cawing. The Librarian was barely visible beneath the black-winged barrage. She fired off shots in every direction, not hitting one bird but sending everyone to the ground or scurrying for cover, except for Eve and Gwen. An invisible Ana dropped from fifty feet in the air, hitting the Librarian on the top of the head with her staff so hard that it sounded like a jolt of thunder. The Librarian dropped to the ground, out cold, as Ana and the birds disappeared into the night.

The men took their time getting up and reappearing while looking at each other and up at the night sky. When no birds reappeared, they pointed their guns at Gwen and Eve again.

"It's over!" Elvis said as he and Lurch pointed guns at the gunmen. It was all so strange.

"What do you think you're doing, man?" one of the men shouted over his shoulder while keeping a gun pointed at Eve and Gwen.

"He's right! This is over! Stand down!" Smash bellowed.

"Ya heard? Lower your weapons!" his tall, lanky friend added.

"Naw, bro! Somebody got to pay us!" the gunman who had anointed himself the spokesman said.

"Ain't nobody getting paid! This was off the books. Any chance of getting paid is laying on the ground with a hole in the head," Smash responded.

"I don't give a..." Ravens suddenly attacked the gunman, then a thump was heard, and the birds disappeared. He swayed on his feet for a few seconds like a sapling blowing in the wind before he stumbled sideways, fell, and didn't move.

"Nope! Not me! Not doing this!" another gunman said as he ran for a car.

"Wait for us!" yelled another gunman as he raced after him.

"Don't leave us!" one of Eve's victims said, still on the ground with a broken leg as he cradled his broken hand. But his pleas fell on deaf ears as the car sped away.

"You kids get out of here. A cleanup crew will be here in a few minutes, so make sure you're ghost by then," Smash said as he yanked Roman up by his collar, cut his ties off, threw him some car keys, and then pushed him forward. Roman turned around like he wanted to fight. Smash looked him up and down, saying, "Boy, I read your files and seen your work, but you don't want it with me," Smash said as Riggins stepped aside to give them room. Roman hesitated, then turned and walked towards Eve and Gwen. First time Eve saw Roman walk away from a fight. She was glad he did.

"This is over, Bishop," Gwen said with finality. "We don't ever want to see you or your friend Erick again." Bishop and Erick's bios were now displayed on Eve's visor.

"Not my call, little lady. Not yours either," the bald man formerly known as Smash replied.

"Make it your call. Go back to teaching hand-to-hand combat in the military, become a gym teacher, get a shrimp boat on the bayou. We don't care. But if we see you again, the feds, police, and newspapers will receive a packet detailing all your extracurricular activities. As will your mother and grandmother in Louisiana…"

"Hey! Don't threaten me, little lady…"

"Threaten you? You're kidnapping kids, Bishop! You're a decorated war veteran and you're kidnapping kids! So don't talk to me about threats! Just know that my sisters and I will do anything—anything—to protect our friends and family. So find another line of work, because if this goes south it's a wrap, you and Erick will be wearing an orange jumpsuit when his pregnant wife comes to visit."

"I said it's not my call, but do yourself a favor and keep my family's name out your mouth because, little lady, if my mother hears about this, I'll be visiting you. And you don't want that smoke. Let's hit it, Slim." Bishop and Erick started loading all the men Eve had injured into both vans. Then they drove off together.

Eve watched them leave, then she thought her visor picked up movement in the hangar, but it was gone as quick as it came. She and Gwen turned towards Lurch and Elvis. Lurch and Elvis looked at them, then laid their guns on the ground. Their faces looked tired. They nodded at the sisters before they drove away. Maybe the Librarian had freed them. Maybe this was their chance for a new beginning. Eve didn't know if she would ever see them again, but they showed their true colors and deserved whatever freedom and happiness they could find.

Aaron and David emerged from the cornfields as the sisters took off their helmets. The night air felt good. But it couldn't console Eve. A dead man was a few yards away. And maybe he was a monster who created other monsters, but there were no maybes about him being dead. There would be no redemption arc to his story. No chance to atone for his sins, and Eve didn't doubt that he had many. His last chapter would read like Dr. Frankenstein's, dying at the hand of his creation. With an assist from the Parker sisters. Eve became overwhelmed with guilt.

Gwen dropped to a knee as she struggled with her gag reflex. She discharged a small amount of mucus, and it almost triggered Eve's gag reflex. Eve fought it. She forced herself to swallow a small amount of bile. She spat to try to cleanse her mouth. It didn't work.

Gwen stood up and spit before turning to meet David and Aaron as Roman joined them. "Good thinking, keeping David hidden. He was our only leverage," Gwen said, sucking in oxygen and coughing it out.

Aaron looked at everyone and the dead body before he responded, "That wasn't the plan. He took off running and I had to catch him and force him back. Didn't think it right to leave y'all like that."

Eve nodded, but Aaron looked and sounded angry and frustrated. She couldn't remember ever seeing him like this. But from what she knew about David, him leaving kids to fend for themselves was on brand.

"He took off running through the cornfields when it was pitch black?" Gwen asked. "How the heck did you catch him?"

Aaron looked down and away, then sighed. "I… uh, have heat vision."

Ana dropped quietly from the sky between Eve and Gwen. She took off her helmet, closed her eyes, and held her face up to the night sky. Eve knew the feeling.

Aaron's eyes got big as he looked at Roman. Roman shrugged. "Yeah, mami can fly."

David looked at the sisters, "But how is that possible? We need to…"

Eve stepped to David and put her finger in his face. "You need to be quiet."

"But I, I…"

Roman stepped between them. "Trust me, Doc, just be quiet for now."

David nodded and then looked around like he was checking for another escape route, but he didn't move.

Eve took off her backpack, removed a shoe, and handed it to Aaron. He looked like he didn't trust her. Like he didn't trust anyone or anything. Then his eyes softened, and he mouthed, "Thank you."

"What do we do now?" Roman asked.

"We go home," Eve said.

Roman looked at the fallen businessman and the Librarian. "What about the bodies?"

"Body," Ana countered. "The Librarian is not dead."

"Should we say a prayer or something?" Gwen asked.

Aaron knelt and tied his shoe. "Pray for kidnappers and murderers? Y'all can miss me with that." His tone was jagged, rough like a serrated knife.

"Let's just go home," Eve said. She was bone-tired and emotionally spent.

Ana knelt and put a one-hundred-dollar bill beneath the foot of the businessman. Everyone looked at her. "I prefer this be his final passage," she offered.

It was odd and not expected, but Eve understood. The money was payment to the ferryman who transported souls across the river. Ana wanted to ensure the businessman did not become stranded for lack of payment and spend eternity causing mischief and haunting the living. He had done enough of that when he was alive.

"We out, fam," Roman said as Aaron and David headed for one of the remaining cars.

Aaron then stopped and turned around. "You Parker girls came through tonight. 'Preciate that, and I won't ever forget it."

It was the most words Eve might have heard him speak. "That's what friends are for," she replied.

Aaron looked at her, then her sisters, before he headed to the car.

Ana flew off into the night sky as Eve's car pulled up using the auto-driving feature. They got in, and as they drove off, someone ran off the plane, helped the Librarian up, and supported her as they both got back on the plane. Eve shrugged. She did not doubt that they would run into the Librarian again, but for tonight she was going home.

"Eve, would... would you mind helping me put the pearls back on?" Gwen asked. Eve put the car on autopilot so she could snap the pearls around Gwen's neck. Then they turned the car back into an ordinary Mustang with the top down and headed home. After driving for a few minutes, Ana dropped out of the sky into the backseat without a sound.

They turned off the dirt road, and Eve asked, "You think the boys will OK?"

Gwen fingered her pearls and shook her head. "No, Eve, the boys won't be OK. And neither will we. Our DNA is invaluable and there a lot of greedy people out there who will risk it all to monetize it. Monetize us. We're walking lottery tickets, so we're a long way from being OK."

"You probably right," Eve said after a long pause.

"I know I'm right. All we did tonight was buy ourselves time, but the risk is never going away. That's our new normal."

"So… so what do you suggest, sister?" Ana asked in a halting voice. Eve looked in the rearview and saw tears streaming down Ana's face.

"We got two options: turn ourselves into the authorities and hope and pray for leniency and that our parents don't go to jail, and Grams' legacy isn't too badly tarnished…"

"What's option two?" Eve asked.

"We just did it. We destroy whoever messes with us as a deterrent," Gwen punched her open hand with her fist as she talked. "We destroy companies, we destroy lives. We make it so painful for whoever crosses our path that they never want to think about us again. We make sure that they understand the risks aren't worth the rewards. But on the real, fam, even that won't be enough. There will always be someone willing to risk it all."

Eve didn't respond. She didn't need to. Gwen was right. The darkness and silence weighed on Eve as she drove. Her vision became blurry once they got to the city limits. She couldn't breathe and had to stop moving, so she pulled over. Eve gripped the steering. The journey from childhood to adulthood was supposed to be gradual and marked with idyllic milestones. Milestones like your first bra, your first dance, your first kiss. The Parker sisters' childhood ending was abrupt and cataclysmic. Their childhood ended with a single bullet and a singular loss of life. They watched a man die a violent death tonight. A death in which they played a role.

Eve's hands wouldn't stop shaking as tears fell into her lap. She squeezed her eyes shut and listened to her heart. She tried to control her breathing, but sobs interrupted her as her chest heaved. Deaths were piling up around the Parker sisters. The deaths circled them like sharks in the ocean as they fought to keep their heads above water.

Doctor Jim, the mercenary, the stadium staff, the businessman. Gwen was right; they were a long way from being OK.

Once the tears stopped and Eve had her breathing under control, she looked at Gwen, who had just stopped crying herself. She then grabbed Gwen's hand and squeezed it. Gwen squeezed her hand back, and Eve let go, reaching back and grabbing Ana's hand, who still had tears streaming down her face. She held Ana's hand until the tears stopped. Then Eve let go and drove home, leaving what was left of their childhood behind at the abandoned airport with the dead businessman.

Chapter Twenty

"Why won't you tell me?"

"Seriously, Stacey, I honestly do not know if Gwendolyn has anything planned. Besides, if she did, I would be the last person she would share that information with." The last day of school had Ana's friends requesting any information she could provide on how Gwen was going to prank the school and who from the faculty was going to get clowned. And the attention was not limited to Ana's small circle of friends. Students Ana didn't usually socialize with asked that she pass on to her sister they were available for backup if needed.

"Hey, Ana, my brother's band is hiring me as a roadie for their tour this summer and you know, if it's OK, I'll text you the info so you can follow online? You know, if you like?"

"We'd love to!" Stacey said, snatching Danny's phone, typing on it, and giving it back to him. "I put both our numbers in there because we're best friends and do everything together. Right, Ana?"

Ana nodded.

"Uh, yeah, you know, the more the merrier. They're doing a gig in the city this weekend, so if you want to come down and meet everyone beforehand… but it's at a bar so you can't stay…"

"We'll be there! Right, Ana?"

Ana smiled and nodded, still searching for her voice.

Danny smiled back. "Cool, cool, I'll text you the info later. Bye." He then turned and ran down the hallway like somebody was chasing him.

"Oh, my gawd! We are going to have so much fun this summer! No fat camp for me! Both our sisters have cars! Ana, this could be the best summer ever!" Stacey said as they walked down the hallway.

"This summer does portend possibilities…" Ana added. It had been three weeks since the school dance, and just the previous night Ana finally made it through the night without nightmares. But her nights of not sleeping had not gone wasted. She made significant headway in her John Henry Artificial Intelligence and nanotechnology project. This was thanks mainly to her spyware/malware project, which had prospered beyond her wildest dreams and freed up a lot of the time that she had previously used looking for bad guys. The malware spread from phones to laptops, to notepads, to desktops, and only her company's software could remove it. Her paid subscribers went from fifty thousand to ninety million. That propelled the small company she had secretly purchased from a small-cap to large-cap as its revenue and stock price increased exponentially. The malware also gave Ana an entry into Massive Dynamic, the dead businessman's company. She corrupted all their data and posted some of their more salacious financials online. Their stock dumped, and Ana made billions because she had shorted it the week before. And, as Gwen predicted, Massive Dynamic hired her software company to assist with data recovery. In the three weeks since the school dance, Ana had netted over seven billion dollars, and her software had infiltrated every level of Massive Dynamic, including the C-suite. Stacey was right; this summer had the potential to be the best ever.

"Hey, there goes Maddy! Hey, Maddy! Oh, Maddy, me and Ana are going to a bar this weekend to listen to Danny's band! Danny from orchestra has a band! You should come with! It's going to be so much fun! And I'm trying to get Ana to tell us whatever it is Gwen is doing so we can help! Isn't Gwen the coolest?"

Madhuri laughed, as did Ana. And Ana was just glad to have Maddy back and didn't judge her to decision to try on other friends for size. Ana also allowed that, by an arbitrary shifting barometer Gwendolyn could be categorized as the most popular, if not the coolest of the Parker sisters. But Gwen, unbeknownst to her fawning classmates, was probably also the strongest person in the world, as well as being immune to small-arms fire. Ana had discovered a virtually impenetrable chitinous exoskeleton on Gwen, built from glucose and protein. It was similar to that of an ironclad beetle, which had the most durable exoskeleton in the animal kingdom. Until now. However, Gwendolyn still bled and bruised, because she had an excessive amount of blood between her skin's epidermis and dermis layers. It was fascinating.

"Oh my God! You know what I just thought of? Guess! You'll never guess! You guys should get horses! It would be sooo much fun! We can all go riding together!"

Madhuri and Ana looked at each other and laughed as seven of Ana's birds flew overhead in V formation. Ana looked up briefly and frowned. She was finished with bird experiments and enhancements. It wasn't right, and Gwen's comments about Dr. Frankenstein hit too close to home. She was happy the birds decided to stay and take out drones, but their brief exodus forced her to recalibrate her thinking. They were not her birds, they were her friends. And she was happy to have them.

"So what do you say, guys? Horseback riding this summer?" Stacey persisted.

Ana gave a noncommittal shrug. She had too much on her plate, and she didn't need to add a horseback riding to it. Besides, Ana was more of a bird person.

***

Gwen had never seen the school so wild. Half the teachers called in sick, and the administration could not get enough last-minute replacements, leaving students unattended and unsupervised. The students took advantage, with a few ambitious ones attempting to prank the staff and school. But they lacked the experience, logistical aptitude, and creativity, so most, if not, all were quickly busted. But Gwen would gladly hand over the prankster extraordinaire title. She just wanted everyone to know that she retired undefeated.

"Hey, girl, got room for me?" Elizabeth asked, standing over Gwen with her lunch tray. The table of misfits had gradually dissolved. Lately, it had just been Elizabeth and a few girls from the basketball team. And Gwen and Elizabeth had started texting each other again. Gwen was relieved. Elizabeth was a good person who got lost in the pressures and games of middle school. Something Gwen could relate to.

Gwen looked up and smiled. "Always, girl," she said, sliding down to make room. Rebecca sat across from Gwen and next to Melissa, who managed to roll her eyes, unbeknownst to Elizabeth. Gwen stifled a laugh. But most students like Elizabeth were trying to figure out who they were and what defined them. Mistakes were made, and resets were needed. Students fought for their identity, but being young meant that could change from week to week. Gwen considered herself lucky. She had her family as her North Star. That made a difference. But Elizabeth would be OK. She just needed space, time, and patience. They all did.

"I like your dress," Elizabeth said to Gwen.

"Thanks, thought I'd change it up a bit. You know, keep 'em guessing." Gwen laughed and winked at her. Elizabeth laughed as well. Gwen kept her starter jerseys in heavy rotation, but a dress now and then wouldn't hurt.

"I think you look hawt!" Javier announced to everyone. Gwen and Javier had experienced a two-week whirlwind romance. They went to the movies, talked on the phone every day, and had a couple of make-out sessions. But after two weeks, Gwen wasn't feeling it, and they settled into the friend zone. However, being with Javier and talking was a good distraction from the night of the dance. Javier might never know it, but he helped Gwen through a rough period.

"Hey, anyone hear what happened to the Librarian? I bet she set that fire and ruined the dance for everyone," Elizabeth said.

"Girl, who cares? Hopefully, the school gets a librarian that can at least read!" Melissa laughed.

Gwen laughed as well while turning to look at Elvis, or Mr. Thompson to use his real name. He tipped his hat, and she nodded back as he continued to watch every student like a hawk. It was a new day for him and Lurch, or Mr. Bassett. They were now full-time employees of the school. Ana's background check also revealed that, like Roman and Aaron, they were orphans in a way. The Army jailed them for trying to cover up their sergeant torturing prisoners. That sergeant was the Librarian. They became pariahs, ostracized by their community when they were released. The Librarian finished her time and tracked them down, getting them jobs with a defense contractor. Multiple science experiments, including genetic enhancements and enough plastic surgery to evade facial recognition, gifted them new identities and new jobs. Now they were starting over again. Gwen was still going to keep an eye on them, but they earned their space for now.

"You cool Gwen?" Melissa asked.

"Yeah, I'm cool, are you?" Gwen laughed as she turned back to her friends.

They all laughed as they left the cafeteria, passing Roman and Aaron. The boys had been ghost for a week then reappeared, saying David had snuck away again. He left a note saying he had to tie up loose ends but would be in touch. How adult of him. But Ana hooked them up with a two-bedroom condo in a nice area only a fifteen-minute walk to school. They refused at first, especially Aaron, but finally relented. And if Aaron was quiet before, he was completely shut down now. He rarely even talked to Roman. Gwen couldn't remember ever seeing him smile. But he was a friend, and Gwen wasn't giving up.

The rest of the day passed without incident, outside of Sammie and Dean starting a water-balloon fight that somehow only got Mr. Little drenched. Gwen sensed her classmates were disappointed. They wanted something big. Motorcycle-duct-taped-to-the-roof-of-the-gym big. Frogs-in-the-cafeteria, hair-remover-in-the-shower-dispensers big. But Gwen couldn't put pressure on herself based on others' expectations. Trying to figure out who she was was complicated enough.

Eve was parked outside after classes ended. Gwen waited for Ana so they could walk together. That had been the pattern since they first fought the Librarian months back, and they never stopped. Before Gwen got in the car, she looked around. She had pulled off some epic pranks, got suspended three times, lost some friends, made some new ones, fought, cried, laughed, all within those walls. But she was going to be in tenth grade next year, and maybe her father was right. Maybe it was time to put aside childish things.

***

"Same arm?" Eve asked.

Amy looked down and adjusted her sling. "Yeah, tripped over a hurdle."

"But you haven't run hurdles since like seventh grade? I remember, because it was the first year you beat me in the hundred," Eve said as Toni joined them, kissing them each on the cheek.

Amy shrugged. "Team's competitive in the sprints, so Coach and my mother said hurdles would be my best chance to make varsity. But I needed a break anyway. You know? Recharge my batteries. This year has been wild. Besides, I've been drilling and shooting with my left hand every day after school. When summer ball starts, I'll be ready."

Eve nodded. "Can't wait to see your new moves, because you know I'm coming to some of your games. And have you heard from Lucia lately? Does she like her new school?" Amy's best friend Lucia transferred after receiving a full scholarship to a private school over Christmas break. It was a twenty-minute train ride from her home and boasted impressive alumni, including a few Ivy Leaguers. Eve knew Lucia would make the school and her family proud.

Amy looked directly at Eve before turning away. "We exchanged texts last week but it's softball season, so she's pretty busy."

"Well, tell her I said hello." Eve felt terrible for Amy. Unfortunately, happiness was not promised, and change was constant. Eve had been changing in ways that made her uncomfortable. She watched a man die, but unlike her sisters, that trauma didn't weigh on her. Eve had a couple of sleepless nights, but nothing like Gwen or Ana experienced. She didn't feel bad about breaking limbs or breaking men. Eve argued her actions were a necessary deterrent. The only thing that still bothered Eve from that night was how slow she was. Eve should have been faster and more efficient. She didn't know what that said about her as a person, so she avoided the question.

Amy half smiled. "I'll do that, Eve. I'll do that. You know, I still think about what could've been if we ever had the chance to play together. I mean we had some fierce moments competing against each other, but I think on the same team we could have been special…"

Eve swallowed. "Yeah, I think about that too, and…"

Toni threw up her arms. "Y'all depressing me! Let's get out of here and do something! Want to hit the city with me?"

"Girrrl, you need to chill and give the city a break from you. Everyone heard about your accident," Eve laughed.

"Pfft, it was a little fender bender. No biggie…"

"But I thought your folks took your keys?" Amy said.

"They did, but Lady Tremaine is in Paris and my father is working like one hundred hours a week, so I doos what I want to doos."

Amy looked at Eve then back at Toni before saying, "Hey, what about coming over to my house? We just got the pool cleaned and we can lay out and catch some rays?"

"Boring! I'm going to the city with some friends. You guys want to come with?"

Eve crossed her arms and shook her head. "Uh, I'm good, but thanks."

Amy adjusted her sling. "Yeah, I think I'm just going to chill."

"OK, I'll call y'all this weekend," Toni said, kissing Amy and Eve's cheeks and walking down the hall like she was a runway model.

Eve watched her go, shaking her head. Toni was the beautiful, rich, white girl who gave beautiful rich white girls a bad name. "I'm going to pray for that child."

"Girrrl, you and me both," Amy agreed. "But the offer still stands. You know, if you want to come over."

"Hey Eve, hey Amy," Tyler said, walking up.

"Hey Tyler. I'll catch you later, Eve," Amy said, turning quickly and walking down the hall.

A lump appeared in Eve's throat as she watched Amy weave in and out of celebrating students before she disappeared around the corner. Eve would give her a call later. Eve needed a friend outside of her sisters. Someone else to keep her grounded, because she felt she was losing herself in violence. Eve's propensity for violence was starting to worry her, because all she could think about was getting better at it. She needed to surround herself with good people worried about everyday things like varsity and boyfriends to stay grounded. Eve needed to call Amy. She needed to sit by the pool. She needed to catch some rays with a friend and reminisce about what could have been.

"So, um, any big plans for the summer?"

"Not really; leaving for London tomorrow with my grams for a week. But that's about it. What about you?"

Tyler laughed. "London, huh? Guess big to the Parkers would be like going to Mars or something. My summer gonna be low-key. Working full-time at your grandfather's shop and he's letting me be flexible, so I don't have to miss football camp."

"No AAU ball?"

"Can't swing it this year, I'm still kind of behind in math so I have to take a summer class."

"But you know you better at basketball than football, right? I mean, have you seen your game tape?" Eve laughed.

Tyler laughed as well. "Girl, you a trip, can't believe you trying to crack on somebody…"

"What's up, soph?" Mike G said as he glided next to Tyler.

"What it do, Mike G?" Tyler replied, dapping him up.

"Hard to believe I'm really outta here," Mike said, surveying the hallways as energetic students bounced off each other while heading for the exits and freedom.

Tyler nodded. "I hear ya, bro, I hear ya."

"Hey, Mike, I never really got a chance to apologize about that thing with my sister…" began Eve.

Mike waved his hand. "Accidents happen, and truth be told Kang should have been starting anyway. He balled out all summer and in practice and deserved a shot. Plus, dude loves football more than I ever did. Coach is just loyal to a fault."

"But… I mean it didn't mess up your scholarships or school choices or anything?"

Mike and Tyler laughed together. "I'm going to Stanford for pre-med, I, um, think I might be alright. Football was more for my dad than anything."

It was Eve's turn to laugh, while feeling guilty about stereotyping and putting people in boxes as she had been put in her entire life. She still had a lot to learn.

"Stay up, soph, and you got my number so hit me up this summer."

"Mos def. And take it easy on them Cali girls, bro." Tyler laughed as he dapped Mike up again before he glided away. "Pretty cool dude right there. You know his father is like a top surgeon? And they use to call him G Minor because he played the piano until he started ballin' out in football and baseball. Just wild, huh?"

"Uh, yeah, wild is one word for it."

Tyler then stepped closer to Eve while rubbing the back of his neck. "So, uh, be cool if I call you when you get back? Maybe we could hang out or something?"

Eve was confused. Tyler broke up with her, and she didn't know what game the boy was playing. Then she looked up at that crooked smile and dimples, and her hand started itching from wanting to touch him. She swallowed and smiled. "Number is still the same." She didn't want to make it too easy.

Tyler stared down at her as his Adam's apple moved up and down. He licked his lips before smiling. "Cool, cool, well, I got to get up, but I'll catch you later…"

"OK, and I know my grandfather already mentioned it, but you welcome to the Juneteenth cookout. You know, if you can squeeze us in," Eve said.

"Girl, you know I'm there. Your uncle got the best ribs in town and… uh, be cool to see your family again. It's been a minute."

"That it has," Eve said as she squeezed his hand to say goodbye. They hugged and walked off in opposite directions.

Chapter Twenty-One

"Foul!"

"Stop crying! That was a defensive foul if anything!" Eve shouted back at Roman as she took the ball out. They had been playing in the Parkers' driveway the last two hours after two hours of sparring, and Gwen was exhausted. The Parker sisters had got back from London three weeks ago and quickly set up up a summer routine. The boys would ride their bikes over in the morning for weight training. Afterwards Aaron helped Ana with tech stuff, while Gwen watched movies or played video games with Roman. Eve chilled in her bedroom doing the typical moody teenager thing. After lunch, they sparred, and then the boys would bounce. Sometimes they would come back later in the evening for more sparring, but those evening sessions got intense.

"Son, she been spinning you like a top all day. I'm embarrassed for you. I mean, at this point your moms wouldn't even claim you for tax purposes. Let me holla at you…" Aaron said as he motioned Roman over. The boys were back to staying in motels. Their neighbors kept calling the police on them to complain about loud parties—parties that involved Sammie and Dean, and other classmates. Gwen didn't even know they had friends, but they got popular as soon as they got a cool spot to stay. Ana had to call in a favor from a cop because the police fingered them for being part of an international drug cartel that had broken into a hospital last year. Now they had to put all their TVs, sneakers, and DJ equipment in storage. It seemed Roman was a sneaker-head, and Aaron an aspiring DJ. Giving two fifteen-year-olds an apartment, money, and no adult supervision didn't work out so well. But they had a good time while it lasted.

Roman threw the ball back at Eve and walked over to speak with Aaron in secrecy. In the last three weeks, Aaron had come out of his shell. It wasn't gradual, but more like a switch went off. One day he didn't talk, and the next day he was cracking jokes. And unlike Roman, he was funny. Ana also confirmed he did have heat vision.

But he couldn't be less interested in his powers, sparring or working out. He just wanted to watch anime and listen to music.

"When you two finish braiding each other's hair can we finish the game? This is game point and then we have to get ready," Eve said, standing with the ball resting on her hip as she wiped the sweat off her brow.

Gwen smiled. Eve could be difficult, but she respected Roman. All the Parker sisters did. He was making strides toward doing the right thing. He had a cellphone now and had reached out to his mother and younger brother and got a chance to see his baby sister. Gwen heard his mother wanted him home, but he refused to leave Aaron. Gwen understood the call didn't end well, but it was a start.

"Do you two need to get a room?" Eve persisted. Gwen, Ana, and Aaron had stopped playing thirty minutes ago after Eve won her fourth straight game and elbows started flying. Gwen didn't need another accidental elbow to the throat. But Gwen stayed alert in case she and Aaron needed to separate Eve and Roman again. Those two went at it like cats and dogs. Roman hated that Eve was better at him in everything, and Eve hated that Roman wouldn't acknowledge that she was better at him in everything.

Aaron whispered one more thing in Roman's ear, and Roman nodded, approached Eve, and threw his hand up. "Check!"

Eve spun the ball on her finger and looked at him without responding.

"I said check, shorty! What, you can't hear me or something?"

"Son, chill. We all heard you. You louder than a pimp's clothes; just finish the game," Aaron said.

Eve threw the ball, so fast Roman almost fumbled it. He recovered, passed it from hand to hand, spun it on his finger like Eve, then sat it down and rolled it to her, crowding her as soon as she picked it up.

"Chill with the elbows, ma!" Roman complained as he reached in for a steal.

Eve ignored him, froze for a second, then when he froze too, she bounced the ball through his legs, spun around him, retrieved the ball, threw it off the backboard, caught it, and threw down a monster windmill dunk.

Gwen, Ana, Aaron fell into each other with their hands in the air, shouting, "Oh, my God! We're not worthy!"

Gwen laughed. Gwen used to try to do everything Eve did athletically. Basketball, track, Tae Kwon Do. But that was a losing battle. Eve was a singular talent, with a capacity for violence that made Gwen uncomfortable. Gwen no longer felt the need to compete or measure herself against Eve. Gwen was unique and special in ways that set her apart. The night of the dance, she started accepting that. Along with being smart, funny, friendly, and athletic, Gwen excelled in logistics and planning under pressure. She was better at that than her ninja super-athlete older sister and child prodigy super-smart younger sister.

Eve threw the ball back at Roman. "Game, Romana."

"Time to get cleaned up! Roman and Aaron, one of you can use the shower in the basement, the other in the guest room, and I already laid out some clothes for you. Let's go! Chop, chop!" the girls' mother shouted from the front door.

Roman glared at Eve while walking to the house, and she glared back like *I wish you would* just as two SUVs pulled up in the driveway.

A short while later, they were all in the backyard chilling. Hot showers and good food smoothed things over, and everyone was happy to relax. Roman managed to shelve his machismo tough guy routine and even blushed when he met Gwen's grandmother. Aaron reverted to old Aaron, meaning he didn't say more than two words and kept his earplugs in.

Gwen was sitting next to her favorite cousin, Walter. His younger brother Emmitt would not stop bragging about how he would dominate the PAC 10 next year as a freshman.

"Dude, how is your mouth not tired?" Antonio asked. "I mean seriously, fam, the only reason you got that scholarship was because I kept feeding you."

"How are you gonna try to take credit for my scholarship?"

Gwen always enjoyed the back and forth between her cousins, but it didn't feel the same today. She and her sisters grew up idolizing them and going to their games. And when Gwen and her sisters started playing sports, their cousins returned the favor. Sports were now over for the girls, and the boys would all be in college when school started. This year the cookout felt like a turning point and not a continuation. Gwen's great-grandmother showing up also spoke to that, and the different paths the family members were taking. Her great-grandmother, the mother of her famed grandmother, was in her late nineties and had Alzheimer's, and seldom left the penthouse in the city.

Ding-Ding!

A few seconds after the doorbell rang, Kang stepped out onto the deck, followed by Amy and Tyler. Gwen's face grew warm, and her stomach started buzzing. Her cousin Walter gave her a severe case of side-eye. She dropped her head. He nudged her, and Gwen shrugged as she got up to meet her friends. It seemed like the Parker family was as good at gossiping as they were at sports.

***

Tyler covered his mouth and coughed. "Seriously, my guy, your pop's Old Spice is burning my eyes and nose hairs."

"Stop hatin'," Kang replied under his breath as they stood on the deck with everyone watching.

Amy wrinkled her nose and laughed. "Tyler is being kind, my friend. Smells you like fell into it."

Kang knotted his brow, sniffed his shirt, shrugged, and said, "Nice dress, Amy. Going to the prom after this?" Amy was wearing a short, light blue summer dress, revealing her toned legs. Her hair was tied into a bun, and blush colored her cheeks.

"Oh, please. Forgot we were coming and had to throw this on last minute," she replied dismissively.

Kang exchanged skeptical looks with Tyler, and they both laughed. Kang had an older sister and knew Amy put in work to get ready, but she got points for trying. However, Kang wasn't here to give Amy a hard time. He was here because he had questions that needed answers. He had been friends with the Parker sisters since they ran track in grade school. His sister, who was also a national sparring champion, became the only babysitter that their parents trusted not to get punked by their daughters. Their lives and families had ties that went back over a decade. His feelings now surprised him like a sack from the blindside.

"Hey, guys, glad you made it, but I thought Toni was coming?" Gwen asked as she approached. Kang had to close his mouth forcibly. Gwen was barefoot, wearing a short, light orange summer dress. She was stunning. She looked like an Amazon warrior princess with muscles and curves. He was shook. He started reciting the alphabet backward in his head to distract himself from looking at her body. He couldn't get past Y.

"Hey, girl," Amy said, hugging Gwen. "Talked to Toni last night and she said she was coming, so your guess is as good as mine. Is that… is that your great-grandmother?" Amy asked, gesturing toward the gazebo at an elderly woman in a wheelchair with oxygen tanks.

Gwen swallowed. "Yes, that's her, she, uh, well, it's been a while since she been out and we're all just happy she's here."

Kang discreetly smelled his shirt again, feeling self-conscious. He stretched, looked at his reflection in the sliding glass doors he just walked through, and grimaced. His chest looked OK, but he should have done more curls instead of push-ups before he came. Gwen's arms were almost as big as his, leaving him feeling intimidated and inadequate.

"Yo dawg, you straight?" Tyler asked, looking at him.

"No doubt, bro, just ain't seen Grandma Jefferson in about ten years," Kang replied. He felt it essential to let Amy and Tyler know—and to remind Gwen—that he had history with the Parkers. That Kang knew they referred to their great-grandmother as Grandma Jefferson and their famous grandmother as Grams or Grandmother Harris. Kang stepped off the deck with everyone staring at him and headed toward the gazebo with as much confidence as he could muster.

Kang smiled while waving to Gwen's parents and her grandmother and grandfather. But in Kang's family, the eldest got the most respect, so that dictated he greet Grandma Jefferson first. He held his breath as he knelt and held the hand of the frail matriarch.

Grandma Jefferson put a hand on his cheek. Kang held it there while saying softly, "Hello, Mrs. Jefferson." Kang saw a flash of clarity in her eyes. A second of recognition. Then it was gone. That was the evil of Alzheimer's. He knew this because his uncle had it. His uncle, who loved Tae Kwon Do and teaching American students about his country, was robbed of that passion. Once his passion was taken away, his condition deteriorated. But his uncle and Grandma Jefferson had lived full lives their families could be proud of. And although history might remember Grandma Jefferson as the daughter of a sharecropper and wife of a Tuskegee Airman, family and friends would remember her as a piano teacher and World War Two nurse who, because she was Black, was only allowed to treat POWs. A visionary who preached the beauty of the American dream while living the ugly reality. Not unlike his parents and uncle, who emigrated here to start a new life and participate in the American dream themselves.

Grandma Jefferson's hand dropped to her lap as the flash of recognition was replaced by uncertainty and confusion. Kang rose and greeted the rest of the adults before joining his friends at the picnic table. Grandma Jefferson, like his uncle, worked tirelessly so their families could benefit from their sacrifice. Karma would see to it that they got to dance in the endzone for their next life.

"Kang! Look out you, my dude, all rocked up. I see you, my guy. I see you!" Emmitt said as Kang grabbed a seat.

"Thanks, Em. Been trying to put in a little work, you know, put on some weight to help me deal with the hits."

"I feel you on the tip, Kang, but don't forget your speed work. They can't hit you if they can't catch you," Antonio added. Antonio was a second-team all-state quarterback. He got a full-ride scholarship to a school in Florida where his mother, who was from Columbia, had family. "And stay in the playbook. You QB1 now. Gotta lead by example."

Kang nodded. The Parker boys were the real deal and state legends. Kang would gladly accept any advice they offered.

"Kang, walk with your boy and let me holla at you," Walter said, getting up and not waiting for a response. Kang followed. "Em right, look like got a little size on you now..."

Kang swallowed. Walt didn't want to talk about his weight gain or gym routine, but he decided to play along. "Yeah, took a pounding last year, so I'm hoping a little bit more weight couldn't hurt."

"I feel you on that tip, but check it—been hearing rumors about you and my little cousin. Know where I'm going with this?" Walt talked while putting food on his plate.

Kang was stuck. Walt had been his idol since he first started playing football. And Kang knew Walt liked him. He even came to a couple of his sparring matches back when he used to compete. But as much as Kang respected Walt, Kang was willing to risk it all. Today he was going to shoot his shot. He just needed to let the Parker boys know that no-one respected his family more than him, and he would never step out of pocket. "Walt, it's not like that, but uh…"

Walter faced him. "Save it, dawg. I'm not her pops and you don't need my blessing or anything. But I'm just saying them girls are special, and you been my boy since day one so you know just… uh, be mindful of that…" Walter then put more food on his plate and laughed. "But on the real, if you trying to bulk up you better put some ribs on that plate. My pops did his thing, besides, you know how Gwenny is if you just get salad, she gonna clown you," Walt said, winking at him.

Kang smiled and piled some ribs on his plate. Far be it from him not to take advice from the Parker boys. Kang sat back down with a loaded plate and noticed the oldest of the cousins, Antonio's sister Antoinette, give Walter the nod. The Parkers stayed locked in and didn't miss anything.

As Kang settled in, Gwen laughed her loud laugh. Kang wanted to laugh without even knowing what had been said. But you didn't need to know why Gwen was laughing. That was the cool thing about her. She could laugh by herself and at herself, whether anyone joined in or not. Today, she laughed at the far end of the picnic table at something the new guy Roman said. Kang needed to know what Roman and Aaron were doing at the cookout. He asked around about them, but outside Roman thinking he was tough, nothing turned up. He might need to take a direct approach to ensure they were not taking advantage of the Parkers. It was about the principalities.

During the next three hours, Kang watched Walter get another plate while Amy innocently took his seat so she could listen to Emmitt and Antonio go back and forth. The extra attention upped their antics. They arm-wrestled, played rock-paper-scissors, played spades, and arm-wrestled again. They were hilarious and exhausting.

The next thing Kang knew, Tyler was tapping him on the shoulder, and his window had closed.

"Time to bounce, dawg." Kang got in the game but didn't even throw a pass.

"I'll walk you guys out," Gwen said, appearing out of nowhere, and Kang felt like doing a backflip off the picnic table. He had done it before. Instead he turned to Amy.

"Yo, Aphrodite, time to hit it!"

"Oh snap! That was cold," Emmitt said.

"Colder than a polar bear's toenails.," Antonio agreed.

Amy looked up, cheeks flushed with color, and shot a glance at Kang that made him glad he knew Tae Kwon Do.

"Kang, you wrong for that. I know you not trying to turn into that guy just cause you QB1 now?"

"Please, Tyler and Amy been clowning me all day."

"Is that what it is? Because I was worried that tight shirt was cutting off circulation to your brain," Gwen laughed.

"Please, I saw you checking out the gun show!" Kang replied, flexing his arms and hitting a bodybuilding pose. They laughed together at his foolishness as they crossed the threshold of deck into the house and new possibilities. Kang was practically giddy. This moment was all he could think of for the last few weeks. And it was everything. "But I know all this is a lot, so I better chill. Don't want to cause any problems for you and Javier, or Mr. New Booty back there."

"Mr. New Booty? Oh, now you got jokes? And I don't know what you heard, but I'm a free agent."

Kang shook his head, laughing. The girl was a trip. "You know, Gwen, since you a free agent and all, it'd be nice if we could hang out sometimes. I mean, nothing serious, maybe catch a flick or something…"

"If you buying, I'm in. And better make it dinner and a movie. I'm carb-loading." Gwen laughed, and one of her hair twists that was tied in a ponytail fell across her face. Before Kang knew what he was doing, he had lightly brushed it away.

Record scratch.

Gwen looked surprised as she tucked the hair behind her ear. Kang took a step back, doubting himself and upset that he overplayed his hand. Kang attempted to play it off. "I got you, but I've seen you put it down so we might have to do a buffet," he said, forcing a laugh as the situation became awkward and uncomfortable.

"Uh, don't want to go all high maintenance on you, but I know you not trying to take me to a spot that has sneeze guards? See this what I've been trying to tell you, you need to work on your game, my brotha," Gwen smiled while folding her arms.

Kang felt relieved as he held up his chin and stood his ground. "For you? Anything, just say when."

Gwen stared back. "What about Toni?"

Kang cleared his throat. He knew this was coming. "Toni and I haven't kicked it in a minute. We don't even talk anymore and, on the real, what happened between me and her is going to stay between me and her. But Gwen, I mean you should probably give her a call. She's dealing with some stuff, and... and could use a friend."

"Aren't you her friend?"

Kang shook his head and glanced away. "I was, but, but— I mean, I don't know. Listen, I probably already said too much, but whether Toni and I are together or not, I still care about her, and I'll leave it at that," Kang finished, wiping the sweat from his brow. The heat had risen suddenly.

Gwen nodded. "What makes you think she'll speak to me? Especially after this."

"I don't know, Gwen. I don't have an answer for you, and if by 'this' you mean us, I just want to hang out. Can we do that? I mean, I enjoy your company."

Gwen laughed. "Who doesn't? But yeah, I could roll with that. Let's just take it slow."

"Wouldn't have it any other way," Kang replied as he hopped in the convertible with Tyler and Amy.

***

Gwen and Eve stood side by side as they watched their friends drive down the street and disappear into the sunset. Turning, she saw her entire family jammed in the doorway, watching. She covered her face with both her hands. *This is so embarrassing.* The door opened, and Antonio and Emmitt tripped over each other, falling to the ground. Emmitt jumped up and shoved Antonio, shouting, "Get off me, punk!"

They started slap-boxing in the front yard until Uncle Benjamin broke them up. Aunt Alicia wasn't happy. "Since y'all got so much energy, load everything up! Now! And you better walk faster, cause PAC 10 or not, you ain't too big for the strap."

Gwen laughed as she linked arms with Eve. She loved her family. Twenty minutes later, the cars had disappeared down the street. Eve playfully hip-bumped Gwen and put her arm around her as they turned towards the house. Gwen hip-bumped her back and then put her arm on Ana's waist, who was on her other side. Gwen smiled. Her sisters. She could not have made it through the year without them. She took a deep breath to keep from getting emotional.

"Hey, after we clean up you guys want to lace 'em and play some more ball? Or maybe get a few more rounds of sparring in?" Eve asked.

Gwen and Ana looked at each other, shook their heads, and laughed. Gwen just wanted to chill, watch a movie, and maybe call Kang. She didn't want to take it that slow. Gwen would also check on Toni. It was the least she could do. "Uh, no, Princess, I think we good," Gwen said as Ana nodded in agreement.

When they reached the front door, their mother shouted past them, "Roman, Aaron, can I see you two in the house, please? Thank you."

Roman and Aaron had been inching for the sidewalk to set out on their afternoon bike ride to the hotel or motel they booked for the night. A few minutes later the Parker family surrounded them in the kitchen as they both looked around nervously like they were about to be blamed for something they didn't do. Gwen's mother twirled her wine while leaning against the countertop.

"My husband and I, along with our daughters, agree that your current situation is untenable. In light of this, we would like to offer you the hospitality of our home while we work together on a more permanent solution. Now, before you respond there are a few rules.

Roman, I will need to speak with your mother. Also, you will have daily chores and if this continues into the school year there will not be any television or video games on school nights. Just so we are clear."

Aaron and Roman looked at each other with opened mouths. The Parkers had had a family meeting before the girls left for London, and all agreed that it was the right thing to do. Unfortunately, the legal side took longer than anticipated, and Ana had to assist by cutting corners.

"Uh, yeah, I've been talking to my mother lately, and I can probably make that happen. But uh… I mean, where would we sleep?" Roman asked as Aaron stepped closer to him. Tragedy and need had bound them together for the last couple of years, and they formed a co-dependency out of necessity. Gwen felt responsible for their predicament. She knew she couldn't pay back or recover what was lost, but they needed to focus on paying it forward, as her father said.

"Roman, this house has over six thousand square feet of living space. We have room, I assure you," their mother replied.

Aaron pulled down his hoody, his eyes red. He sniffled, looked at Roman, and nodded. Roman looked back at him with questions. Then he shrugged, looked at Gwen's mom, and opened his mouth to say something. Nothing came out, and he nodded his confirmation.

The household collectively exhaled. "Y'all get started on the kitchen. I'm going to put on some music. What you young men know about Miles Davis?" the girls' father asked, because he was always ready to torture somebody about jazz, football, or grilling.

"Pops, please! You already trying to scare 'em! Ain't nobody got time for all that!" Gwen laughed. She then threw a dishcloth to Roman. "Yo, Romana, the big pans don't get clean in the dishwasher. You wash and I'll dry."

Made in the USA
Coppell, TX
21 October 2022

85036941R00115